Family Sins

Inez Asher

BOOK EXCHANGE
BREEZEWOOD SHOPPING CENTRE
10643 COURTHOUSE ROAD
FREDERICKSBURG, VA 22401
(703) 898-8063

PINNACLE BOOKS   NEW YORK

This is a work of fiction. All the characters and events portrayed in this book are fictional, and any resemblance to real people or incidents is purely coincidental.

FAMILY SINS

Copyright © 1981 by Inez Asher

All rights reserved, including the right to reproduce this book or portions thereof in any form.

An original Pinnacle Books edition, published for the first time anywhere.

First printing, July 1983

ISBN: 0-523-41186-3

Printed in the United States of America

PINNACLE BOOKS, INC.
1430 Broadway
New York, New York 10018

Darkness has dawned in the east
    On the noon of time:
The death-birds descend to their feast
    From the hungry clime.
Let Freedom and Peace flee far
    To a sunnier strand,
And follow Love's folding-star
    To the Evening land!

—Percy Bysshe Shelley
  "Darkness Has Dawned in the East"

To Enid

FAMILY SINS

CHAPTER I

Martha, knowing her face was slightly flushed, tapped on the crystal goblet, the traditional summons for attention at the family monthly Sunday dinner. The family was seated on either side of the long table, and they looked up in unison. This was the first time since Paul's death that she had asked for time for an announcement, and she had confided in no one her intention.

Thinking the problem over all morning before coming to Aunt Beulah's, she had finally decided it was better to tell the family at one fell swoop rather than have the news leak out. This way no one could be hurt at not having been the first to know. Among as sensitive a group as the family, this was very important. Martha weighed this fact against the momentary discomfort of having the family coalesce, as they always did, into a solid opponent when someone started to speak. A moment after the announcement was concluded, Martha knew they might divide among themselves to discuss her plans, weighing, arguing, contradicting, affirming.

Looking at their faces turned expectantly toward her, Martha felt a wave of repugnance. She dreaded these monthly gatherings of the clan. They had become more than a social tradition; over the years the meetings had taken on a kind of Christian form of ancestor worship, since the older relatives, with almost masochistic glee, talked about the members of the family, close and on the periphery, who were no longer present. To the elders this was a way of preserving the memory of the deceased, as well as providing a topic for conversation, but Martha had heard the younger ones complain. To a member who had recently lost a beloved one, it was crucifying.

* * *

Marha had seriously considered leaving Indiana and moving to Chicago after Paul's death. The family, in its protective cloak, was suffocating. But she felt the children needed the security which the family brought, not only in its solicitude but in its important position in the community, a position stemming from wealth and its attendant prestige extending generations back. So she stayed in Springfield and attended the Sunday dinners.

For the ten months since her husband's death she had forced herself to attend these monthly tribal ceremonies, because Paul had loved them. She used to tease him that he had missed these gatherings more than anything else, including her, when he was in the service in Korea. Paul never denied it.

Now for the sake of his memory as well as for the joy of the children, her daughter, Kate, and her son, Jimmy, Martha came. The children themselves loved the occasions so much; ten-year-old Jimmy had even called a succession of dogs "Sunday Dinner" after the thing he loved best.

Martha waited a second before speaking, almost to catch the beat as the family either replaced their coffee cups on the saucers or reluctantly pushed away the dessert plates with the last fragments of strawberry shortcake. Aunt Beulah always managed to serve the first berries in the market, regardless of price.

The sounds subsided, and Martha started to speak. Her hands clutched at the large, white, heavily monogrammed damask napkin resting on the tablecloth. "I . . . I have something to say. As you know, at least some of you knew, Paul and I . . . we had been planning to go to the Orient this fall. Well, I just want to say, I . . . I'm going this summer. With Kate," she added with a smile, looking toward her fifteen-year-old daughter. "With Kate as chaperon. Jimmy will stay with Grandmere and Aunt Alice." Martha sat down.

The reaction was audible. The relatives, ignoring her, talked to each other, talked across the table. From the startled expressions and confusion, Martha felt as if she had just announced she would be shot into space next week. To some of them the Orient was a kind of earthly equivalent, far removed from Springfield, Indiana.

Actually, she realized as soon as she had made the statement, no one except David had really known of their proposed trip to the Orient. The two of them had been planning it quietly until details were completed. Paul had wanted her to see where he had spent those years away from her; he also wanted to see what rehabilitation had taken place since the war. It would have been their seventeenth anniversary celebration. There was nothing to prevent their long-awaited vacation, since the children were old enough to leave with Grandmere and Aunt Alice, and they finally had the money saved. Nothing except death, which had seized Paul at a football game in the fall. One moment Martha had seen him shouting his team to victory; the next second he was keeled over. In her confused mind all Martha remembered of the exact moment was a chrysanthemum that a slightly inebriated woman in back kept waving in Martha's face as the woman bent over to see what had happened.

From the end of the table Uncle Bolton stood up. "When are you going? Where are you going? The Orient's a big place, you know."

Knowing this would unloose a flood of questions, Martha rose to her feet again. She did not grasp the napkin this time. The opening gun had been the most dreaded. "I guess I had better fill in some details. We're flying from San Francisco." She did not let a gasp from someone stop her, but hurried on. "We'll go right to Tokyo, some side trips, Hong Kong, Bangkok, Philippines, Honolulu, home."

"Picking up a loaf of bread at the supermarket on the way," Sally said. "You make it sound so . . . casual."

"Sounds to me like she's got it pretty well worked out." Uncle Bolton, having been in the Navy in the First World War, albeit no farther than the Great Lakes Training Academy, felt a kinship with anyone dealing in faraway places.

An aunt spoke out. "Martha, I agree with you that you should take a trip. I can respect your desires to follow Paul's wishes, but sometimes one must be practical. Going out to the Orient with a husband is one thing; two women traveling alone is quite another. If you feel you must get away, why not a nice, leisurely trip to Europe on one of the bigger steamers. You'll have a chance to meet congenial people."

Sally interrupted, "Congenial people means *men*. We've all decided behind your back, Martha, you should get married again." Everyone was so used to hearing Sally's outspoken comments, they were no longer embarrassed.

Martha answered quietly, "Well, this can be your summer project, Sally. Find someone for me. Keep him in the deep freeze till I get back."

Sally made a face. "One of these old goats around here?"

Uncle Edward stood up. "I for one am not in favor of this trip. Too risky. I would recommend to Martha to think it over very carefully." There was a ripple of agreement.

Martha looked at them, those on one side of the table, then the other. "I want you to know, first, how much I appreciate your deep concern, but I *have* thought this trip over carefully. I . . . I have discussed it with David, and, well, I'm making my plans accordingly."

As at a tennis match, all eyes now turned toward David Fletcher. Throughout Martha's startling announcement David had kept his eyes averted, looking down at the figures he was doodling with his fork on the white-damask cloth. His handsome face had an even sterner quality than usual. Now he looked up slowly.

Sally turned toward David, her husband. "Thus spoke Zarathustra. If David says it's okay, so be it!"

David said almost sotto voce, "We have discussed it, Martha and I. I can see no reason why she shouldn't take the trip. Travel, even flying, to the Orient is quite common these days, and Paul had wanted to go—"

Sally broke in, "Better than the Hindu way of the wife's throwing herself on the funeral pyre of her husband. What's it called? They do it in India." No one bothered to answer her.

The dinner was concluded. Any announcement about a summer camp for one of the brood of small cousins or even talk about a new car seemed too trivial to mention. Besides, the family couldn't wait to discuss Martha's plans among themselves.

Leaving the dining room, Claire, one of the more progressive cousins, confided to an aunt, "Personally, this is simply an escape, a widow's trauma. I think Martha should see a psychiatrist."

Aunt Beulah said, "The Villa d'Este at Lake Como would be ideal for her. I always love it!"

Aunt Tillie shook her head. "No, Beulah. For all her quiet ways, Martha has a definite mind of her own. Don't you remember she wouldn't keep Paul's casket open at the services. Said he had always been too vital." But Aunt Beulah had walked over to join the small group surrounding David.

Martha watched David talking to them, reassuring them of the safety of the trip for Martha and Kate. Last week she had said to David, "You were best man at our wedding, Dave, and it's a role you have filled remarkably ever since." David had patted her arm in thanks.

What would happen if David revealed the real reason for her trip. They would be as disbelieving as she had been when David had first called her into his office to discuss Paul's will. At the time, she had considered it quite natural for David to summon her to his downtown office. Later she realized he had deliberately chosen the impersonal setting of his office.

That morning in his office Martha had jokingly commented on how pale David looked, asking him if Sally was neglecting to give him organically grown carrot juice. They both had laughed, knowing what a food fadist Sally was. In a few moments Martha knew why he was pale. She suffered for him as much as for herself that he had to be the one to tell her.

David explained carefully the condition of Paul's estate. Martha knew Paul had been successful, though in a much less spectacular way than David, who was one of the most prominent lawyers in the country. Paul had gone into a brokerage firm. As Paul had laughingly said many times, "I've enough wealthy clients within my own family to keep any broker going."

Paul had had several interruptions: World War II, where he had served in the Pacific, even staying on with occupation forces in Japan after the armistice, and again, in Korea from 1950 to 1952. Martha had been so proud when he had come back a full colonel. Even so, he had left her reasonably comfortable, if not rich. She could maintain their lovely house and one servant. A trust fund for college in Kate's name had been set up, which she would use in the next few years. There was also one for Jimmy's education. If Martha was not extravagant, which she certainly was not, and if inflation, didn't skyrocket, she could manage nicely.

"Financially, Martha, as long as I'm living—and to even a great degree if I'm not—you need never worry," David had told her.

"I know," was all Martha had said.

Martha remembered that David had gone over to the window and begun to knot the cord on the Venetian blinds. Martha recalled the flat quality of his voice.

"Paul also left certain charitable bequests," David had said after slight hesitation.

"Good."

"He had one bequest in mind that . . . that is not mentioned in his will. He, Paul, that is, had been contributing a monthly sum to an orphanage in Korea, in Seoul."

"How . . . how wonderful of him! Paul was funny, you know, David. Sometimes I wonder if I really knew him at all. He must have had a deep sensitivity for the destruction in Korea."

"Paul's son is in that orphanage," David said plainly, but Martha knew she could never forget the expression on his face.

"Paul's son is in that orphanage, Martha, and that is why he wanted to go to the Orient, to Korea, to see the boy."

Martha had been stunned. She'd felt as she had that day at the football game when the woman, leaning over, had waved the chrysanthemum in her face—numb and sick. Her husband dead. Now this.

David continued, "Paul was afraid to tell you. I kept telling him he was wrong, that you would understand."

Marthat replied, "I don't know. I don't know if I can understand."

David continued, "The boy's mother was a nurse, a Korean girl, educated, kind, gentle. She died over a year ago, and the boy was placed in an orphanage. Paul had sent the mother money; he then sent it to the orphanage. Paul had wanted to meet the boy, who is eight, nine years old, thereabouts."

Martha said, "He's younger than Jimmy."

"Paul wanted to see if maybe, maybe some other arrangements for the boy couldn't be made. Bring him to this country perhaps." Not knowing what else to say, David had reached into the top drawer of his desk. Then, as if it were too apparent that he had set the stage with the photograph right on top, he had pretended to rummage through the drawer. But Martha was seeing nothing.

"Here . . . here is a picture of the boy. His name is Johnny." David had handed her the photograph of a little boy about three years old. Martha took it, trembling. She looked at it.

David said quickly, "I believe it was taken a few years ago."

Martha looked at the snapshots, then, slowly, she said, "Johnny . . . Johnny must look . . . like his mother."

David had replied, "He goes by his mother's name—Kim, Johnny Kim."

Martha sat silently for a few moments. Then she rose to go.

"May I drive you home, Martha?" David had offered.

Martha took his hand. "I . . . can make it. Thank you, David, as always." She went out the door.

David sat silently at his desk. He fingered the picture of Johnny Kim. He looked idly at the photograph of his brood, the six children, three boys and three girls, which Sally had borne. He thought of the moment he had introduced his cousin Paul to Martha. David had been in law school, but he and Paul, a year or so below him, had been roommates. The introduction had been all Paul had needed, David soon realized. With his gayer, exuberant manner, his good looks, Paul was too much competition for David. David wondered if it would have made any difference if he had told Martha he was in love with her. He didn't then; he couldn't now.

About a year after Paul and Martha married, David

met Sally Schaeffer. She was "hashing" in the student union. Sally's barbed tongue and brittle manner was a complete contrast from the quiet humor and gentleness of Martha. At first Sally kept him amused. After they were married, it kept him annoyed. After they were engaged, David had found out that Sally was wealthy, extremely wealthy. She had worked her way through college as a protest to her parents and so she could feel no one was marrying her for her money. Now married, she made full use of her large income. Believing that those who could afford it should have large families, she was bent on matching her income with progeny. Like little steps, six children had overwhelmed David with their noise and boisterous manners. The Fletchers had bought a huge estate, and David concentrated on his practice, leaving Sally to whatever else she wanted—horses, station wagons, pre-Columbian art, anything.

David returned the snapshot of Johnny to his desk. As a lawyer, he was frequently confronted with the problem of clients' illegitimate children. Paternity suits, blackmail, all were usually sordid. This child of Paul's was different, he knew. He had begged Paul, as he had argued with his other clients, to confide in his wife. He knew Martha would be compassionate. If not at first, then later. But Paul was obstinate and refused to speak to anyone but David. Paul certainly had not expected death to be the tattletale.

Leaving David's office, Martha knew she would never be the same woman who had entered less than an hour ago. Paul had died ten months ago; in the past half-hour part of her died also.

She drove directly home. Somehow she realized she was stopping on red lights, going on green. Once, she applied her brakes to avoid hitting a small boy on a bicycle. The boy was younger than her own Jimmy, maybe a little older than Johnny Kim. She wondered if Johnny rode a bicycle.

Martha went through the motions of dinner. The prattle of Jimmy and Kate both vying for her attention kept bringing her back to her immediate tasks. After dinner she helped Jimmy prepare for his Cub Scout meeting. Then she helped Kate dress for the Thalian's spring dance at the high school. Martha realized Kate had grown up in the ten months since Paul had been gone, from a gangling fourteen-year-old to a pretty adolescent. As she did almost continually, Martha kept wishing Paul could see her and that Kate could receive the compliments so necessary from a father.

When the house was finally quiet, Martha sat down on the sofa in the living room. She did not know how long she sat there. She was filled with waves of anger, of frustration. Who could quarrel with a memory? Who could argue with the dead? Paul had had no confidence in her. He had been so unsure of her love that he thought this tragic incident would have driven a wedge into their relationship. Did it mean he did not love her enough to trust her? Or did it mean he did not feel she loved him enough to forgive him?

How could one live with a man for years and yet not have any idea of so great a secret? Was she so naïve that she did not even perceive any signposts? Paul had not dismissed the child from his mind, ignored his existence, since he sent monthly contributions. But her husband had hidden his secret—he had dissembled his devotion. Her hurt was deep.

She had gone over these facts, but she found no answer. Then she went to her room, opened a small drawer in her desk and took out his letters, carefully cataloged as to dates. She read the ones from Seoul over one by one. She tried to detect from his letters when he might have first met Johnny's mother. Perhaps what she had recognized as his ability to adjust to conditions over there might simply have been his fondness, then love, for this girl. The letters said nothing; Paul was not much of a correspondent. Maybe if she held the pages over a candle, the way children do to decode secret messages written in lemon juice, she might find a clue. But there was no candle strong enough to give the answers.

Which letter was written when he had first made love to her? What was her name? What was she like. How old was she? Was she in her twenties, older? How much younger than Martha's thirty-eight years. But when Paul was in Korea, Martha was younger too. . . . Where did the conception take place? Martha knew the relationship must have lasted over a period of time, otherwise Paul would not have felt this deep obligation to the child. This had been no one-night affair. Did that make it better or worse?

While Martha was home at night, sleepless, pacing the floor, filled with loneliness and longing and hunger for Paul, he had been in the arms of another woman. No, that was not quite correct. There was a difference in time. It was while Martha was probably driving the car pool to school that Paul and the girl had been in bed somewhere. She knew from stories she had read, gossip she had heard, many men overseas found someone. But it had never occurred to her that Paul might have been like them, that he would have fallen in love with someone else, that he would have created a child with someone else. In all the seventeen years of their marriage she felt there had never been another woman for Paul. But she'd been wrong. She wanted to understand. She wanted to forgive him, but she couldn't. Not now.

Jimmy came back from his Cub Scout meeting, excited at the thought of an overnight hike. Could he go? Tommy's father would take care of him too. Please? Martha kissed him, giving him permission. She knew she would have to make up for many overnight hikes without Paul.

She glanced at the empty bunk bed in the room, which Jimmy kept when a friend slept over. Then suddenly she imagined the face of another child, dark, almond-eyed, different contour to his little face. Jimmy's half-brother—Johnny Kim—a baby who, like Jimmy, had no father. But Johnny had no mother either, no loving grandmother, no Sunday Dinners. A child her husband had caused to be born out of love.

She turned out Jimmy's light and went back to her room. An idea was forming. She realized she could not let her own frustrating anger at Paul's silence affect the destiny of this child. She, too, would go to Korea to see him, to provide for him. If this is what Paul had wanted, she would carry out his wish.

The thought came swiftly. Maybe in this traumatic fashion Paul would have revealed to her the existence of Johnny, not by meaningless words, but by the boy's actual presence. This must have been what Paul had in mind in planning the trip. But she knew deep in her heart this was not so. She doubted if he would ever have told her.

Martha could hardly wait for morning to see David and tell him her plans; she and Kate would go to the Orient. Jimmy could stay with Grandmere and Aunt Alice.

At first David was violently opposed to the idea. She need not subject herself to such an ordeal, he kept repeating. "This child is certainly not your responsibility, Martha."

But Martha was adamant. "I must go. I could never be satisfied if I felt a child of Paul's . . . was in want."

So, three months after she'd heard about Johnny Kim, Martha had finalized her plans, even to the date of departure. Only the reason for the trip was not revealed when she made the announcement at Sunday dinner.

A day or so before their departure Martha and Kate were busy packing the last few articles. Martha found it impossible to stay at the task more than a moment, before another relative would drop in, bringing useless presents and equally useless advice. But, with prodding, Martha and Kate were most gracious in accepting both.

In one hilarious moment Kate put a large, elaborate basket of fruit and delicacies, all adorned with wide ribbons and a gilt "Bon Voyage" sign on the scale. Kate giggled. "Mama, we can take this present from Aunt Tillie, but we'll have to leave our baggage home. It weighs a ton."

Martha peeked at the scale, and she, too, laughed as she saw the weight appear against the arrow. "Aunt Tillie is thinking in terms of the train and boats, dear." Then she uttered, "Goodness, where did I put the list? I want to keep a check to write thank-you notes to everyone."

Kate was vehement. "Well, I'm not going to spend my time writing letters. I want to go sightseeing."

Martha was surprised to see David arrive unexpectedly in the middle of the day. He handed her a large Manila envelope with the plane tickets and typed itinerary. As they were talking in the living room, they heard Kate's radio, upstairs, turned full blast to one of the local AM stations.

David glanced up toward Kate's room. "One thing bothers me, Martha," he began. "How can you keep Kate from knowing about Johnny Kim?"

"Simple," Martha replied. "For one thing, Kate is too involved with her own problems—clothes, makeup, the rest—to pay too much attention. She's not inquisitive anyway. I'll just tell her that, as a member of some social-service board here at home, I want to inspect an orphanage in Korea." She smiled wryly. "Don't worry, David. If a wife who *is* inquisitive didn't suspect all these years, a child certainly won't."

David continued, "Martha, I know you. Don't make any rash promises to the orphanage or the child. Don't get carried away."

Martha put her hand on his arms. "You mean don't airmail him home. I understand. I promise you, I won't do anything rash."

"And, Martha, if problems of any kind come up, will you cable? Phone me? Promise?"

Martha nodded her head. "Den mother's honor. I promise." She touched his arm. "Really, David, I'm a grown—I hope—mature woman." Then, seeing Kate come in the door with several voluminous petticoats, she added, "Besides, I will be well-chaperoned."

Kate sighed and thrust the petticoats toward her mother. "Mom, I simply can't squeeze another thing in. Can you possibly find room for these? They don't weigh much."

After David left, Martha took the envelope he had given her. It loomed large and heavy. She tried fitting it into her traveling handbag. It was too big. Where could she carry it? She panicked. Suppose she lost the plane tickets, the return tickets, the itinerary, the traveler's checks! She suddenly realized now what she was embarking on. For seventeen years she had relied on Paul to make all the arrangements, to steer her through the details of travel. She had scarcely been away during her entire marriage with Paul—a few trips to Chicago for concerts, shopping, once to New Orleans to visit a college roommate. Each time, she had been met at the airport or depot. Now she would arrive in a strange land, with an incomprehensible language and different customs. She felt she must be out of her mind to take this trip. Maybe Cousin Claire had been right. Maybe she did need a psychiatrist. Maybe this was a delayed reaction to Paul's death.

She went to the phone to call David, to confess her fears, ask him to return the tickets, cancel the reservations, wipe the slate clean. Later in the year she could take the steamer to Europe, maybe even Lake Como and the Villa d'Este. Martha dialed David's office number. His secretary said he was not in. "Is there any message, Mrs. Montgomery, for Mr. Fletcher?"

Martha wanted to say, "Yes. Tell him I'm not going. I've changed my mind." Instead she replied, "No message. I'll talk to him later."

"I hope you have a wonderful trip and a safe one."

"Thank you, Miss Townsend. I'm sure we will." Martha hung up the phone. She would tell David later of her change of heart.

But she did not.

CHAPTER II

"*Kangei!* Welcome aboard!" The Japanese stewardesses in their colorful kimonos greeted Martha and Kate at the end of the red-carpeted runway. Looking back a few hundred feet to the towers of the San Francisco Airport, Martha felt she was already straddling two worlds. The majority of other travelers were Orientals. Martha couldn't tell if they were Japanese, Chinese, or what. They all looked and sounded alike to her.

"Aren't they just adorable." Kate nudged her mother, indicating the stewardesses. Kate was disillusioned to learn that one hostess was named Mary Jane. But Martha's daughter recovered when Mary Jane offered her a happi coat to slip on. "Pinch me, Mom. I can't believe it's really me."

Martha hugged her. She was now delighted she had chosen to fly Nippon Air Lines, in spite of the family's objections. Her relatives distrusted strangers and foreigners, particularly in an emergency. But Martha didn't want to be cheated of one moment in a foreign environment.

"Look how much Japanese I know already. This is called *o shibori*," Kate boasted as the stewardess handed them each a hot damp towel for their hands before serving the meal.

Martha laughed. "Good thing it isn't Jimmy with his grubby little paws."

"So soon," Kate exclaimed as the Japanese gentleman in the seat in front pointed out the first sights of the Hawaiian Islands. Martha and Kate looked down at Koku Point and Diamond Head. "Have you ever seen such colors as the water down there—blues, green—and the color of those little boats." They could see brightly colored catamarans near the coast, with their pink, white and yellow sails representing the resort hotels.

During the several hours' stay on the island of Oahu they drove around Honolulu. Kate would have foregone the entire trip to remain on Waikiki, learning how to handle a surfboard. She did manage to wheedle a promise out of her mother. "All right. I promise. We'll stay a few days on our way back, and you can practice surfing." Kate was delighted, and Martha knew the girl would keep reminding her often of her words.

They boarded the plane. They saw the Hawaiian Islands recede. Now the plane trip to Japan stretched on. Martha watched Kate writing post card after post card. "Not homesick, are you, Kate?"

"Nope, but I hope there's mail waiting for me. I told everyone to write ahead of our leaving so I'd be sure to have some letters when I get there."

And then, after what seemed to be an endless wait, through a break in the clouds, they saw Mt. Fuji, symbol of Japan. Moments later they were landing. Martha and Kate carefully walked down the high steps leading from the plane to the ground. Kate planted her feet firmly on the blacktop, exclaiming, "Our first steps on foreign soil!"

Martha felt herself take a gulp. She looked around, shifting her overseas bag and coat to her left arm. Obviously they must follow the other passengers to the air terminal. A middle-aged Japanese man dressed in a dark-blue uniform with a neatly embroidered name indicating "Forest Travel Agency" on his right-breast pocket approached her. "You Mrs. Montgomery?" he asked, and Martha, surprised, nodded.

The guide introduced himself as Mr. Furokawa, representative of the Forest Travel Agency, and bowing low, his arms on either side, said he was here to aid her in her journey. He knew all about her, that she was going on to Seoul, then returning. David had taken care of her right from the start.

Martha let him guide her with majesty and magic through customs. Although she saw the officials examining the baggage of her companions on the flight, she was pleased to see their luggage was given a pat and stamped.

Again, Mr. Furokawa asked her to follow him, this time to the stand where her baggage would be checked until the time for the plane to Seoul, Korea, six hours later. Martha sighed. She thought that distances and time on a travel folder in Springfield were one thing; experienced in a foreign country, they were quite another. The airport, according to the agent at home, who had been no farther west than Chinatown in San Francisco, was only nine miles from Tokyo. Time to run in for a few hours and then return. Now Mr. Furokawa told her that although it was only nine miles distant, because of traffic it would take at least ninety minutes each way. The alternative would be to remain in the airport for the next six hours.

Martha had an idea. She asked Mr. Furokawa if it would be possible to stay overnight in Tokyo and continue their flight to Seoul the next day. She hadn't realized how tired they were.

Mr. Furokawa looked extremely puzzled. He shook his head. "It is impossible to get rooms at the Imperial on a moment's notice. They are arranged long in advance." Frankly Martha wondered about this, but suggested perhaps some other hotel. Mr. Furokawa looked despondent as he explained, "Any first-class hotel always booked in advance." He paused. "In addition, it would be extremely difficult to change tickets on another plane to Seoul, since they, too, booked in advance."

Martha knew she had no choice but to accept what he said, whether or not she believed him. Thinking out loud, Martha asked Kate what they should do about going in to the city now. There was no doubt in Kate's mind: Tokyo, by all means. Martha shrugged. They followed Mr. Furokawa to the auto entrance, where he skillfully guided them on to a bus that would take them directly to the Imperial Hotel.

They took their seats, and he bowed low, wishing them a good trip and saying he would meet them at the gate for their plane.

"But aren't you going with us?" Kate asked.

Again bowing low, Mr. Furokawa assured them nothing would give him greater pleasure, but he had other friends to meet and arrange for.

Kate was unhappy. She said she felt as though she and Martha had lost their one friend—a friend shared by many. Martha knew exactly what she meant.

Martha felt safe in the large bus as she looked out at the phantasmagoria of Tokyo traffic. She felt it looked like an old movie comedy in which the speed of the film was increased for a laugh.

Martha chuckled. "Kate, do you suppose we'll be brave enough to go out in these crowds?"

Kate didn't answer. She was looking out the window. All she could do was point to the crowded sidewalk and motley assortment of people: tiny women in bright kimonos, moving as quickly as crowds would permit; less-shy ones in Western dress; old gray-haired men with gray pointed beards in old gray kimonos; young men in immaculate Ivy League cut; schoolgirls in blue-and-white middy uniforms; black-clothed schoolboys; young women wearing bobbysocks and carrying babies on their backs; Japanese teenagers; girls with pony tails, long hair, or baby-doll hair style complete with bangs. Few of the adolescent boys wore coats. They had on white shirts, or sport shirts that were even gaudier than those at home. A few wore hot-rod leather jackets. Weaving in and out of the crowds were men with advertising signs front and back. Kate uttered, "How do they breathe, so many people?"

They walked into the Imperial Hotel, with its older wing, landmark of Tokyo, and its new addition, modern and Western. Martha whispered to Kate, "You pinch me. See if it's real. For years I've heard about this hotel. It's even more wonderful and exciting than I ever could have imagined."

They lunched on the cafe terrace and were intrigued by the Japanese dishes. At the time, both Martha and Kate thought they were being initiated into the delicacies of Japanese cuisine by ordering such familiar names as sukiyaki; rice; daikon, or radishes; and, of course, *cha*, Japanese tea.

With only a little time to spare, they went to the entrance for a taxi to the airport. The doorman was calling out, "*Takushi! Takushi!*" Hailing a taxi, he motioned to Martha and Kate.

Suddenly, Kate screamed out that she had left her pocketbook in the dining room. She darted back so quickly, Martha had difficulty trailing her. They arrived in the dining room, but it had emptied. The headwaiter was gone. Martha saw one waiter and went up to him, asking if he had found a pocketbook, describing it at the same time with her hands.

"Eigo-wa hanashi mosen—no English." The waiter shook his head. Martha found no one who could understand her.

Kate, too, was having difficulty in making anyone understand. In a shrieking voice, as though sound would convey meaning, she cried, "I lost my pocketbook!"

"Wakali-masu." And the tiny busboy bowed very low.

Realizing everyone who spoke English had gone from the dining room, Martha and her daughter looked for the table they had occupied, but the busboys had moved the furniture around in order to clean. Kate wanted to go to the "Lost and Found," but Martha insisted there wasn't time, adding she would write a letter from Seoul, asking the hotel to hold the purse until their return. They again rushed to the taxi entrance. "Taxi for the airport now, please," Martha said.

The doorman nodded. "Taxi be along in minute. Very busy time now." Then he shouted, *"Takushi! Takushi!"*

A limousine drew up. Kate, reasoning it was a taxi, since the man getting out paid the driver, shouted, "Here's a taxi, Mom!"

She started to jump into the car, but the doorman gently held her back, saying, *"Sumi-masen*—sorry," as two men came up from behind. Both were Japanese; one was short, the other tall.

Kate said, "We were here first."

The doorman bowed again. "Sorry. These gentlemen order taxi special." He started to put the men's luggage in the front seat of the taxi.

Marth stepped up. "But we must get to the Tokyo International Airport right away. We have to catch a plane."

The taller of the men spoke in Japanese to the doorman. Then the doorman again bowed low to Martha and Kate. "Gentlemen say go to Haneda, if you care share auto."

Kate was impatient. "Mom, we're not going to Haneda. Tell him we're going to the International Airport."

The doorman nodded, smiling. "Haneda niko-jo is Tokyo International Airport."

The two men stepped back as the doorman assisted Martha and Kate toward the rear seat. Kate was worried. She whispered in a penetrating voice, "Mom, do you think it's safe, strange men and all?"

It was an awkward moment, but Martha was already in the back seat, and Kate had climbed in next to her. Martha handed the doorman a tip. Then, turning to the two gentlemen, she thanked them. The shorter one bowed very low; the other nodded his head briefly.

The two men occupied the small jump seats. They were speaking Japanese. Kate was subdued. She was worried about her purse. "To lose my pocketbook in the first few hours on foreign soil is too much."

After riding for several blocks, Kate leaned over to her mother and said in a low voice, "I thought the Japanese were all small. The one guy is as tall as Dad."

Martha motioned her to be silent, but Kate prattled on. "It's safe. They only speak Japanese, Mom."

Tired, but entranced by the sights en route to Haneda, Martha and Kate fell silent. They felt that the two Japanese men speaking rapidly to each other in a language completely incomprehensible seemed to be background for the scenery.

At the passenger entrance of the airport the limousine stopped. The two men stepped out first, the taller one bowing in apology to Martha and Kate. He then paid the driver the entire fare. Martha felt foolish; she had her hand outstretched, offering some yen to the driver, but the chauffeur smiled, motioning that the fare had been paid.

Embarrassed, Martha said to the driver, "Tell the kind gentlemen we thank them very much, but I couldn't possibly accept it. I insist upon paying our share."

The driver turned to the men and spoke in Japanese. The taller of the two smiled and said to the driver in flawless English, "Please tell the lady the honor is ours. We were going in the same direction, and the fare is the same for all of us."

Kate blurted out, "He speaks English!"

Martha was too flustered to know what to say. She turned toward him. "I won't begin to thank you, but we are so very grateful to you both, not only for sharing the taxi but for the fare."

Again, the smaller of the two bowed low, and the spokesman tipped his hat, saying, "That's quite all right."

A guide directed them to the check stand. There they found their friend, Mr. Furokawa, waiting. He was frowning. "Not much time for everything."

Martha smiled pleasantly. "I know, but we had difficulty in getting a taxi."

Mr. Furokawa shrugged. He felt vindicated, for he had always told his neighbors, "These Americans, they never seem to know what they are about; yet they somehow manage to come out all right."

Now he skillfully guided them through customs, through passport validation, and saw them safely on the plane to Seoul. Martha pressed some yen into his hand. She wasn't sure how much, but it was the money she meant for the taxi plus a few extra bills. Bowing very low, Mr. Furokawa thanked them and wished them a good voyage and a safe return. *"Go-kigen yo,"* he said, and then he was gone.

Suddenly remembering the expression, Kate stood up in her seat, turned back and called to him, *"Sayonara,* Mr. Furokawa." The she sat down again, beaming. "Remember Marlon Brando's picture you wouldn't let me see." She sighed. "It was great, but the real thing is better."

Telling Kate to fasten her seat belt, Martha started to look for the left side of hers, when, seated across the aisle, she noticed the two Japanese men with whom they had shared the taxi. She didn't know whether to speak or not. But they were busy talking; so she decided not to interrupt them.

The plane was aloft, when one of the two men, the spokesman and obviously the only one of the two who spoke English, stood up and said to Kate, who was seated on the aisle, "See Fuji-yama—Mt. Fuji—over there."

Now standing in the aisle, Kate looked out the window on the opposite side. "Can people climb Fuji, like the Matterhorn?"

He replied, "They say there are two kinds of fools: those who have never climbed Fuji, and those who have climbed it more than once. Most school children, some time or other, try to climb. Pilgrims plan to be on the summit at dawn to admire the *goraiko*, or sunrise."

Kate turned back to Martha. "Can we do it, Mom? Please?"

Martha smiled. "I'll meet you on the summit. There must be a train or taxi."

The gentleman smiled and said, "Tell your mother there is only one way to the top, by foot, although in summer there is bus service halfway."

Landing at Kimpo, the airport for Seoul, Martha's first impression was of the contrast between the very modern and efficient service at Haneda and this. They looked around, but there was no friendly Mr. Furokawa to meet them. They went through customs and had their visas checked in what seemed an interminable length of time. Martha felt she had never been so tired, and she knew if there was any more delay, she would burst into tears. Kate was pale, and fatigue had made her speechless.

Somehow they managed to get to the entrance, where they stood, waiting for a taxi, surrounded by their luggage. Martha was too tired to give the baggage more than a casual glance to see if all was accounted for. She glimpsed the two Japanese gentlemen also looking for a taxi. She and the taller man smiled at each other in remembrance.

He asked, "You are going to one of the hotels?"

"To the Bando Hotel, I believe it's called."

He nodded. "Then may I suggest we drive together. We are going quite near there." He directed them to a taxi he had hailed, an American model at least twenty years old. He motioned Martha and Kate into the back seat. Again, he and his companion took the jump seats.

Martha closed her eyes for a brief moment, almost reveling in the fact that this stranger was, for the moment at least, taking care of them, lifting the pressure of being completely on her own, halfway around the world. When she opened her eyes, he happened to look back. "Tired?" he asked gently.

"Unbelievably so," she replied.

"Don't try to sightsee too much. Better rest tomorrow," he advised.

"You're right." She nodded. She was aware that their benefactor was a very attractive man, gentle but with the authority of one accustomed to being in charge. She wondered who he was.

Wearily, Martha and Kate got out of the car when it stopped in front of their hotel. Martha said, "I'm really too tired to apologize for all the trouble I've caused you."

"Please, do not mention it. We have all been going in the same direction."

Martha turned to the chauffeur, offering him some money. "Will you accept Japanese yen, driver? I haven't Korean money yet."

The same gentleman interrupted. "Madame, we have the correct amount of *hwan* right here."

Martha was again flustered. Kate nudged her, saying, "You simply can't let them pay for us again, Mom."

The gentleman turned to Kate. "When I come to America, you can reciprocate."

Martha replied, "It will be our pleasure, but I'm afraid visitors don't care to come to Indiana. I'm Mrs. Montgomery, and my daughter, Kathleen—Kate for short."

The gentleman inclined his head. "My colleague, Dr. Yamazuki, and I'm Dr. Tanaka."

Martha started to offer her hand, but instead of taking it, Dr. Yamazuki bowed very low. Dr. Tanaka, however, quickly gave her a warm handshake, which covered up her embarrassment. Thanking the two doctors most profusely, Martha and Kate went into the Bando Hotel.

Martha was annoyed upon awakening the following afternoon to find that she and Kate had slept not only the whole night but until two o'clock. They had had nothing to eat and she hadn't unpacked anything but her night clothes. She wondered if she had time to go to the orphanage, but decided against it. She hadn't the strength for the emotional upheaval that she knew such a visit would cause. She concluded there was nothing to do but count their first day lost.

Early the next morning Martha awakened, dressed and

had breakfast sent up for the two of them. Then, after making Kate promise not to leave the hotel room, she took a taxi to the orphanage, an old brick Western-style building. The neighborhood belonged to the yesterday that was Korea, untouched by any modern influence such as one saw in Tokyo or even in the downtown sections of Seoul.

A young Korean girl of about eighteen had let her in when she arrived at the orphanage. Now the girl bowed low. Martha asked her if she could see the matron or head of the orphanage. Having continuously thought over the visit, Martha had decided not to phone for an appointment, since she hadn't known quite what to say. An institution such as an orphanage, Martha felt, was accustomed to having people come unannounced.

The girl smiled shyly, obviously not understanding her, and bowing again, disappeared. Martha felt awkward standing there, alone. She looked around. The interior of the building was spotless, but the hall seemed empty. And, as in so many like institutions at home, there was no sound of children. The entry of any home like this always seemed devoid of purpose, until one crossed the threshold. Martha knew of such places, because she had served on an orphanage board in Springfield.

In a brief moment or two an older woman came up to Martha. She was dressed in black, with rimless glasses, and her hair was pulled tightly back in coils. Her manner was gentle, patient and tired. Martha had seen her counterpart at home, dedicated women whose lives were circumscribed by their work, their faces etched with sorrow lines caused by the tragedies with which they were constantly confronted—if not the individual cases then the sum total of all whom they had tried to help.

"I am Mrs. Lee, the matron. Did you wish to speak to someone?" Her precise English was delivered in the softest tones Martha had ever heard.

"Why, yes," Martha replied. Then she stopped. She had come this far. Could she take the next step? After a brief pause she continued, "I . . . I am Mrs. Montgomery, Mrs. Paul Montgomery from Springfield, Indiana. My . . . my husband had been interested in . . . this orphanage when he was living." Martha felt she was starting to sway. She took a deep breath to steady herself.

Mrs. Lee, nodding her head, asked Martha to come into her office. Martha entered a small room, also immaculate, but sparsely furnished with an old Western-style desk in one corner and a table on which were a few Korean dolls, a ball and some yellowing photographs. Mrs. Lee brought up one of the two chairs in the room, a weather-beaten oak chair, straight and uncomfortable. She motioned Martha to be seated. She then drew up an older, even more decrepit reed chair. But the motions had been made with such dignity that Martha forgot the appearance of the furniture.

Mrs. Lee said quietly, "You say when your husband was living. He is no longer living?"

Surprised at the question, Martha answered, "No, he died suddenly last fall. You didn't know?"

Mrs. Lee was deeply moved. "I did not know. I offer you my deep sympathy." She rose slightly from her chair, but then sat down again. "You see, we continue to receive the same monthly gift of a money order."

Martha was confused. "A monthly money order? Who sends it?"

Mrs. Lee replied, "A gentleman. Mr. David Fletcher. I believe he was Mr. Montgomery's lawyer. He has never missed a month, nor is it ever more than a day or two late."

Martha said softly, "Mr. Fletcher has been very kind. He . . . he didn't want to trouble me." With great effort Martha continued, "I believe my husband was particularly interested in a little boy—Johnny Kim. I . . . I would like to meet Johnny." Martha's fingernails dug into her palm.

The matron, in her unhurried way, rang a bell. The same young girl appeared. The matron spoke to her in Korean. Bowing low to both women, the girl left.

Mrs. Lee turned to Martha. "We will have some tea. You have had a long journey."

Feeling drained and grateful for this respite, as Mrs. Lee tactfully knew she must be, Martha answered, "Yes, a very long journey, too long. My daughter and I flew directly here from the United States. We did not realize it would be as long and tiring a flight. My daughter is resting at the hotel."

"How old is your daughter?"

"She is just fifteen. I also have a son, who is ten years old. He is staying with his grandmother while we are away."

Mrs. Lee nodded her head. "You would like to meet Johnny Kim. He is a nice little boy, a good boy, and very intelligent." She rang another bell. This time a Korean boy of about sixteen entered. Mrs. Lee spoke to him, and he left, also bowing low to both women.

"What wonderful young people those two are," Martha remarked.

"They have been living here since they were small ones, since 1951. They have known no other home. Soon the boy must leave, and I shall feel sad. I have so many who grow up to leave the nest. The girl will remain as a helper. It is not easy for young people to find jobs. Costs are high, and salaries are so low. Education is compulsory here in Korea, but at the same time one must pay. The orphanage can afford to send children to lower schools, but it can not pay for higher education. Korea is one of the world's oldest civilizations, but it is also one of the world's poorest. War has done that. These are our problems; I must not inflict them on you."

The young girl returned with teacups, teapot and other accessories on a lacquer tray. The matron poured a cup and offered it to Martha. Sipping it, Martha said almost inadvertently, "This is so good." The matron quietly refilled Martha's tiny porcelain cup, reserved for use by honored guests only, Martha felt sure.

It wasn't long before the older boy returned, holding by the hand a very little boy of about three years of age. Martha saw the small child and spoke quickly, "But that can't be Johnny. He's too young."

Mrs. Lee shook her head. "*Aigo!*" Then she said something to the older boy, who was visibly embarrassed. Mrs. Lee turned to the small child, opened her desk and offered him a sweet tidbit. The two boys left the room.

Martha smiled. "Just like a pediatrician with lollipops."

The matron apologized, "I am so sorry, this error. We have several Johnny Kims. Kim is a common name in Korea." Mrs. Lee then turned to a large black-lacquered box. She took out some files, American style. Searching out the one she wanted, she read it carefully and then closed the file.

Martha didn't know what to say. Should she ask questions? How much does Mrs. Lee know? How much was Martha supposed to know? Could she come out and say, "My husband is the father of this child, but who or what was the mother like? Was she pretty, smart?"

Her silence was broken by the return of the older boy with another Johnny Kim, this one, her husband's son. Martha's heart was beating so fast and so loud, she wondered if Mrs. Lee and the others were aware of it. Martha knew she must not stare at the child, but she ached to look at him with more than a passing, casual glance.

At first impression he looked like any other Johnny Kim, a small Korean boy, dark-skinned, Oriental features—this little boy with one-half his being in roots thousands of miles away, and the other half, thousands of years away. Standing there before her, his little head bowed low in shyness as well as custom. Martha yearned to reach out and clutch him to her as befit the half-brother of her own fair-skinned, blond Kate and Jimmy. Suddenly Johnny Kim looked up at her. There was something startling about him, Martha realized, and the shock was electrifying. Johnny's eyes were round. They were not almond-shaped or heavily lidded and slanted. Martha looked quickly at the older boy, at Mrs. Lee. Their eyes were dark and oblique to match their skin and Mongoloid features. Johnny had Paul's eyes in an Oriental face.

The young boy was so very shy. This was probably the first time he had seen a lady with such a white face and such blond hair. Mrs. Lee spoke kindly, gently to him in Korean. Then Johnny bowed very low to Martha. As if Johnny could understand every word she was saying, Martha said softly to him, "How do you do, Johnny? I am very glad to know you."

The child stood there. Somehow there was a presence about him. He was almost poised. To break the awkward moment, Mrs. Lee reached into her desk and brought out a sweet. She offered it to Johnny. He hesitated, and Mrs. Lee said something else to him. Then he accepted the candy, bowing low, but when his little face came up, it was in smiles. Oriental or American, little boys weren't so different when it came to sweets.

Martha hoped her words spoken in English would reach across the barriers to the boy. "I hope I see you again, Johnny."

Mrs. Lee spoke to the older boy, who took Johnny by the hand and left the room. At the door Johnny, almost impulsively, turned and bowed low to Martha.

Martha could not speak for a second, then in low tones she said, "What a wonderful little boy."

Mrs. Lee poured another cup of tea. Martha regained her composure. As steady as she could speak, Martha asked, "The boy's mother is dead, I believe?"

Mrs. Lee looked at the chart she had taken from her file, although Martha felt sure the woman knew the case history of each child by heart. "Yes. She died over a year ago, the result of an auto accident. A friend, a Miss Yang, brought the boy here. The friend felt she couldn't care adequately for Johnny. Miss Yang is also a nurse." The matron looked at Martha kindly but steadily. "Mrs. Montgomery, ordinarily we would not open our files, but I believe this situation is an exception. That you would be interested to come this distance to meet Johnny Kim proves what an extraordinary person you are."

Mrs. Lee continued, "Painful as this visit must be for you, I should like to continue." She looked up for permission from Martha. Martha nodded her head, her eyes were filled with tears.

"Korea, unfortunately, is a land of orphans, of children orphaned by the direct ravages of war. These little ones are forgotten people. The orphanages cannot possibly take care of all, only a handful, really. We took in Johnny at a time when we were already overcrowded. We were pleased to have as fine a child as Johnny, but there are so many fine children. We were also pleased to have the contribution of money that went with Johnny. This may seem harsh, but it is also true. Our funds are so limited.

"I shall write out on a card the name of the friend who brought Johnny to us. She is a nurse at the Chosen Hospital. You may wish to speak to her. She can tell you things perhaps you would wish to know. Johnny is a remarkable little boy. The few tests we have at our disposal show him already to have a fine little mind. He had the advantage of leaving our premises two weekends a month to visit with Miss Yang, a very kind lady."

"What a wonderful person she must be."

"There are many wonderful people, Mrs. Montgomery, like your husband, yourself. I do not know what Johnny's future will be. I realize you have obligations to your own little family. You have already done more, as has your husband, than anyone I have ever been privileged to know. In most instances those responsible turn their backs on the little ones. I can see now why Johnny is as he is."

Martha took out her handkerchief; she could no longer hold back the tears.

Mrs. Lee occupied herself writing the nurse's name on a card. She handed it to Martha. "This is the name of the good friend, Miss Helen Yang. She is a nurse at the Chosen Hospital. I have written down the address."

Martha opened her purse. "Mrs. Lee, I just want to assure you, I shall not forget this . . . this orphanage or your kindness." Taking out some money, she handed it to the matron. "Will you buy some extra sweets for that desk?"

Mrs. Lee accepted the gift graciously.

Martha hesitated, then asked, "Mrs. Lee, would it be possible for Johnny to visit me at the hotel? I . . . I wouldn't feel as awkward as I do, well, just standing here looking at him."

Mrs. Lee replied, "By all means. I shall be glad to cooperate in any manner you wish, Mrs. Montgomery."

Martha told Mrs. Lee she would like to meet Miss Yang at the hospital now, in fact, since their time in Seoul was limited. If Mrs. Lee guessed that this American lady was anxious to get on with her mission, she gave no evidence. She rang again for the older boy, who escorted Martha out of the orphanage and then hailed a taxi for her. He then instructed the driver to take the lady to the Chosen Hospital.

Martha realized she was clutching the card so intensely, her fingers ached. In a few moments she would meet Miss Yang, who had known her husband's mistress. But would she have known Paul too? Would she have warned Johnny's mother against the liaison, or would she have condoned, even encouraged the liaison? What had she thought of Paul?

Her speculations were stopped by their arrival at the hospital. It was a Western-type building, but old and dark. As at many hospitals, hanging about on the outside steps and just within the entrance were small children waiting for someone visiting inside. Martha looked at the youngsters, cute, friendly little Oriental faces. Little girls with bangs and pigtails, little boys with straight black hair hugging their heads like skullcaps. All resembled Johnny Kim, but with one significant difference: Their eyes were oblique; Johnny's eyes were round.

Within the hospital Martha approached a receptionist seated at a desk. Martha asked if it was possible to talk with one of the nurses, Miss Helen Yang. The woman smiled and said something rapidly in Korean.

Martha asked, "You speak English?"

The woman shook her head, smiling. Martha handed her the card Mrs. Lee had written. The girl studied it, then she smiled again. She looked at a schedule posted near her desk. Then she bowed and motioned Martha to follow her. The elevator doors opened, and a crowd exited. Martha glimpsed Dr. Tanaka, taller than the others. He saw her, but the crowd pressing forward pulled him into the corridor. Martha, too, was propelled into the waiting elevator. She asked the receptionist, who, still smiling, was accompanying her, "That tall gentleman—Dr. Tanaka—do you know him?" The young woman shook her head, motioning with her hands, obviously indicating she could not understand.

Excusing himself from the other doctors with whom he was talking, Dr. Tanaka rushed back to the elevator. It was a few moments before the elevator came down. When the door opened, he asked the elevator operator if he'd seen an

American lady and, if so, on what floor did she get out? The elderly elevator man shook his head. "Too many people to remember." A colleague came up to remind Dr. Tanaka they had an appointment. Reluctantly, Dr. Tanaka left the elevator, which had already filled and was ready to go up again.

On the third floor the receptionist walked to a nurse's station and asked for Miss Yang. Martha looked around at the busy corridor, the Korean nurses, the groups of people, families talking together. No one seemed to be alone.

In a few moments Miss Yang came up to the station. She was tiny, immaculate and pretty, with a gentleness about her that was not shyness but a quiet competence. The receptionist spoke and handed Miss Yang the card that Mrs. Lee had given Martha.

Miss Yang nodded, then, turning to Martha, she said in English, "How do you do, Mrs. Montgomery."

Martha said hesitantly, "Mrs. Lee at the orphanage was good enough to give me your name. I thought we might have a little talk about Johnny Kim."

If Miss Yang was surprised to meet Martha, she gave no indication as she added after looking at her wrist watch, "I shall be finish at three o'clock. You join me for tea?"

On her way back to the waiting room on the first floor Martha passed the phone booth in which Dr. Tanaka was talking. His back was to the door. He didn't see Martha, and Martha, of course, didn't see him.

Dr. Tanaka had phoned the Bando Hotel and was talking to Kate. He asked discreetly how she and her mother were getting along. Kate prattled on that her mother was shopping, and she was busy writing letters home. They were fine. How was he? He replied he was busy, but to please give his kindest regards to her mother. When he hung up, he mused that obviously Martha had not told Kate she was going to the hospital. Why not?

Joining Miss Yang for a cup of tea, Martha found herself even more tense than she had been with Mrs. Lee. Here, face to face, was the one person who'd known Johnny's mother, perhaps Johnny's father as well. Martha wasn't quite sure how to begin this traumatic conversation.

She hesitated and then said, "I met Johnny Kim." Pausing slightly, she added, "He is a wonderful little boy."

"He is very bright boy. That is why I feel so fortunate to get him in the Ewha Haktang Orphanage. Ewha Haktang mean 'Pear Blossom.' I search carefully for proper place after his mother die."

Martha felt her voice was coming from the next room as she asked, "You knew Johnny's mother?" Martha suddenly realized she didn't even know her name.

Miss Yang looked down at her teacup. "Yes, I know her very well. We were roommates, sharing apartment after Johnny was born."

Martha forced herself to ask, "Did . . . did you know Johnny's father?"

Miss Yang looked up. "No. I know Fay only after . . . afterward." Then she suddenly spoke to Martha in a far different tone. "Mrs. Montgomery, please don't hold unkind thoughts about Fay, or your husband. They both very, very lonely. Fay was a wonderful person, gentle, kind, most intelligent. You, living in America, can not understand what it means for a girl from poor family to get an education here in Korea. She work very hard to become nurse. You can not imagine how hard.

"After Johnny's birth she and I have an apartment. She continue as a nurse at hospital. She pay an old lady to come watch over Johnny. She could not go back to her family, to live as they live. You can not believe those villages, poor, dirty, same as a hundred years ago.

"When Fay know she was dying, after the accident," Miss Yang went on, "she talk with me about Johnny. She have such fine, beautiful hopes for him. We decided orphanage be best for his education. He can not just go in the streets as so many little ones do; no one guard them, hungry, learning to be thieves or worse. Now we not know whether orphanage will still get gifts of money.

Martha spoke softly, "I told Mrs. Lee that I shall continue sending money to the orphanage, and if you feel you need extra for Johnny, write me." Then, with difficulty, she asked, "Did Fay ever talk about . . . about Johnny's father?" She realized she could not say husband, or even Paul.

Miss Yang looked at the teacup. "Naturally. She talked a great many times about Johnny's father. She showed me photographs of him, very tall, handsome. Fay was very proud."

"Was she angry at him when he left?"

"Oh, no. She had Johnny to love." Looking at her watch once more, Miss Yang said, "I must go quickly. I am glad you like Johnny Kim."

Martha asked, "Miss Yang, would it be possible for you to bring Johnny to the hotel? I would like to see him again, but it's so hard for me to find my way. Mrs. Lee has given her permission."

Miss Yang hesitated. "Day after tomorrow. It could be arranged. I shall bring Johnny to the hotel."

Martha added, "We're at the Bando Hotel. My daughter, Kate, is with me. She is fifteen years old. She knows nothing . . . nothing about Johnny. I will tell her simply that you are a friend. . . ."

"It is better so, if you wish. I will say nothing."

Martha then asked, "Tell me, did Fay know about me?"

Miss Yang looked at her. "I do not know. I never ask."

The next day Martha and Kate hired a car and chauffeur to go sightseeing. The hotel porter had difficulty finding a driver who could speak English, but at last one came. After seeing the usual places of interest, such as Duksoo and Changduk palaces, Martha asked the driver, who spoke a limited English, if it would be possible to see any of the battlefields where American troops had fought. Surprised, the driver asked, "You, lady, want to see battlefields?"

Martha assured him she wanted to go. Shrugging, the driver said, "Okey-doke. We go."

A few miles out of the city Martha felt she had gone back thousands of years. In the background were the famous mountains whose names had been datelines during the war. But the villages amazed Martha. Rectangular houses of stone and mud with straw-thatched roofs were built close together. All roads but the main one were muddy, and everywhere walked poorly dressed people, particularly the children, who wore scraps of different materials. Some brown, heavy clothes Martha and Kate identified as being made out of GI blankets. Nearly all Korean girls of about ten years and up were carrying a smaller brother or sister on their backs.

Kate remarked, "At least when I baby-sat for Jimmy, I didn't have to carry him around on my back."

"By the way, Kate," Martha said calmly, "a friend, or rather a friend of a friend, is bringing a little Korean boy for lunch at the hotel tomorrow. Her name is Miss Yang."

"*Miss* Yang? Not her son, I hope?" Kate laughed.

"No. The little boy lives in an orphanage. Miss Yang is like a godmother to him, like Aunt Sally."

Kate said, "And not like our Aunt Sally, I hope?"

Martha laughed. "Quite different. That reminds me, I better write Sally."

Kate remembered, "Speaking of reminding *reminds* me. I forgot to tell you, that kind Japanese doctor, the one who paid for all the taxis, called yesterday to see how we were. Wasn't that nice?"

Martha said, "My, that was very thoughtful."

Suddenly they felt a lurch. Cursing, the driver opened the car door. The car was stalled in thick mud. Upon seeing what had happened, the chauffeur began mumbling something under his breath. He tried unsuccessfully to budge the car as the sticky slush oozed from behind the rear wheels. "I go for help," he soon announced. Opening the windows, he left Martha and Kate marooned in the hot, muggy interior of the car as he walked off toward the nearest village.

Martha said, "Your father used to write how hot and uncomfortable it was, but who could imagine 7,000 miles away what it was really like? This isn't even a small taste of it."

Kate and Martha began slapping at the mosquitoes that thrived in the heat. "The Korean kind sure grow big," Kate said. Large welts were appearing on the exposed areas of her arms and legs.

"Look at your arms. I know it's hot, but you better put on your sweater."

Kate, fretful and unhappy, said, "Wouldn't it be great if our nice Japanese Lochinvar came by on a white steed to rescue us?"

"A Greyhound bus would be more comfortable than a white steed," Martha replied.

But no one came. Their discomfort was acute. They were both dripping-wet and covered with mosquito bites. At length an old truck rambled up. Their chauffeur jumped down from the cab. In a short time their car was pulled out of the mud and on the road again. Martha asked the chauffeur how much she owed the truckdriver. The chauffeur translated the question, but the truckdriver shook his head and gestured an emphatic "No."

Their driver said, "He no charge American. They help during war. He glad now to help."

When Martha opened her purse to give him some money anyway, their chauffeur shook his head sternly. "No! No! No! He want to help."

Seeing a package of cigarettes in her purse, she offered that. The truckdriver accepted it, grinning, and bowing many times.

The following day Miss Yang brought Johnny Kim to the hotel. He was dressed immaculately in a little dark suit, quite outgrown but clean. His straight black hair was combed; his face was scrubbed. Martha could scarcely resist squeezing him. Kate, too, was captivated, particularly by his eyes, which grew wide as saucers when he got two dishes of ice cream for dessert.

Miss Yang was quiet but so gentle and kind that Kate was won over completely. The nurse was concerned about the mosquito bites on Kate's arms and legs, which were more swollen than Martha's. She insisted on ordering baking soda from the kitchen, which she applied to the sores.

While Kate happily showed Johnny about the hotel, Martha and Miss Yang talked. Martha said, "I've fallen in love with Johnny. He's a precious little boy." She paused. "Miss Yang, whatever I can do for Johnny, I will."

Miss Yang hesitated. "If you ever hear about American family who wish adopt Korean child, you keep Johnny in mind, please? It is mostly chance now that child adopted. I love Johnny Kim very much as like he were my baby. I hate to lose him to America, but I think also of his future. He is American as much as he is Korean. But he has no future, no big future in Korea. Maybe in America."

"Tell me what he will need, Miss Yang. I'll send as much as you feel he needs."

Miss Yang said softly, "You are very kind and wonderful. But there are other things. Johnny is alone. He must leave the orphanage when he is still young. To go where? To do what? You see, Korea is still in afterward of terrible, terrible war. Jobs are not many. No big factories left. Someday, not soon.

"And," she continued, "Johnny has great, great problem. He is only one-half Korea. America part shows in his eyes. Korean people now do not like Americans, even though they come to help us. They do not like American soldiers because of what they did—make children."

Miss Yang saw the expression in Martha's face. "Please, please, Mrs. Montgomery. I did not mean. . . ." She stopped. "Your hus . . . Johnny's father . . . and Fay. No. I meant those soldiers who only cared for a good time, not love." She stopped abruptly, as she realized she was saying the wrong words.

"I understand, Miss Yang, what you are saying." Martha marveled at the control in her voice, in contrast to the turbulence she was feeling.

"Korea filled with orphans running the streets. Johnny is not one of them. But Fay wanted him to have good future. So I."

"We all do," Martha said. "Perhaps there will be an American family when I get back. I'll see."

"I love Johnny Kim, but I want him to have good home."

After Miss Yang and Johnny left, Kate insisted upon talking about the boy. "Don't laugh, Mom, but you'll never guess who he reminded me of—Jimmy, our Jimmy. There was something about him. Or maybe I'm just homesick."

Martha tried to keep her voice under control as she said, "All little boys have a great deal in common, Kate, regardless of the color of their skin or their features."

Kate continued, "But his eyes, they were so round!"

Suddenly a thought came to her. "Mom, do you think, could it be that Johnny's father was an American?"

Martha hoped her pause was not too revealing. "Why, I don't know. It certainly could be possible. There are many Korean children whose fathers were American soldiers."

Kate was emphatic. "I think it's awful for people of different races to fall in love."

Martha said slowly, "I suppose they are lonely . . . and need each other."

Kate said, "Well, I, for one, don't approve. When you see those peasant villages we saw yesterday, the people don't have anything in common with us. It's another world, and I don't see how we can accept each other."

Martha said, "Love and affection recognize no color. Frankly, Kate, you and I don't know what we would do if we were put in such a spot. I don't think we can judge."

Her daughter replied, "It's just a matter of self-control, after all. And having a sense of pride for your family and all. Just suppose, for example, how out of place Johnny would be at our Sunday dinner. I'm certainly glad Daddy was like he was."

"How is that, Kate?" Martha tried to sound casual.

"Well, I remember the time Jimmy and I wanted that cute little multicolored poodle, so tiny and white with little black ears? We wanted him so badly, but Daddy said one should buy only thoroughbreds. He said all others were misfits."

Martha felt herself getting angry. "Kate, you are still very young. How dare you compare a precious little boy like Johnny to an animal?"

"Gosh, Mom, don't get so mad. I think Johnny's adorable."

The phone rang. "Who knows us here, way out in Seoul." Kate hurried to get it. "Oh, hello, Dr. Tanaka. How are you? Yes, she's here now. I'll call her."

Martha went to the phone and said hello to Dr. Tanaka.

"We missed each other by seconds at the Chosen Hospital," Dr. Tanaka said. "I was worried when I saw you. I hope nothing is wrong."

"I was visiting a friend, Miss Yang, who is a nurse there," Martha replied.

"Look, I've got a few extra minutes. Could you and Kate meet me for a cup of tea downstairs?"

"I'd be delighted. Thank you."

They arranged to meet in front of the elevators. Kate begged off, as she had some post cards to write, and she was feeling tired.

Dr. Tanaka was waiting for her. He towered above the others. They went to a small table in a corner of the dining room. Dr. Tanaka smiled. "You told me to drop in on you in Indiana but that's a big state. I need better directions. Is your home on the banks of the Wabash?"

"No, the other part of the state. I'm from Springfield. I'm sure you've never heard of it."

"Wait, wait. Springfield, that's not where Lincoln was from. That was Springfield, Illinois," he said.

"You know your American history very well."

"I should," he replied. "I had most of my education in the States. Tell me, what are you two doing in Korea, in Seoul?"

Martha explained as simply as she could. "My husband was stationed here during the Korean War. We had planned to come, he and I, before he died. I just decided to fulfill one of his wishes. He was very anxious to take the trip."

The doctor interrupted her, "You're a widow."

She nodded. "A little more than a year."

"I'm sorry. You and Kate are really, well, I'll say brave to come here. Someday this will be a tourist attraction like other cities, like Hong Kong, but that's a few years hence."

"Maybe I'm more foolhardy than brave," Martha replied.

The doctor's years of taking case histories from patients told him she was not telling the whole story, and he quickly changed the subject.

Their brief visit was soon over. He made no mention of seeing her again when Martha said good-bye.

As she walked down the corridor toward her room, she felt an overpowering sense of loneliness, of aloneness.

CHAPTER III

Disturbed by the impact of the Korean trip, Martha, with no objections from Kate, decided to leave Seoul several days ahead of schedule. They were both anxious to return to Tokyo. Once back at the Imperial Hotel, Martha and Kate felt they belonged to a world they could at least recognize. Kate's first mission was to seek out the "Lost and Found," where she discovered her bulging purse intact.

Remembering their motor trip through the Korean countryside, Martha said, "Hereafter we shall join a group of tourists. If we're going to be stuck in the mud, at least we'll have company."

Leaving a call to be awakened early in the morning, Martha woke up, dressed and then tried to arouse Kate, who sleepily wanted just a few minutes more. Martha told her they had a wonderful tour planned for the day: the Imperial Palace with its willow-fringed moats, the Diet Building, the Meeiji Shrine, lunch at the Chinzano Restaurant. Martha read off the alluring details from the tourist folder.

Kate slowly got out of bed and started to dress. She looked peaked. Her mother suggested postponing the trip, but Kate laughed as she said if she were going to write any more letters home, she'd have to see something new to write about. She'd already covered Seoul.

Martha and Kate climbed into the large sight-seeing bus and found a friendly, older couple across the aisle. The elderly gentleman said he was from Washington State, adding, "All my life I've watched the sun set in the Pacific, and all my life I promised myself to follow that sun before my own sets. And here we are."

His wife volunteered this was the first step in her husband's retirement, and although she would rather have gone to Virginia to visit the grandchildren, here she was too.

The tour director in his Japanese pidgin English, exaggerated for effect, described the buildings as they passed. He pointed out the famous Library of Tokyo, explaining that not only are the Japanese the most well-read people, but also the cleanest, since they must wash their hands with water and disinfectant before they can read books.

Martha laughed. "A good idea for some of your friends, Kate." But Kate sat rather tensely.

The guide continued, "We pass through Ginza, main shopping center. They clean you here too—your wallets, pocketbooks. So much to buy, poor husbands can't carry all home. Ladees, you see silks, you buy Haori—that is coat worn over Kimono. Porcelain, first ceramic came from Korea."

Martha nudged Kate. "Maybe we better go back to Seoul." Kate smiled wanly.

The bus stopped as the guide in stentorian tones explained, "Imperial Palace, center of city, moat built in Seventeenth Century. People used to bow low. Now *demokuraru* not to bow. We get out here. Camera fans, you up your alley. One word caution: Don't fish in moat. Sign says, 'Love the Fish.'" The tourists filed out of the bus and started walking around. The camera enthusiasts were immediately busy.

"Wouldn't you know?" Martha said to Kate. "I left our camera at the hotel."

But Kate didn't answer. Looking at her, Martha was startled to see how pale her daughter looked. She saw a nearby bench and took Kate by the hand. "What's wrong, Katie?"

Kate shook her head. "I don't know, Mom. I feel awful."

Martha put her hand on the girl's forehead. "You are warm. We'll get a taxi back to the hotel. We can go on the tour another day."

Kate started to get up. "I'll be all right." But she quickly sat down again.

Martha said, "We'll wait near the bus for a taxi. I'll tell

the driver. We don't want the guide to think we're lost in the wilds of the Imperial Palace." Kate didn't smile.

At that moment the elderly gentleman came back. He said jovially, "Say, I missed you girls. No gold-bricking so early in the tour." Upon looking at Kate more closely, he asked, "What's the matter, young lady? Too much sake?"

Kate replied, "Maybe not enough."

He said, "That's the spirit—pardon the pun." He sat down on the bench next to Kate. "Let me take a good look at you." He looked at Kate's eyes, felt her pulse. Turning to Martha, he said, "I think you better take Junior Miss home and put her to bed for the rest of the day."

Martha said, "That's a mighty professional look you gave her, Doctor. Am I right?"

He grinned. "Sssh. I'm retired."

His wife came up, saying, "I just had an idea where you were."

Martha said, "Your husband is very kind."

His wife smiled. "Kind? He's been bored the entire trip. No children to look after. He's been a pediatrician since they invented the word. He whispered to me your youngster looked kind of peaked."

Martha, putting her arm around Kate, said, "We'll get a taxi and go right back to the Imperial."

The doctor nodded. "Good idea. Take it easy; take it light. Keep her in bed."

In the hotel room Martha put Kate to bed. She took her temperature and found it to be over a hundred. In a low voice Kate asked her mother to turn the light off. Her eyes hurt.

The phone rang. Martha answered to hear the jovial voice of the doctor. "Remember me—Doc Stevens from the bus? I'm in the lobby. Mind if my wife and I come up?"

Martha was dumbfounded. "But the tour?"

Dr. Stevens chuckled. "Got bored seeing fancy little parks with fancy little trees and little bridges. We're on our way up."

In a moment Dr. Stevens, carrying a stethoscope and a small flashlight, walked into the room. Mrs. Stevens followed him. She nodded toward her husband. "Frankly, my dear, he was just itching to get back here."

Dr. Stevens sat on the edge of Kate's bed, looking at her out of the corner of his eye while he talked. "Well, see one Buddha statue, see them all. How's my friend here?"

"How . . . how did you know our names, where we were staying?" Martha asked.

Mrs. Stevens smiled. "Dr. Josh asked the tour guide. He had a list of the herd."

Meanwhile Dr. Stevens was examining Kate, completely checking her throat, eyes, glands and pulse. Gently he lifted her head and tried to move it back and forth. Her neck was rigid, but Martha was unaware of the condition. Dr. Stevens stood up. "Mrs. Montgomery, I really can't practice medicine here in Japan. I think you should call in somebody who can. Do you have any doctor here in Tokyo to call?"

Martha shook her head. "No one."

Kate said in a low voice, "You know Dr. Tanaka."

Martha smiled. "I don't even know if he lives in Japan, much less Tokyo. He's another very kind doctor we met briefly in Korea."

Dr. Stevens asked, "You came from Korea? How'd you like it?"

Martha replied, "Well, it isn't like Japan at all. At least not Tokyo. It's older, less Western and terribly poor." Then she asked intently, "Doctor, what do you think it is with Kate?"

Dr. Stevens was rummaging in his pocket. "Hard to say. Maybe flu bug. We doctors usually call it that till we know it isn't." He opened a small booklet and rifled the pages. "Tokyo, Tokyo. I like to carry this around, medical directory." He smiled. "What do you know? Here's a gent I used to meet at coast meetings of the AMA, a Japanese doctor. About my age. If he's still living and practicing, well, we'll soon find out." He went over to the phone. He asked the operator to get him Dr. Nishimura at the address indicated in his directory. He turned to Martha and asked, "Kate had polio shots?"

"All five of them," she answered.

In a moment Dr. Stevens was connected with Dr. Nishimura's office. He spoke to the nurse, then nodded his head at Martha. "Still living, all right. Even practicing."

Briefly, he told the nurse, who spoke excellent English, that he wished to talk to Dr. Nishimura. "An old friend from America calling. Dr. Josh Stevens, from Washington State." After a pause Dr. Stevens began shouting greetings. Obviously Dr. Nishimura was on the phone.

Mrs. Stevens said, "They have phones here in Tokyo, Josh."

Ignoring her, Doc Stevens continued talking in a loud but jovial voice. "Yep, she's with me. Still telling me to shut up. Say, Dr. Nishimura, I have a little sick friend here at the Imperial Hotel. She and her mother are traveling alone. Just came over from Korea yesterday. Probably picked up a bug or two. Can you drop in and see her? I don't have a hunting license for Japan. Ask for me—Room 235." After a second he added, "Thanks. I'll see you." After he had hung up the phone, he told Martha that Dr. Nishimura would be over shortly. They'd meet him in their own room. Taking his wife by the arm, he went to the door. "Come on, Ma. Kate'll be wanting to doze off. Be seeing you in a while, Mrs. Montgomery. You'll be in good hands with Dr. Nishimura. He's not got a whizz-bang of a personality, but he's competent all right."

In their own room Josh told his wife, "That's a pretty sick little girl, Ma. I hope Nishimura caught on when I said 'Korea.' That's when I really got scared."

"Why Korea, Josh?" his wife asked.

"Well, according to the papers, they've been having quite an epidemic of encephalitis—sleeping sickness—in Korea this summer."

CHAPTER IV

Martha scarcely had the time or desire to look around the wonderfully clean hospital room with its Western-style furnishings, old and outmoded by modern standards, but spotless and worn with constant scrubbing. Later Martha found out that the hospital was one of several international institutions. This one, called St. Thomas, was founded by American missionaries but now was staffed completely by Japanese. She also discovered that Kate had one of the limited number of private rooms, since most patients were in wards of twelve beds. But upon her arrival with Dr. and Mrs. Stevens in a taxi, which had followed the ambulance to the hospital, Martha was only concerned that Kate was being well-cared for. One competent Japanese nurse after another tiptoed in to administer to Kate.

Dr. Nishimura, an elderly Japanese with exquisitely polite manner and quiet demeanor, spoke to Dr. Stevens out of deference to him. In turn, Dr. Stevens addressed Martha. "Dr. Nishimura says he would like to take a few laboratory tests, if you give permission."

Martha, dazed, said, "Whatever Dr. Nishimura and you think advisable."

Dr. Stevens grinned. "Already given permission for you." Then, hustling Martha out the door of Kate's room, where Mrs. Stevens was patiently waiting, Dr. Stevens said, "You two girls wait around the corner somewhere. Can't have visitors taking up all the oxygen in a sickroom."

Mrs. Stevens, with her usual competency, had discovered a quiet alcove and now led Martha by the arm in the direction of the small room used for scales and other nonantiseptic equipment. From somewhere she had one of the nurses produce a couple of straight-back chairs. "Not exactly overstuffed, are they?" Mrs. Stevens drew up one for Martha. "But I found out the sitting room for friends is on the main floor, and I figured you'd rather be uncomfortable up here."

Martha nodded.

The nurses were busy for the following several hours. Dr. Nishimura ordered a lumbar puncture, which a younger doctor in conventional green surgical gown administered. Meanwhile competent nurses took blood tests. Dr. Stevens watched them closely. "These nurses have either got mighty good training, or else they're mighty smart." He nodded. "See how quick they get to the veins, almost without a pause."

At six o'clock in the evening Dr. Stevens and Dr. Nishimura both came up to Martha. A nurse's aide had brought Martha and Mrs. Stevens a small tray with a teapot and two cups and saucers. But Martha merely held hers in her hand, Dr. Stevens spoke. "I'm going to let Dr. Nishimura here tell you in his fancy terms. Then I'll fill in."

Dr. Nishimura bowed slightly, and then in his beautifully modulated voice said, "Mrs. Montgomery, I feel a woman as intelligent as yourself would like to know the truth. Your daughter has a virus that we call encephalitis. Sometimes it is more popularly called 'sleeping sickness.'"

Martha could hardly believe what she heard. "My God! How? Where?"

Dr. Nishimura continued, "That is not of importance. I would like to call in a colleague who is an expert in this disease—one of the world authorities—if I have your permission. I feel my own knowledge is too limited."

Martha was numb as she said, "Please call him as soon as possible."

Mrs. Stevens pulled Josh to one side. "Josh, see if you can get Martha a room. And give her a sedative."

Over Martha's protests that she wanted to stay with her daughter, Mrs. Stevens and Josh reasoned with her that she must eat something and rest for an hour. Martha castigated herself. "The family, back home. They were right. I shouldn't have come. This is my fault. Kate will get well. She will get well, won't she?"

Mrs. Stevens soothed her, "Of course, she will. Kate will

be in the best medical hands. The way you can help right now is to get some rest."

Dr. Nishimura told Dr. Stevens as they proceeded to the doctors' reception lounge on the main floor, "I hope Dr. Tanaka is in the city. He travels a great deal."

"What do you think, Dr. Nishimura?" Josh asked. "Kate pretty sick?" Dr. Nishimura nodded his head.

Kate was in a comatose condition when Dr. Tanaka, with Dr. Nishimura and Dr. Stevens, came in. Dr. Tanaka looked at her. "Why, I know this child. She's traveling with her mother. I ran into them in Korea." He spoke softly to Kate as he sat on the edge of the bed. "Hello, Kate." There was no answer or recognition. He rubbed her chest to stimulate a response.

Kate opened her eyes slowly. "Hello . . . Dr. Tanaka. Are you . . . in Japan?"

He laughed softly. "Very much so, fortunately." But Kate had dropped off to sleep. Dr. Tanaka picked up one of her arms and examined it. Then he looked at the other one.

Dr. Nishimura volunteered, "She has mosquito bites on her legs too."

Dr. Tanaka turned her arms over. "How could she possibly have got all these if they just stayed in Seoul? They've cleaned up the breeding place of mosquitoes."

Dr. Stevens replied, "I can guess these two girls didn't miss a thing."

Dr. Tanaka added, "Unfortunately." Then he examined Kate more thoroughly. "There's been quite an epidemic in Korea; that's why I flew over there. A little different course, more acute onset, shorter period of incubation, abrupt rise in temperature, a different form of encephalitis than the lethargico, or 'sleeping sickness.' We call this type Japanese B. Curiously, much of the population in Korea and China are immune. They have built-in antibodies. But with the repatriation of so many who've lived in Japan, there's quite an epidemic this summer."

"Wars, politics, viruses go together," Dr. Nishimura said softly.

Dr. Tanaka nodded. Then he spoke gently to Kate. "Open your eyes, Kate. Look at this light." He held a pen light, moving it in front of her. Kate did not open her eyes. He spoke in a louder tone, but she did not respond. Again he rubbed the center of her chest gently with round motions to stimulate her. The girl opened her eyes, but closed them almost immediately. Dr. Tanaka dictated to the nurse, who took down all he said, "Pupils react sluggishly to light." He examined her neck, felt the muscle, moved it gently back and forth. "Rigidity of neck." Running his hand deftly over her body, he continued dictating, "Absence of abdominal reflexes." Then, as he felt her limbs, he added. "Rigidity of upper extremities."

He walked to the end of the bed, took a key ring from his pocket and, selecting a key, ran it along the sole of first the right foot, then the left, as one might draw a line down a piece of paper. Kate's toes curled down. The doctors were pleased. Dr. Tanaka took the chart from the nurse and read it over quickly at first, then turned back a page and reread, "I'm glad you've done a spinal already. Kate's fortunate to have had such prompt and expert care."

Dr. Nishimura bowed, then, nodding to Dr. Stevens, he said, "My colleague alerted me even over the telephone."

Dr. Stevens breathed deeply. "I dunno, that sudden onset, rigidity of the neck, ocular disturbance—I didn't like it. Felt we better call in somebody connected with a hospital here. Then when the mother said they had just returned from Korea, that really threw me." Dr. Stevens took out a handkerchief and wiped his nose. "I read on the plane coming over, there was an epidemic in Korea this summer."

"You were right on the ball—isn't that the expression?" Dr. Tanaka asked.

Dr. Stevens nodded, then he asked, "Any connection between the cell count and the prognosis of the disease?"

Dr. Tanaka shook his head. "Curiously, we have discovered there is no relationship between the two. Recovery is possible with a higher count, or fatality with a lower. According to this spinal report, there's been some minute hemorrhaging, traces of fresh blood, not unusual." He then spoke in Japanese to one of the nurses, then turning to Dr. Stevens, he said, "I've ordered an IV—she won't be able to take nourishment—and also a catheter. We don't want the bladder playing tricks. Besides, we can keep a measurement."

Dr. Stevens shook his head. "Poor baby, poor baby." Then he asked, "No serum for this bug yet?"

"No," Dr. Tanaka answered slowly. "Not yet. We're working on one. We're lucky to have a convalescent serum. I'll start it on Kate later. Meanwhile there isn't much we can do. I find intramuscular injections as effective as intraspinal, and not as much discomfort for the patient."

The two Japanese doctors were discussing various solutions to use, when Dr. Stevens broke in, "Gentlemen, I'll leave the pharmacology to you experts, but we have to tell her mother something. What can we say?"

Dr. Nishimura looked at Dr. Tanaka. Dr. Tanaka spoke slowly, "I know Mrs. Montgomery wouldn't want us to mask the truth, and as a point of fact, what is the truth? No one knows. The next weeks will be critical. After that, if we're lucky, we'll try to lessen the possibility of the development of the chronic state." He paused, then added, "Sometimes damaging psychological condition sets in; sometimes worse. I've seen broken minds, broken bodies, both. But we can't stop trying, because in some instances there is no residual. We can't tell now; we simply can't tell."

Dr. Stevens's sigh was heavy. "In all my years of practice I've never run into an acute case like this."

Dr. Nishimura said, "We've had epidemics before in Japan, but I always call in an expert."

Dr. Stevens's voice was practical. "I wonder if Mrs. Montgomery has any close family back in the States. She's a widow—the expense and all."

Dr. Tanaka replied quickly, "The expense will be the least of her problems. After all, I feel fortunate to be called in at this early stage—diagnosis, prognosis. As far as hospital and nursing services, that won't be much of a burden either. I'll see to it."

Dr. Stevens said, "I like these two girls. They're spunky. Now, my own plans are to shove off in a few days, finish up Japan. My wife's been screaming about seeing Kyoto, Osaka, the rest. Then we plan to see Hong Kong, Bangkok, you know, the works. But I certainly hate to leave a nice little lady alone."

Dr. Tanaka replied earnestly, "Dr. Stevens, I promise you I will do my utmost for them. I know Dr. Nishimura will also. After all, you are strangers also to Mrs. Montgomery and Kate. You could not be expected to alter plans of, I dare say, many months' planning."

"Months? You mean years, a lifetime," Dr. Stevens said. "But if I didn't believe she was in the best hands, I wouldn't budge."

Dr. Tanaka continued, "However, I agree we must speak to the mother. There may be someone—sister, brother, someone—she may want to notify. She could be here for weeks or even months. . . ."

While the doctors were talking outside Kate's room, Martha came up. Mrs. Stevens was holding her arm. Martha was somewhat dazed from the sedative, and when she saw Dr. Tanaka standing there, she could hardly believe her eyes.

Dr. Stevens spoke, "Mrs. Montgomery, looks like our expert is not only about the best authority in the world, but he's also an old acquaintance of yours."

Dr. Tanaka put his hands out, just as Martha grabbed both his arms. "I can't believe this," she managed to utter. "I can't believe it. The one person I could possibly know in all Japan."

Dr. Tanaka said, "I could hardly believe it when I saw Kate was the patient."

Martha looked at him almost pleadingly. "She's sick, isn't she? Desperately sick?"

Dr. Tanaka replied, "I never dissemble to my patients' families. Yes, Kate is very ill now, but I don't think she's in too much discomfort."

Dr. Stevens spoke up, "But looks like you'll have to rearrange some of those sightseeing plans for a while—postpone events and change your reservations. I can take care of the details if you'll give me your itinerary."

Martha, almost not hearing, looked up at Dr. Tanaka. "How long will she be hospitalized?"

He shook his head. "I couldn't even attempt an answer. Sometimes several weeks, sometimes several months."

In an almost inaudible voice Martha said, "Sometimes—"

Dr. Stevens cut in, "Sometimes measles can throw a child for a loop."

Dr. Tanaka added, "As a matter of fact, Mrs. Montgomery, encephalitis occasionally accompanies or follows measles, scarlet fever, whooping cough, even chicken pox. The word *encephalitis* is frightening, because not too much is known about it or its prevention. It takes various forms: Kate has one kind, which is an epidemic encephalitis. Korea had an epidemic this summer. One time St. Louis had it—1933, I believe. Certain sections of the West, New England. Now, I suggest since Kate is comfortable, you go back to the hotel to rest."

Martha shook her head. "I couldn't. I wouldn't leave. But perhaps I should send a cable home to say our plans have changed."

In spite of the excellent nursing care given to Kate, Martha refused to leave the hospital room. When she first saw Kate, lying rigid, with the holder for the intravenous beside the bed, the transparent tube leading to Kate's almost childlike hand, and then when she saw the plastic bag attached to the other side of the bed for the tube of the catheter to drain into, Martha wanted to cry out, grab Kate and run with her from the room. Martha had often seen such equipment when she had visited a hospitalized member of the family, and in a group as large as the clan at home, some member always seemed to be recovering from some surgery. But those patients were older. This was a child, her child.

Kate's face was pallid. The healthy-looking suntan had already begun to fade since they had been away. Now her face was colorless, even the lips were thin, drained of any coloration. As she looked at Kate, Martha noticed the only movement in the child's face was an occasional involuntary twitching of her lips, which Dr. Tanaka had explained was one of the symptoms. Sometimes in the illness, he had explained, the whole body convulsed, but with Kate, her body was almost immobile. The girl's blond hair was tousled and matted. The saucy ponytail, no longer confined, hung stringlike around her face. Sensing Martha's reactions, the nurse gently moved Kate's hair away from her face. "Later we fix it." She smiled sweetly at Martha, who, at that time, did not consider it unusual that the nurse spoke English. She was to find out that Dr. Tanaka had combed the hospital for English-speaking nurses.

Martha sat in the darkened room. She had no idea of the passage of time, nor were her thoughts even distinct. She was numb, almost as catatonic as her child.

At midnight Dr. Tanaka came in to check over Kate for the second time that evening. He gave the nurse some instructions in Japanese and then asked Martha to join him in the doctor's lounge for a cup of tea. Martha looked toward the bed. She started to protest that she was quite all right.

"Kate is fine, Mrs. Montgomery, I can assure you. Besides, we won't be more than a few steps away."

Martha nodded her head and rose to follow him. Just before leaving the room, she looked back at the bed, but Kate had not changed her position.

"Mrs. Montgomery, Kate will be exactly like that for some time to come, except when the nurses turn her." Martha couldn't answer.

The lounge was a combination of Japanese decor and Western comfort. A nurse's aide brought in the tea tray and slivers of buttered bread. "At home it's called a coffee break, is it not?"

Martha nodded. Suddenly she said, "I can't believe that of all the people in Japan, it should be you—the only person we've ever seen before—out of all these millions of people."

"Westerners call it coincidence of travel, or small-world department, I believe. In the Orient we are inclined to think differently." Dr. Tanaka refilled the teacup.

"I cabled the family," Martha said. "I didn't trust myself to phone. I was afraid I couldn't handle that."

"True. You can say less more emphatically in a cable." He paused. "Tell me about the family. Is it your family? Your close family, what?"

Martha smiled. "I guess another name would be 'clan,' since there is Scotch ancestry—Scotch and English. I couldn't say 'tribe.' But it's a family of aunts, uncles, cousins of all ages, a closely knit group. It was originally Paul's family, but it is mine now too. They accepted me from the very first time Paul introduced me to them."

"Smart clan." He smiled.

"Thank you. I have no parents. They died while I was growing up. The family are truly wonderful, wonderful people, loving, kind, but opinionated. Very. They have great security not only of wealth and position but in the support of each other in a crisis. Almost all of them opposed this trip. They wanted me to go to Europe. They were right."

He looked at her. "Who can say what is right?"

Martha was silent for a moment, as if her thoughts were in a hundred different directions. Suddenly she asked, "Doctor, there was a little boy, a ward of Miss Yang. He was visiting us at the hotel, playing with Kate. Could he catch this?"

He shook his head. "No, it is not infectious in that sense of the word, nor even contagious. Nor is everyone susceptible to the disease. It's tricky. Maybe that's why it's always interested me."

"How long have you been working with . . . with this awful disease?"

He shrugged. "Since the war, the prisoner-of-war camps."

"Oh, I see." A chill ran through her. He might have been in charge of a prison camp where Paul could have been interned. Those dreadful stories of Japanese prison camps Paul used to relate always made her shudder.

Dr. Tanaka continued in prosaic tones, "I wondered why one man would get it. The next one would not. Both lived under the same conditions, the same approximate state of health—or ill health, I should say—the same lack of nutrition."

"But if it's not infectious or contagious, how is it transmitted?"

Dr. Tanaka offered her a cigarette, lit hers, then one for himself. "We feel it's carried by wild birds and, in turn, by mosquitoes."

Martha turned white. "Mosquitoes? Kate was badly bitten!"

Dr. Tanaka said, "Yes, I know. I was surprised to see

the bites. I thought the mosquitoes had been cleaned out in Seoul . . . the virulent variety at least."

With tortured voice she told him about the drive in the countryside, being marooned in the swamp, how Kate wished Dr. Tanaka—their official rescuer—would come along on a white steed, or a Greyhound bus. Martha finally broke down, as she felt it was in every sense her fault. She should never have taken the motor trip in the country.

Dr. Tanaka crossed over to the other side of the small tea table. He took her arm gently. "Please, Mrs. Montgomery, you must not crucify yourself like this. It is not your fault for coming to the Orient, Korea, instead of Lake Como, for taking the drive outside Seoul. If one had the power to foresee what an action would bring and then act accordingly, there would only be a vacuum in the world. Few actions are altogether good or bad. But I know you will not believe me." He sat down again. Martha stared straight ahead without speaking.

CHAPTER V.

At breakfast, at dinner Sally and David Fletcher talked about Martha. Sally read aloud the letters and cards received from Martha and Kate. But David did not tell Sally about the mail he was receiving at the office, in which Martha described her meetings with Johnny Kim and her pronounced reactions to the child.

David was already in court the morning Sally received the cable announcing Kate's illness. There was no way of reaching him until noon recess, when he would check in with his office.

It was early afternoon when David received the news: Kate was ill and hospitalized. He immediately put in a call to Tokyo for Martha. He tried the hotel; he was advised she was at the Hospital St. Thomas.

The waiting between connections was trying. As he reported to Sally later, all he seemed to get was "Moshi-Moshi," whatever that was, and there was far too much of it. At last he heard Martha's voice. She was in a noisy reception room. The whole phone call was must unsatisfactory. But however faulty the connection, however far the distance between them he knew Martha was in trouble. He told her that he was in court on a case, but that he was asking for a continuance so he could fly out to her. In spite of her protestations he insisted he would come, if only for a few days. He added that he would suggest that Sally accompany him, but the twins were ill, and Sally was recovering from a bad case of the flu.

As soon as the court reconvened for the afternoon session, he asked the judge for a continuance. The judge was most sympathetic, but the final decision, of course, rested with the opposing counsel. David spoke to the other attorney. Eager as he was to accommodate David, he explained there were witnesses coming from Washington, D.C., who had rearranged busy schedules. David pleaded for just a few days recess to take care of an urgent matter in Japan. The lawyer agreed for a continuance. As the opposing attorney said later, "Anyone as desperate as Dave Fletcher was to go couldn't be refused. I wouldn't want it on my conscience."

Rereading the cable announcing David's arrival, Martha had an eerie feeling that it could not be real. It did not seem possible that David Fletcher, emissary from her life at home, would soon be with her. He was part of another world, a secure world. At the time of Paul's death, there were comforting friends and relatives. Now she felt suspended in time and space. Day had no beginning; night, no ending. There was only a blending of one into the other. What was it Kate had said when she'd crossed the international date line? How can one live and breathe and still not have it count on the calendar as a day lived?

For the first night and day, Martha had remained at the hospital, dozing off to sleep at infrequent intervals. Then, when Dr. Stevens and his wife had pointed out that she was doing Kate no real good and only injuring her own health, particularly at a moment when she must keep going, she'd agreed to return to the hotel for a few hours' sleep at night.

She had worked into a routine of arriving at the hospital early in the morning, leaving late at night to return to the hotel for a night's sleep, however short the duration. In this manner she was able to shower and put on clean clothes at the hotel.

She had asked Dr. Stevens if there was any possible way to take Kate home. He had questioned Dr. Tanaka and Dr. Nishimura, and both had agreed it could be fatal to move the child. She needed the constant supervision available only in a hospital—the suction tubes, oxygen, blood tests and chemistry, urinalysis. Dr. Stevens had inquired himself if a ship's hospital could provide the necessary care, since many of the boats now carried completely equipped hospitals even for the most difficult surgery, but with a disease like encephalitis, no ship would accept her.

In the final analysis Martha realized she had no choice but to stay in Tokyo and to try to maintain a semblance of self-control. She experienced, in fact, a kind of hypnosis induced by the routine of her now-contracted living. She felt she was a donkey working in a mine deep under the ground, following a circular path. Her path led from the hospital to the hotel and back again.

Somehow she managed to say the right things. She urged Dr. Stevens and his wife to continue their trip. She explained that her devoted friend, her husband's cousin, was flying to Tokyo. She did not tell them it was only for a few days. She knew that out of the pure goodness of their nature, they had already pared several stops from their itinerary.

Dr. Stevens and his wife came by the hospital on their way to the airport. Martha realized it was considerably out of their way and required an extra hour at least to fight the additional traffic. Dr. Stevens handed her a page on which he had written their itinerary, making her promise that if she needed them, just phone.

Deeply touched, Martha threw her arms around Mrs. Stevens. Then she kissed them both. "No one has ever been kinder than you two. Bless you both."

Dr. Stevens patted her on the shoulder. "My dear woman, I always said in pediatrics that the only bad part of the practice was the mothers. Believe me, in all my years I've never seen a pluckier one—or one more intelligent about the whole thing."

Martha shrugged. "What else is there to do?"

Dr. Stevens replied, "I dunno, but some of those damn fool women I knew coulda thought of something." Then they were gone. Martha felt her own heart descend with the elevator arrow as she stood in front of the elevator door.

Mariko Ikeda, a tiny nurse who spoke English and who had been speaking to Martha as they would pass in the halls, came up to her. "Montgomery-san, may I offer you a cup of tea, perhaps?"

Martha shook her head. "Thank you very much, but I think not. I . . . I'm quite all right."

The little nurse bowed her head and then looked up at Martha. "Montgomery-san, everybody admire you very much. You are so brave, with your little girl so sick so far from home."

Martha touched the white sleeve of the nurse. "I'm not really brave, Mariko, not really. But all of you in the hospital are so kind and thoughtful, I can't burden you more." Not understanding every word, but comprehending the general tone, Mariko bowed low and hurried off, wiping away her own tears for Montgomery-san and her daughter.

Martha meant it when she said she was not being brave, she was merely numb. Whatever she said or did was a reflex action left over from a more tranquil period of her life. She had tried sometimes in the hotel room to recall her reactions when Paul had died. She had been dazed then, stricken, but in normal surroundings and encircled by the love and devotion of friends and family. She had been able to carry on. Whatever nuisance the family was in normal times, in periods of tragedy their combined love was like a blanket protecting the sufferer. Now she felt she was on the edge of an abyss, looking into a bottomless pit that could magnetize her to leap into it; yet she knew she must keep her balance for Kate's sake.

Martha was particularly concerned several evenings later at Dr. Tanaka's unexpected return to Kate's room. He had been there just an hour before, and, except for the first few critical days, he rarely returned to the room within such a brief period of time. Martha looked anxiously at the bed. Kate was asleep, in the same motionless coma. The intravenous had been replaced by feedings through the nostril, since Dr. Tanka had explained a week or so before that they felt she must receive more-solid nourishment, and it was impossible to feed her by mouth. Martha had even grown accustomed to the sight, so frightening at first.

Seeing Martha's apprehension, Dr. Tanaka quickly reassured her this visit was nonprofessional. He had just remembered the date, and he had something of interest to show her. At her reluctance to leave the room, he added that she wouldn't have to step outside the hospital.

Taking her by the arm, he guided Martha to the elevator and then, to her amazement, to a roof garden, she did not even know existed on top of the hospital. On one side was a parklike garden with miniature pine trees, dwarf cypress and a small arched bridge over a tiny pool made of sand, not water. In another corner of the roof was a small Shinto shrine. Dr. Tanaka explained the small shrine was often found on the roofs of many department stores and buildings. Originally, since the hospital had been founded by missionaries, there was no such shrine. But over the years, since the hospital had become completely Japanese, the shrine, replica of a larger and ancient one, had been built. In the case of the hospital, families came up to pray for the recovery of their ill relatives.

Martha saw a Japanese family approach the shrine. The woman clapped her hands. Dr. Tanka informed Martha that this was to get the attention of the gods. Then the woman struck a gong. The man opened a colored *furoshiki*, a cloth for carrying packages, and took out some seeds and plants—sacrificial offerings.

Dr. Tanaka led Martha to the far side of the building. There in the distance she saw a spectacular fireworks display. He explained this was the Grand Fireworks Display on the Sumida River in celebration of the opening of the river in summer. Many leading firework manufacturers participate. He gave her a pair of binoculars through which she could see the thousands of people on the embankment of the river, watching the show. "It's too bad we could not visit one of the restaurants along the river and watch the display. It's one of the highlights of summer," the doctor said.

"Why, it's just like Fourth of July," Martha remarked. "In July and all."

He smiled. "Funny, when we were in the States and used to see the fireworks on the Fourth, my father used to say, 'Ah, just like the opening of the Sumida River.'"

"Does it have the same kind of significance as our celebration?"

"No, but it does date back to the early Eighteenth Century, somewhere in 1730, not too long before American

Independence. The original purpose was to clear the depressing atmosphere brought out by a terrible famine that swept the country, killing thousands of persons." He stopped. "Now, like so many other customs, even Fourth of July, people are apt to lose sight of the origin and remember only the festivities. My father, however, always impressed upon me the importance of the independence of the Fourth."

"You know a great deal about the United States. And you speak English with no accent at all. You once said you were educated in the States." They had walked away from the spectacle, over to a stone bench apart from the shrine, where they sat down.

"I was born in Japan, but I was raised in the United States. My family took me there when I was about three years old. My father was a professor of Oriental languages, and he taught at several American universities. He purposely selected several areas of the country so he and my mother could know the whole of the United States: the South, at the University of North Carolina, some years at the University of California; and then the Midwest, University of Chicago."

"You probably know more about the United Sates than I do," she replied.

"Well, I went through all my schooling in America. I attended the University of Pennsylvania Medical School. As a matter of fact it was debatable whether I would return to Japan at all, but my family wished it. After I interned and took my residency in Chicago, I came back." He started to continue, but was interrupted by a call over the public-address system for one of the doctors. He was silent.

Martha remarked, "What a paradox. A public-address system along with other new, scientific devices, and yet the shrine with the gong sounding just as it did hundreds of years ago."

Dr. Tanaka replied, "Modern Japan often wears a mask to cover its true feelings. In public institutions it brings many problems, the conflict of the old and the new." He paused. "When the conflict comes within a family, the problem is insurmountable." Then he looked at his watch and quickly rose from the bench. Martha knew he was upset, but she wondered what it was he had left unsaid.

Back in her hotel room, for the first time Martha thought of something besides Kate's illness. There was so much about Dr. Tanaka that was American, but there was so much else that was Japanese. Was it this combination of two cultures that made him so different from Paul? He was much more articulate, but at the same time reserved. He had an air and attitude of authority, but he was gentle and caring about Kate. Martha realized she had never known such attentive medical care for a patient . . . and such solicitude for a patient's relative. She felt she probably would have fallen apart had some less considerate doctor been taking care of Kate. In the midst of all the horror she could be thankful they had met Dr. Tanaka.

CHAPTER VI

Martha always remembered the day of David's arrival. Several memorable events occurred that day, events which, upon looking back, Martha felt were peaks if she could have charted the days.

After Dr. Tanaka had introduced her to the peaceful roof garden, she found herseld drawn there, preferring it to the visitors' lounge. During each of the succeeding visits she managed to remain tranquil while viewing the panorama of the city below and on the horizon, and watching families paying homage before the small shrine. Japanese families always seemed to be together, young and old. Martha smiled, wondering if the Irish word for kin, "sib," could be applied to the Japanese. If one member of the family was ill, the whole family crowded the corridor outside the patient's room. She had been told by one of the nurses that in a smaller hospital the families were obliged to take over the nursing care. Some member of the family would literally move in with the patient to provide meals and whatever attention, other than medical, that was required. Now, here at the shrine, the families attended en masse. The family devotion accentuated Martha's aloneness. It was the kind of tribal devotion the family at home would offer, but in a more sophisticated form.

After a particularly difficult night for Kate, Martha went up to the sanctuary of the roof garden. She chose a stone bench a little apart from the others, the one she and Dr. Tanaka had selected the night of the fireworks. She sat down, and suddenly she started to pray. In almost-biblical fashion she offered up a sacrifice: If Kate recovered, she, Martha Montgomery, would take full responsiblity for little

Johnny Kim. She would bring him to America, to her home, where he would assume his position, if not title, as half-brother of Jimmy and Kate. She would give him love and care.

She thought for a brief moment that perhaps Kate's illness had been a punishment for turning her back on the boy. Sending a few dollars each month, as she had promised Helen Yang she would do, was no sacrifice. But by adopting the child, she would help atone for Paul's mistake of having kept him hidden all these years. She realized it was not his infidelity but his deception about the affair, that bothered her. She might have forgiven the liaison, which brought about the birth of the boy, Johnny Kim's existence was pardonable. How could Paul have betrayed Martha, or Johnny Kim by keeping the secret?

Martha was deep in thought when she became aware of a shadow blocking out the sunlight. Looking up, she saw David Fletcher standing there. She could hardly believe her eyes. It was even more incredible that he should arrive at such a tense moment in her own thinking.

David said quietly, "The nurse told me I'd find you up here, Martha."

Without saying a word, Martha rushed into his arms and kissed him, starting to cry at the same time. A Japanese family turned its back in modesty. Martha herself blushed. "I'm afraid I've embarrassed that sweet family. Some Japanese still don't approve of kissing or public display of affection." She hugged his arm. There was so much to say, she could say nothing but cling to him with a tight grasp. Then she stood back to look at him. "David, I . . . I didn't expect you until tomorrow, but, oh, I'm so glad you're here today."

He looked at her, hiding his great concern over her haggard, gaunt appearance. "I took an earlier plane."

"Have you seen Kate?" Martha asked.

David replied that he had just poked his head in the door, and the cutest kind of a nurse had come out and told him, "Montgomery-san on roof garden."

Gaining her composure, Martha brought David up to date on Kate's illness, describing the great and overwhelming kindness of strangers: Dr. Stevens and his wife, and now Dr. Tanaka, who had been devoting himself to Kate. Without him, Kate would not still be breathing.

David in turn told her all was well at home. He had seen Jimmy at Sunday dinner, and he looked particularly well. Grandmere and Aunt Alice were doing their best to spoil him. As for his own immediate tribe, Sally was annoyed she couldn't have come too, but one of the twins had just developed measles, gophers had burrowed into the rose garden, and the main water pipe had burst. David added, smiling, "You know, the usual kind of day for Sally." He did not add that he had discouraged Sally from coming. In such a moment of crisis he could not have endured Sally's too witty banter and biting humor.

They returned to Kate's room. David stood at the foot of her bed, looking down at the comatose figure of the girl, the masklike quality of her face, a characteristic of encephalitis. Kate seemed to move her head. David wanted so desperately to reach across the chasm of unconsciousness that he repeated Kate's name several times, concentrating with all his strength, calling her name, each time a trifle louder. "Kate . . . Kate . . . Kate, dear. Hello. . . ."

Then Kate turned her head in the direction of the voice For a second she tried to focus her eyes on David, but she quickly closed them as if the effort were too much for her. Whether it was the sound of his voice or that brief glance, no one knew. But in almost-inaudible tones Kate said, "Hello, Uncle Dave." Then her voice trailed off, her eyes remained closed, her face impassive. But in that second the nurse was at her side, beaming, shaking her head incredulously.

Martha was too overwhelmed to speak for a second. Then she whispered to David, "This is the first recognition of anyone, anything for days now."

Dr. Tanaka came in within a few minutes. He looked around at the beaming nurse, at Martha crying softly. In answer to his unspoken questions, the little nurse excitedly turned toward him and rapidly spoke in Japanese. Then she looked at David and apologized for speaking Japanese. "It just came out," she said.

Martha, whose tears of joy had subsided for the moment, turned to Dr. Tanaka and introduced him to David. The two men shook hands warmly. David was taller than Dr. Tanaka. By comparison to the other Japanese men whom she had seen in the hospital and in the hotel, Dr. Tanaka had seemed much larger than he actually was. However, when both men stood at the side of the bed, they towered over the tiny nurse, who had to tilt her head up to look up at them. Each man intuitively respected the competency and authority in the other. Each man commanded respect.

While Dr. Tanaka examined Kate, Martha and David waited in the corridor. Martha was still overcome by the miracle of the moment, that Kate should have unhesitatingly recognized David. "You were always Kate's favorite, even though she said you were really an 'un-uncle.'" Martha smiled.

In the room Dr. Tanaka, after giving Kate a neurological examination, found that there was no change in her condition, apart from the second of recognition. She was in a deep coma again.

Later Martha and David met with Dr. Tanaka in the doctors' lounge. A quick glance around showed David that he and Martha were the only Caucasians in the room. Unlike Martha, who by now was not even aware of this fact, David felt an overpowering feeling of sadness and frustration at being so far from home and in so strange an environment.

David questioned Dr. Tanaka as if he were cross-examining a witness. Dr. Tanaka in turn respected this competent and professional approach. He told David that there was no question that Kate's recognition was of the utmost significance. It meant she had powers of speech and of recognition, both visual and auditory. Above all, she had evidenced memory. Looking at David, Dr. Tanaka added, "Where there is recovery, it usually evidences itself within fifteen days." Dr. Tanaka then suggested that he drive David to the Imperial Hotel to check in. Martha excused herself, preferring to remain with Kate in case she should awaken. Dr. Tanaka pointed out gently that Mrs. Montgomery must not be too optimistic or expect too immediate signs of recovery. "We must accept this one episode of recognition and be grateful for it," he said. Eager to talk to Dr. Tanaka without Martha, and feeling from his own long experience of examining witnesses that the doctor had been circumspect in answering him, David welcomed the ride to the hotel.

At the entrance to the hospital Dr. Tanaka called a taxi. "My car is here, but I feel we have much to talk about, and in Tokyo when one drives, one concentrates on the traffic, not on conversation with a friend."

Once in the taxi, Dr. Tanaka offered David a cigarette and then said seriously, "I was quite aware that your questions in front of Mrs. Montgomery were quite as guarded as you expected my answers to be. That is why I suggested this short visit alone." The doctor leaned forward and thoughtfully moved the valise and briefcase, which were pushing against David's feet and which he was too tired to notice. David nodded his head in thanks.

Dr. Tanaka began, "Kate has contracted one type of encephalitis. It is caused by a virus. It could be carried by humans, but it is usually transmitted by mosquitoes that have been infected by wild birds. She had many mosquito bites when I first saw her."

David sighed, "I know. Martha wrote me from Seoul."

Dr. Tanaka paused before saying, "But I know you are more interested in the prognosis than in the symptoms." Seeing David nod he continued, "And I know you want the truth, as I would in a similar situation. The mortality rate in this infection is high, very high. About fifty to sixty percent. But we have two factors working for us: The longer the case goes on, the better from the fatality point of view. Plus Kate's youth is the real bonus factor. The older the patient, the darker the picture."

"Have you any idea of the length of the illness, the length of convalescence?" David interrupted.

"None. Absolutely none. Recovery can come quickly; it can be protracted. We have no way of knowing. There can be disturbances of mobility, even complete paralysis. A catatonic state can last months. Then the patient may seem to be recovering, but weeks, months, even years later a mental disturbance can manifest itself."

"Without any previous warning?" David asked.

"Without any previous warning. Sometimes after a hard case of measles or other infectious disease that may be accompanied by undiagnosed encephalitis, the child shows personality changes. Those who know the child attribute this change to the fact that he has been spoiled during the illness, too much attention during his sickness and convalescence. But this is not true. There has been definite nerve and brain damage due to encephalitis that has gone unrecognized. Those of us who specialize in the disease have a crusade to alert physicians to the possibility of encephalitis in many so-called harmless childhood diseases, and to look out for it particularly where there have been radical personality changes."

"Can the changes be diagnosed if it occurs months or years later?"

Dr. Tanaka continued, "There are tests we can perform that enable us to see if there are sclerosis and calcification of the walls of small blood vessels, as well as deposition of iron-containing material. With Kate, we know she has suffered acute encephalitis, and we will be aware of any problems. Let us hope there will be no need."

"Meanwhile," David sighed, "is there anything you can do for Kate to shorten the course of the disease? I know that's almost a ridiculous question to ask."

"Only the answer is ridiculous, because there isn't anything. We try to make her comfortable, to prevent complications. For example, we give her intravenous feedings. It is too risky to give food by mouth to a person in a coma because of the difficulty in swallowing. We must also watch out for bladder and bowel functions. Kate has no voluntary control."

"And there's no way of knowing how long this condition will continue?"

"None at all. Diagnosis in this disease is relatively simple by comparison to its cure."

David did not answer. He looked vacantly out the taxi window. After a pause he spoke, "In addition to my great concern for Kate, there is also her mother. You know, Mrs. Montgomery lost her husband a year ago. She has had one trauma after another. Let me ask you, must Kate be completely cured before she can be moved?"

Dr. Tanaka replied slowly, "No, I don't think she must have a complete cure, but certainly the acute and critical stages must be behind us. I wish I could say when. But as soon I feel it is safe for Kate to travel, I will let you know immediately."

David nodded. "I feel so helpless, so frustrated, leaving them here."

"I promise you, Dave, I shall do everything in my power for both Kate and Mrs. Montgomery."

"She was blessed to have found such a doctor and friend as you," David sighed.

David stretched his visit to several extra days, but the moment came when he could no longer postpone his return. At the thought of David's leaving them, Martha felt herself more acutely alone than ever. There were only minutes before he would leave for Haneda, the airport, the "field of flying wings."

"There is one matter we haven't even mentioned, Martha," David's voice was quiet and gentle. "You've told me nothing about Seoul, about Johnny Kim. I know only what you wrote in your letters."

Martha looked at him, and then she gripped his arm as if she were afraid he wouldn't stay to listen. "David, this is important. The other day when you came up here on the roof garden, when you had just arrived in Tokyo, something had just happened within me. Call it hysteria, anything you will, but I must try to make you realize how I felt at that moment, at that very moment." She paused an instant, then, in a restrained voice, she continued. "I saw Johnny Kim in Seoul several times, as I wrote you. He is a precious child, bright, a wonderful little boy. He has Paul's eyes—round eyes, not slanted, not heavy lids, even though his skin is a different color, and his little features are entirely Korean. Imagine Paul's eyes in an Oriental face. This gives him a different look than the other Korean children.

"I made arrangements with the orphanage and with Helen Yang, his friend and a nurse, to send money. But money is not enough, David. Money is not enough. Here is a little boy without parents, without really belonging anywhere. He's entitled to a future. You can't erase his being alive as an accident of war, a mistake. He's here! Alive! I know there are other war babies all over the world, but this is Paul's child. And I want to do everything for him I can."

Her voice dropped so low, David had to strain to hear her. "That morning you came up here," she explained, "I had just made a vow, a promise, a bargain. If Kate would get well, I would take Johnny Kim into my own home as a member of our family, another child. Then, at that exact moment, you came, and we went downstairs to her room. You saw the miracle of Kate's recognition." Martha continued, "Since then, I realize how unfair such a bargain is. It's almost immoral to bargain Kate's life for Johnny's. I must have been hysterical."

David put his hand on her arm. Even though they were sitting in bright sunlight, she was trembling as if she were cold. "Of course, you were hysterical. But understandably so."

Martha placed her free hand on David's. "One has nothing to do with the other—Kate and Johnny. It is sinful to want to bargain with God. I am determined now to adopt Johnny without any terms or bargains. I shall make arrangements to bring him to the States as soon as I can."

David looked at her. "Martha, when you said you were hysterical, you were quite right. When you said just now Kate and Johnny have nothing to do with each other, I am glad you can see that too. But, Martha, you can't adopt this child, bring him to your home. What about Kate, Jimmy? People may be suspicious. Perhaps they'll figure out he's Paul's son. You're not living in the Orient, you know, but in a conservative Midwest town.

Martha replied, "I can't help it. That's not important now."

David continued, speaking quickly, "Take it from another point of view, that of the child. Johnny's cute now, little and appealing. But what of his future? Will he be accepted as an equal when the novelty of his being a child wears off? What then? Adolescence in a town like ours? Then, eventually, will he be able to make friends? Isn't he better off here, among his own people?"

Martha shook her head. "No, David, there is no future for an orphan like Johnny in Korea. I want him to have a good education. He's very bright. Maybe someday he will have a contribution to make to his country, but even if he's just a good citizen in American or Korea, that's important too. But our environment will have to accept him. He's Paul's child. The family will have to accept him."

"Martha dear, Paul confused gratitude with love. He was living under chaotic conditions. He was lonesome. Such a, well, an affair probably would never have taken place under normal circumstances. You have no obligation to this child, legally, morally or any way. If Paul had lived, this would have been a problem he could have worked out. As Paul's widow, you need not take on his burden."

Martha looked up at him. "David, you disappoint me. Of all the people in the world, I thought you would understand. I thought you would help me."

"Help, I will always give. 'Understanding,' as you call it, I cannot pretend. Just promise me, Martha dear, you won't act hastily now. What you are experiencing, you may not feel later at all. These are not normal conditions. Don't do anything now you will have to regret later."

Martha smiled slightly. "I promised you before I left, I wouldn't send Johnny Kim home airmail. I won't."

David purposely changed the subject. "Martha, I've asked Dr. Tanaka to keep me informed. But phone me if you need anything, or if you get too lonesome. I'll put some extra money in your account."

Martha's eyes expressed her gratitude. "Thank you, David. I'll pay it back later when I get home."

David laughed. "You're a good risk. Martha, my leaving you here alone in this, this city, would be almost insurmountable except for Dr. Tanaka. What a remarkable man! Do you know anything about him?"

"Very little. He started to talk to me one night, but I had a feeling he didn't want to continue." Then she added, "David, you speak of understanding. When Dr. Tanaka mentioned that he was first interested in this dreadful disease in a prisoner-of-war camp, I had to fight myself to overcome my prejudices. Paul used to describe how terrible these Japanese camps were—"

David interrupted, "But he wasn't connected with a Japanese prisoner-of-war camp. He was a prisoner in one of ours in Saipan."

"Then he should be resentful of us, of Americans. He should be full of hate," Martha said.

"No, to the contrary. He holds no bitterness. He says the commandant of the camp was a former classmate at the University of Pennsylvania. He had many privileges to do research. You know, he nearly remained in the United States after he finished his medical internship, but his father wished him to come back to Japan. It was his ultimate duty. He called it *giri*—obligation to the emperor. Too deep for me to understand. All I know is that George is not at all bitter. He felt the Japanese warmongers were to blame for the war."

"George? I thought his name was Joji?" Martha asked.

"Japanese for George. Do you know about his wife?"

"Frankly, I didn't know whether he was married or not."

"He is married, but his wife, particularly since the war, has reverted to old Japanese thinking, religious customs, everything. She will not accept anything Western. There is a terrible schism between them. He hasn't seen her for a number of years."

Martha smiled. "David, you've found out Dr. Tanaka's whole history, and I imagine it didn't take you more than a half-hour. Heaven help the poor witness in your hands. I've known Dr. Tanaka all this time, and I, well, we never discussed anything at all about our personal lives."

David looked at his watch. "Martha, would it embarrass your Japanese friends here too much if I kiss you goodbye? I'll have to hurry to the airport."

Martha sook her head. "I'm sure this case is an exception." Then, as he kissed her, she started sobbing, "David, your visit here has been a dream. Now you're going. I can't be brave about it. I don't feel brave. I just can't pretend."

David held her tightly. He hoped his arms would express all he wanted to say to her, but they never had and couldn't now. "Martha dearest, I'm going to make arrangements for another attorney to handle my case. I'm going to be back just as quickly as I can."

Martha tried to regain her composure. He could feel the physical effort she was making, "David, no. You can't do that. You have a family, Sally, the children. This might even be months. . . ."

"It doesn't make any difference. Martha, you need me

more than Sally or all my clients. I'll let you know as soon as I can make arrangements."

"Maybe things will be better. Maybe Kate will be able to travel soon."

"Let us hope to God. Do you want me to send Sally or Aunt Beulah until I can get back?"

She shook her head. "No, it will be easier this way."

David managed a smile. "I think I know what you mean. They're not as flexible as you. I'll be back as soon as I can."

"David, how good you are . . . how good."

In a second, David was gone. Martha sat down on the bench. She was numb. Her body felt heavy, as if she had planted herself on the ground so firmly to resist being thrown over, she was almost like a piece of stone. Even to move physically from one spot to another was an ordeal. She didn't believe she would have strength enough to walk. But she got up slowly from the bench. She knew she would keep going, because she had no other choice.

On the plane going back, David had no idea of time. Almost before he realized it, they would be landing in San Francisco. He had laid out his plans for returning to Tokyo; he had selected the names of several attorneys with whom he could associate the case. Sally would have to accept his decision to leave, and he would have to discourage her from coming along. Then, from out of nowhere, he recalled Martha's words: "How good you are, David!" This was how she felt about him, how she had always felt about him. It was not enough.

CHAPTER VII

Martha felt it might have been easier for her if David hadn't flown over at all. The void after his brief visit was even greater. She remembered that when one left a sick pet at the veterinarian's, the hospital requested that the owner not visit. It was much harder on the animal after the master had left. Martha smiled to herself at the comparison, but she knew now what Dr. Harvey had meant by posting such a sign in the foyer of his small-animal hospital.

The monotony of the days at the hospital were broken only by Dr. Tanaka's visits in the morning and again in the evening and sometimes in the early afternoon. These calls set the pattern of the day for Martha. Once, Dr. Tanaka had been in to see Kate earlier in the morning than usual. Martha was so disappointed she had missed him, she had actually gone into the corridor to control herself. She was acting like a schoolgirl. He had phoned in later in the morning to explain that he had had an emergency and was forced to make hospital rounds at six o'clock that morning instead of the usual eight o'clock visit. Although Dr. Tanaka assured Martha that the physical findings were greatly improved, she was constantly disappointed that Kate had no other intervals of recognition since David had left.

Then one day Kate moved her head and opened her eyes. She did not speak, but Martha was confident the girl recognized her. That same morning the nurse excitedly beckoned Martha to the side of the bed. At first Martha couldn't grasp what the nurse wanted to point out, as Kate was lying on her side, apparently deep in sleep or coma. "Montgomery-san! Kate rolled over." The nurse's face was shining. "Alone, by herself."

Then Martha realized this was a voluntary act on Kate's part. Previously the nurses had been turning her from one side to another to prevent bed sores and to give her some kind of movement. Kate had a long way to come back. Even a newborn baby has motion, but until this moment Kate had been immobile. Then, just as Dr. Tanaka had explained, the physical findings were improved, as the body salts were stabilizing themselves, the blood pressure was up, and the while-blood-cell count was slowly going down. So within the coming days Martha could see changes in Kate's condition. Not all the improvements were pleasant. Kate opened her eyes on several occasions, only to close them hurriedly, moaning with discomfort. Dr. Tanaka explained that Kate was suffering from diplopia, or blurring and double vision, characteristic of encephalitis. The fact that she could moan and notice the discomfort was gratifying.

Approximately a week after David's visit Dr. Tanaka suggested to the nurse that Kate be given water through a straw to see if she could swallow. He remained by her bed as the nurse experimented. At first Kate made a sucking sound, as a nursing infant. Then, as she felt the liquid coming through the straw, she sucked eagerly. Even her expression seemed intent, her brows wrinkled, her eyes half-closed. She looked much as she did when Martha had nursed her as an infant. The nurse tilted the glass upward to prevent too rapid a flow, and automatically Kate raised her right hand to steady the glass.

Dr. Tanaka was pleased and encouraged. He told Martha they could now try liquids by mouth, as Kate seemed cognizant enough of what she was doing to swallow. And one morning not too long afterward, Martha was overjoyed to see the nurse feeding Kate spoonfuls of porridge.

On the doctor's orders, the nurse began massaging Kate's arms and legs more vigorously than before. Martha had to turn her head. Her daughter's arms and legs were pale, thin, almost emaciated by comparison with the robust Kate who had always seemed tireless—the girl with a built-in machine for renewing energy, Martha had often said.

But for the first time Martha had hope. Before she had had only prayers. She immediately cabled David relating Kate's progress and telling him not to disarrange his plans, that there was no need to hurry over.

CHAPTER VIII

Martha stood, quietly watching the setting sun suffuse the area with a pinkish glow. It was the dinner hour, and there were no families at the shrine. She walked over to the edge of the building and looked at the uneven skyline of Tokyo, at the skyscrapers alongside the roofs of squatting buildings. She saw in the distance the high radio tower, tall as the Eiffel Tower. Martha was too far above the ground for the strident street noises to reach. In addition she was on the side above a comparatively quiet street. The stillness of the scene gave it the one dimension of a colored post card. She felt disembodied, as if she were looking at herself pictured on such a card.

From the time she'd received a cable from David informing her of his change in plans, she had had only one thing left to look forward to. Since he would not be returning to Tokyo, she lived just to see Kate's progress from day to day—however painfully slow it may be. And now, standing here, she had no sensation of belonging to the scene or even of being alive. So often since the moment of Paul's death had she experienced this same detached feeling. She was standing there motionless, in a vacuum.

She was aware of someone walking toward the niche where she was standing, but she didn't have the energy or even sufficient curiosity to turn her head or look up, until she heard the voice of Dr. Tanaka greeting her.

"If one could see far enough, Mt. Fuji would be at the right," Dr. Tanaka pointed out as he came up to her. "At dusk she is difficult to see. They say she is getting ready to retire for the night and is too modest. No one talks about dusk on Fuji; they only speak of the dawn. Pilgrims who climb Fuji always want to be on the summit to admire the *goraiko,* or sunrise."

"Yes, I remember you spoke of Mt. Fuji to Kate on the plane. She wanted to climb the mountain." Martha's sigh was almost a sob.

"Kate is much improved today," Dr. Tanaka said. "That is why I feel I may ask you now, for I am sure you would not have considered this invitation before. But believe me, Kate is well enough for you to leave her for a few hours. Would you allow me the privilege of showing you a little of Tokyo, something beside this hospital? I have tickets for a Noh play tomorrow night. You might find it interesting. We could have dinner first." Dr. Tanaka had not given Martha a chance to catch her breath.

"You're very kind. But the truth is, I've become so accustomed to the routine of the hospital, back to the hotel, then the hospital, I don't know. I think I feel like a mule on a train in some mine. I go forward, backward, neither right nor left."

Unsure as to whether she wanted to decline, the doctor waited before he continued. "I think the change would be just what the doctor should order."

She smiled. "Frankly, I was thinking what dreadfully stupid, dull company I would be. I'm sure I'm far too tired to concentrate on the play."

He laughed. "You wouldn't be the first American who couldn't concentrate at a Japanese theater."

Martha hesitated, then said, "Yes, I think I should like very much to go. Thank you."

They stood for a moment, looking at the skyline. "There's a great deal more of Tokyo. It's a wonderful, an exciting city when you know it."

Martha looked up at him. "I'm sure it is."

He took her arm in a fashion she had grown to know as characteristically his. He slipped his hand along the inside of her wrist in a gesture that was warm and reassuring, yet could be completely impersonal. He led her over to one of the stone benches and offered her a cigarette. "One of your newer cigarettes. I saw them advertised."

She took one, then looked at the brand name. "They had

just come on the market, and I didn't get around to trying them. I'm not one to change—same brand all these years."

He opened his lighter for her. With a flick of the finger his lighter opened, and the flame showed. Martha was intrigued by the fragility and efficiency of the lighter, and he handed it to her. It was silver and almost razor-thin, but on one side was a copy of Dr. Tanaka's signature—Joji Tanaka. "The lighter is a copy of a famous British make." He smiled. "You know, we Japanese are great copyists. If you'll let me have your signature, I'll have my friend make one for you. He's a metallurgist of note, and he does this for a hobby."

Martha laughed. "I'd like one very much. With a signature on it, one can always tell from whom the lighter is borrowed. I didn't know until David told me that *Joji* was Japanese for George."

"I like your friend Dave Fletcher. He's most competent and capable. In fact, part of the time I felt he was interrogating me. I enjoyed it! I always like to watch a pro in action."

"He said the same thing about you—a 'pro in action.'"

"Thank you." Then he hesitated. "Mrs. Montgomery, in asking you to the theater with me tomorrow, I feel it is only fair to tell you I'm married."

Martha looked at the lighter still in her hand. "Yes, I know. David told me."

"He is quite an interrogator." George Tanaka held the cigarette in his fingers. He added, "Dave may also have told you my wife and I are estranged. She hasn't lived in Tokyo for a number of years. Akiko prefers to be with family in Kyushu. I would protest, and demand that she occupy my home, because her continued absence is contrary to all Japanese custom, but, well, I guess I'm too Western to submit her to what she feels is the agony of Tokyo.

"We are not divorced, because that, too, is uncommon in Japan among the higher-status groups, to put it bluntly. Since the war, however, it has been more accepted. But for me to initiate divorce proceedings against Akiko would force her family and herself to accept the cruelest kind of scorn. You see, in Japan a man and his family could have the right simply to say, 'This woman does not please us,' meaning please his family as well. That is sufficient reason to divorce. They used to call the divorce certificate the 'three-and-a-half-line note'; it could all be said in those few words."

"Couldn't the woman divorce the man, or would it take more than three-and-a-half lines?" Martha asked.

"Considerably more, because for a woman to divorce her husband would, in the past, have been unthinkable. Today, of course, it is different, but it is still not widely accepted."

"If . . . if your wife doesn't live in Tokyo, are you just separated?"

"Yes, separated by hundreds of miles, decades in time, and a world apart in thinking." Dr. Tanaka paused. "In our marriage Akiko and I never loved each other. It was no *ren-ai-kehkon,* or what Westerners call a romantic match. Our marriage was arranged, as Japanese marriages usually are. My family was attuned to Western culture, it is true, but there were still certain Japanese traditions they followed."

Martha was puzzled. "Your marriage was arranged. I don't understand."

Dr. Tanaka explained, "Before the war—and everything I say seems to be prefaced by stating, 'before the war'—let us say, before the MacArthur constitution and the acceptance of Americanized thinking, marriages were arranged by persons called go-betweens. The go-between could have been a close friend, relative, a boss or a professional go-between. The go-between approached the families separately and assured each one the marriage was worthy of the family. Usually it was, for the selections were carefully made, even by a professional, who couldn't be influenced by bribes and have expected to stay in business.

"A Japanese marriage was as carefully worked out as a campaign—maybe merger would be better. This was done at all levels of Japanese living, but the higher the social level, the stronger the demands for family background." Dr. Tanaka stopped.

"And you mean the young people had nothing to say?" Martha shook her head in amazement.

"Well, in years gone by, the parents might have betrothed the children before they were born, or immediately after birth, as soon as the sex was noted."

"I can't believe this. It's not done today, is it?"

"Curiously, there is a trend back to it. You know, the pendulum of custom is always swinging. I would say there is more pretense that it has been abandoned than is actually the case in the final analysis."

Martha looked at him. "You . . . you didn't know your wife before you married her?"

"I insisted upon seeing her, and alone. Almost revolutionary, but the families accepted it. My family was pleased with Akiko, and I guess I was too. She was everything a bride should be—dainty and well-educated in Japanese custom. Her family was an honorable Samurai line."

"Then your family must have been too," Martha commented.

"Let us say her family approved of me. Akiko was an excellent housewife, managing our home, our servants. Nothing else was demanded of her, as in America, where one expects a doctor's wife to help her husband in his career."

Martha said, "There ought to be a special school in America for doctors' wives! Entertaining, contacting, not offending patients, all that."

"In Japan none of that is expected of a professional man's wife. Japanese culture is structured entirely different in its home life." Dr. Tanaka continued with great effort. "We had a baby, a son," he said quietly.

"I didn't know. How old is he?" Martha asked.

"He isn't living."

Martha put her hand on his arm. "Oh, I . . . I'm sorry."

"He was five years old." His voice was now so low, Martha had difficulty in hearing him. "We had sent him with his nurse to a safe place during the war. To the island of Kyushu, where my wife's family was living during the war. Near Nagasaki."

"Nagasaki! Oh, my God, no." Martha could feel a chill down her spine.

"The nurse had taken him to a doctor there for some minor ailment. He was in Nagasaki August 9th, 1945."

88

Martha was horror-stricken. She could hardly speak. "The second atom bomb! How . . . how could you stand it? How could you live?"

Dr. Tanaka shook his head. "I do not believe in hara-kiri. I had my work to do."

"But your wife, could . . . could she? . . ." Martha scarcely finished the sentence.

"My wife couldn't stand the shock. When she was feeling better, I made her promise she would not kill herself. She has kept the promise. I thought with time we would have other children. But Akiko became so . . . so bitter, she turned against me as well as everything Western. Because I was not pro-military, as the rest of her family, she turned against me too. I became a symbol, I guess, of America."

Martha said sympathetically, "But it must have been so terrible for her, the loss of her child, feeling as she did about you . . ."

Dr. Tanaka was silent for a while before he proceeded. "Now Akiko has reverted back to the most traditional in religion, with its complete obedience to ceremony prescribed by ancestors hundreds of years ago. She has refused to accept any concept of the world in which we are now living."

"She escaped into the past," Martha sighed.

Dr. Tanaka nodded. "Completely. She has retreated into a world of her ancestors. She hasn't even been in Tokyo for more than five years."

"But I can understand how bitter, how unhappy she must have been."

Dr. Tanaka looked straight ahead. "I couldn't understand. I failed her. I don't mean immediately; when our baby died, as a matter of fact, I was out of the country, in a prisoner-of-war camp in Saipan. But when I came back after the war, when I tried to resume a semblance of a normal life, I couldn't break through to her. In the months, the years that followed, we grew farther and farther apart. Akiko couldn't understand my point of view, that the warmongers here in Japan were to blame, that the atom bombs had saved millions of lives on both sides, even though our own family was shattered.

"Instead of being patient with her, I was impatient. Instead of being tolerant, I was intolerant. I buried myself completely in my work, in my new medical interest—encephalitis. I shut the door on her. I drove Akiko back to the welcome sanctuary of her ancestors. The rift between us was a thousand years.

"When I finally realized how much the fault was mine, it was too late. We had nothing to rebuild." He stopped for a second. "I think of the two of us and believe perhaps she has found more peace of mind. She has always had her religion."

"You have your career," Martha said slowly.

"Yes, but with all its heartbreak. I have often wondered if it hadn't been for the war, what might have happened to Akiko and me. But that, of course, is self-indulgent speculation."

"Then this was a double disaster for you—your son, your wife," Martha stated, rather than asked.

He spoke hesitatingly, "Yes, except that in reality my wife was never entirely part of my world. She didn't understand; she didn't really accept my life or my work. Just before the war I was offered an exchange status at Johns Hopkins University. But Akiko was adamant against it. She had no interest, no desire to go to the States. My mother, on the other hand, had always been eager for my father to know all cultures. She had urged him on. She used to say, 'To know many peoples doesn't make you a traitor to your own.' It is, in the final analysis, a matter not of race or of people, but of individuals."

Martha spoke softly, "Yes, you are right. Some are rigid; some are flexible. The family—Paul's family—can't accept change readily."

"I know their attitude is difficult for you too, Martha." Neither was aware at the moment that this was the first time he had called her Martha. "David Fletcher told me why you went to Korea." He looked at her.

Martha flared up. "Oh! I didn't want him to. He had no right to tell you."

"But he did have a right," the doctor replied. "I asked him what you and Kate were doing traveling in Korea. It's not part of the grand tour."

Martha persisted, "He didn't need to tell you."

"Dave wanted me to protect you from yourself, from any rash move you might make in a feeling of hysteria."

"But this is not hysteria. Johnny Kim is a creation of war, just as, as your baby was a victim. I cannot ignore his presence. I just can't turn my back on him. Don't you understand?"

George Tanaka was silent for a second before he answered. "You are asking me a very difficult question, one to which I have already given a great deal of thought. What you propose to do, accept into your family one whom you might well hate, is remarkable." He smiled slightly. "You know, it's almost Oriental. Curiously enough, it used to be accepted in Japan that one would bring the husband's illegitimate child into the home to be raised with the legitimate members of the household. But unfortunately you live in America today, not in Japan in the past."

"I guess maybe I'm an anachronism then, a transplanted one."

George was serious as he continued, "But Martha, what about the boy himself? If you take him to the States, you take him to problems he would certainly not meet in Korea. I realize, of course, on the other hand he would not have many opportunities in Korea."

"From what I understand, he could not even receive a decent education," Martha said. "I can provide that for him, and a good home with security and love."

George looked at Martha. "If you are willing to fight his battles of acceptance, shield him until he is old enough to accept the challenge for himself, then he may be able to bridge the gap at least until he matures. Eventually, it is hoped, he can find a place for himself. Who knows what the future could bring to an educated person? He may decide to come back to Korea, as I did to Japan, to serve his native land. But he will have trouble adjusting, even as an adult." George paused. "Living in two cultures, he will have problems of double loyalty. It's not easy to straddle two civilizations."

"Perhaps by that time there won't be the same conflicts of culture you have had."

"Perhaps not." George smiled. "The whole world seems

to be becoming Americanized, at least in superficial aspects." Then he was serious. "But apart from Johnny, it will not be easy for you. Some people may even suspect your interest in the child is not just a passing fancy. They may see a resemblance to your husband. They may figure the age of Johnny. There could be gossip. Your own children may be affected by the presence of this child—even ridiculed because of him."

When Martha replied, her voice was firm. "My children will have to mature into responsible adults. Maybe this will help."

"You are willing to risk the weight of public opinion and the family's opposition to your proposal?"

She nodded. "I'm used to family opposition. They are inflexible in their own way. I can't be governed by their own tight prejudices. I must do what I must do. I can't desert that child."

"Let me say again, my advice to you is to wait, wait until after you return home and then for some time. If you feel you can stand the strain of additional problems, then send for the boy. But it won't be easy for any of you."

"You just mentioned additional problems," Martha said anxiously. "Do you think Kate will be all right? Can you tell this early?"

"Martha, I can't honestly tell so soon. I can make no promises. I think her convalescence will be slow. I must admit, there might even be problems, physical, even behavior problems. No area of the brain can be inflamed, as with encephalitis with even its minute hemorrhage, without running the risk of some damage. But I sincerely believe now, unless some complication comes up that we do not suspect, she will recover. Two weeks ago I couldn't even have made that statement."

"What would have happened to Kate and to me if you had not been here in Tokyo?"

He smiled. "Someone else would have taken over. There are many good doctors in Tokyo, as everywhere else."

"That isn't quite what I meant." She looked at the cigarette, at its glow, and realized for the first time that dusk had segued into night. A chill ran through her, for the night had become cooler.

"You're cold." He touched her arm.

"I . . . I had no idea it was so late." Martha looked up at the sky, which was filling with stars, and at the sliver of moon showing in the right-hand segment of sky.

"Would you like my jacket?" George asked.

"I think I'd better go down to Kate's room." She refrained from asking the time. She didn't want to embarrass either one of them. And because it was one of the few times in his busy life that he didn't want to think about the passage of moments, he, too, refrained from looking at his watch.

They walked toward the elevator. In the half-light Martha did not see the small step leading to the elevator. She started to trip, but he caught her. She steadied herself, although he was still holding her. He turned toward her, leaned down and kissed her. The elevator came to a squeaky stop, and the door opened. Without saying a word, they got in. He pressed the button for Kate's floor.

CHAPTER IX

"Now my loneliness following the fireworks. Look! A falling star!" George read over the tiny verse form by Shiki. In moments of anxiety and tension he frequently found solace in the exquisite haiku, the seventeen-syllable form in which Japanese poets had been working for hundreds of years and which is so crystal clear to the Japanese mind, yet so fantastically incomprehensible to the Occidental.

After the evening talk with Martha on the roof garden Dr. Tanaka had returned to his apartment in one of the modern buildings erected since the war. He had opened the door and entered the apartment. The manservant, who had already left for the day, had turned on several lamps, and George looked around the comfortable, attractively furnished rooms. He would be proud to show them to Martha, if he could ever bring her to his apartment, which was not likely. The chairs, tables, lamps, desk—all were Western and selected in good taste, many being English imports. Every time George had visited the homes of many of his Japanese friends, he was appalled at the lack of taste they evidenced in Western furnishing. Their own knowledge of Oriental art might be superb, but somehow it did not translate itself to Western furnishings. They bought expensive overstuffed sofas and chairs, furniture upholstered in henna-colored mohair and sickly blue friezes. He often wondered why so many people thought if something was imported, it was automatically in good taste. Just as he knew so many Americans would select inferior lacquer or clumsily made ceramic ware to take home as souvenirs.

Looking around the living room, he knew Martha would approve of his fine English imported furniture, the warm tones of the Persian rugs, the interesting collection of rare Imari bowls, which he had placed on occasional tables. Yes, Martha would admire the apartment, as he did. What was her home like? No doubt it was large and well-furnished, but in what style? What colors? She showed excellent taste in clothes. Yes, he felt he could show Martha the apartment with pride.

He often reflected that Akiko would have cared little for his apartment. In fact, he knew such Western decor would have been impossible had they still been living together. Their home had been traditionally Japanese, which he used to tell Akiko was suitable for a summer home, such as his mother's in Miyanoshita. But he would argue there was no reason to put up with the cold, bare floors, drafts from the sliding doors, and futons on the floor in place of comfortable beds. No doubt, he always concluded, he would have kept a room in Western style in the home he and Akiko shared, or perhaps he would have maintained a small Western apartment elsewhere.

George went directly to his bedroom. He stripped, took a shower, and selected from his closet a dark-brown, heavy, silk kimono, the finest and most expensive from his collection. He walked down a corridor. At the end of the hallway he unlocked the door of the meditation room, the only room he had kept traditionally Japanese. Stepping over the threshold, he knew he was stepping over the boundaries of culture. He felt himself now to be every inch Japanese, and he knew this was necessary tonight to be able to think clearly. He shut the door behind him.

The only concession to Western living in this retreat was electricity. The lighting fixtures were suspended from the ceiling, white spheres encased in bronze latticework, ancient fixtures that he had modernized by wiring. But before flicking on the light, he looked up at the small window high on the wall. He could see one star through it. When the manager of the building had first shown George the apartment, he was impressed by the "room for sewing," the manager had called it. With his quick eye for detail, George had noticed a small window, which would let in sufficient light and air. But he hardly ever used the room during the day, since it was usually at night or dusk when he found need of the sanctuary. Sometimes a sliver of moon showed through, but tonight it was a single star.

First, he went over to the *tokonoma,* or alcove, the place of honor in a Japanese room. He stood there silently, finding solace in his close examination of the scroll hanging above the low, lacquered table. He had not changed the scroll since he was last in the room several months ago. Now, for the moment, he decided not to exercise even the physical and mechanical motions of taking down the painting, rolling it carefully, enclosing it in its old case of magnificent brocade and selecting another scroll to hang in its place. He did not want to divert his mind from the original purpose of seeking this retreat—to purify his own thoughts. He looked carefully at the beauty of the hanging picture in front of him. He wondered if Martha, sensitive as she was, could appreciate it in the same degree.

Then from the cupboard he had built into the wall he took out an exquisitely printed small book of haiku. Remembering the evening when he had first visited with Martha on the roof garden and had shown her the fireworks display on the Sumida River, he selected the volume that included five lines by Shiki about fireworks. He read and reread it. Then he continued reading another, still another haiku. Could Martha understand these verses, or those of Basho, a student of Zen, or the equally superb craftsman Buson? He doubted if the Western mind, with its practical application to everything, would understand the beauty of these often-incomplete statements in which the reader becomes a co-creator by adding his own associations and imagery to the poems. *"Butterfly asleep, folded soft on temple bell . . . Then bronze gong rang. Thus too my lovely life must end, another flower to fall and float away."*

George closed the small book, his fingers delicately caressing the binding with its embroidery so fine, one could scarcely feel the threads. Some day he must read aloud these poem forms to Martha for her reactions, although is any language so difficult to translate because of abstract concept as is Japanese? Was he anxious for her reactions to see if she was able to understand not only the haiku, he wondered, but the essence of Japanese culture? Was he now probing himself to find out how important and necessary this was for him to know?

Always able to examine his own reactions, George knew he was experiencing a growing affection for this charming *gaizin*, this American, this stranger. He looked forward to being with her, inventing excuses to come to Katie's room. Should he stop now, or allow himself the indulgence of continuing? Western as he was by culture and even by temperament, he realized he was still Japanese in many aspects of his nature. His parents, Western as they were, had imbued him with all the best in thought and philosophy his own culture had to offer. He knew that no Westerner could spend hours sitting quietly on a tatami, legs folded under him, as he was now doing, being revitalized by reading simple little five-line verse, or standing before a scroll or flower arrangement, seeing every detail, every vein on a leaf or petal.

He knew this was the paradox of his life: He was an American superimposed on a Japanese body and inheritance. He had been taught to reason as an American through his schooling. He knew he had the forthright, direct, logical approach to problems and certainly to speech, without any of the ambiguity and evasion of the traditional Japanese. He had always felt this was advantageous in his profession, disadvantageous in dealing with his colleagues.

He had long ago concluded that he bore a nationalistic dichotomy. Now he realized all of Japan, particularly urban Japan, was becoming a victim of this split in personality. But he knew his variations were on an intellectual level, whereas the Japanese of today were accepting the surface of Americanization without a rooted understanding of what or why. George used to argue with some of his close friends—professors at the university or important businessmen—about how the Japanese could expect to know and feel democracy without being educated for it from childhood on. Either a person would be in awe of the new freedom or would become too rapidly familiar with it, accepting the outward trappings while abusing the privileges, as the rioting students had done against Eisenhower's proposed visit. To accept democracy as part of living and breathing required more than a score of years from the day when a five-star conquering general handed over a ready-made constitution, and a radio broadcast announced to ninety million people that their leader was not a descendant of the sun god.

A man opening a door for a woman so that she may precede him into a room, or allowing the woman to walk alongside him rather than follow respectfully in the rear, these new ways might be revolutionary for a Japanese, but they did not make him immediately democratic in thought, George would argue. Taking away the essence of Japanese thought and philosophy and replacing it with surface Americanization without a fundamental understanding of what or why was creating a national vacuum of spirit. Once when he was expressing his views, one of his colleagues had interrupted, "Why, Joji, don't you go back to the States?"

George had answered with a grin, "Can one transplant a pine tree?"

"Yes, it's been done," his friend had answered.

But George knew differently in his heart. He knew he could not be happy in a land where he would be in the minority, where his own people lived either in a Japanese ghetto or were forced to accept inferior housing in too many areas. But out of loyalty he couldn't talk about the tarnish of the democracy. He had thought about Europe or Hawaii, but with his medical practice established, there had been no real reason to leave Japan.

Now the past weeks with Martha had brought to the surface all his feelings about America and Japan and had italicized his own problems. When he was with Martha, he was no longer wholly Japanese on the one hand, but on the other hand he was more Japanese, because he realized Martha was truly American. In an American woman like Martha, he felt, was the personification of real American democracy. The new political freedom, the act of voting could not give the Japanese woman the assurance Martha was born with. He knew Martha accepted herself as a man's partner, neither as his toy nor slave, such as a Japanese woman might. Decisive in her actions, clear in her thoughts and speech, emotionally able to stand the trauma she had known, feminine enough to cry (which a Japanese woman would never permit herself to do in public), in all of this, Martha personified security. The years of a changing social code would certainly alter the sociological differences, but George wondered how many generations it would take to create a Japanese woman in the mold and spirit of Martha.

He looked down at the mat—a love mat, it was sometimes called. He allowed his mind to imagine love-making with a woman as secure as Martha, as unfettered in her thoughts, as unsubservient. This would be a new experience for George. It would be unlike the experiences with a courtesan trained in the art, or even of a mistress who knew she had to please him. It would come about because Martha herself would desire him and feel the shared moment of joy.

He thought of his wife, Akiko, and of her modest, obedient surrenders. He remembered the shock when he first saw her lying on the *futon*, nude. Her figure was waxen, like a statue, with no evidence of any axillary or pubic hair. She had reminded him of a "doctor's doll," a small ivory replica of the female body that the Chinese women, in their unbelievable modesty, used in going to a doctor. Rather than undress and expose themselves, they would point to the portion of the anatomy on the figure to show where their pains were located. Akiko resembled one of these figurines.

He had been almost afraid to touch her, she seemed so young. Although a graduate medical student, he had grown up in the United States. Curiously he did not know, until he had delved into the subject, that this marblelike appearance was not too unusual among Japanese women, just as a heavy beard and body hair were not too common among Japanese men. That wedding night, embarrassed and frightened as he had been, all such anatomical thoughts had fled, and he wondered if Akiko was ready for marriage.

Now for the first time in his life George knew he wanted a particular woman. He wanted Martha. But in Japanese tradition he recognized that Martha was a mother, not only of his very sick patient but the mother of a son in America. A woman like Martha was inviolable.

He realized, too, that he wanted more than just a fleeting love experience. He wanted the challenge, the stimulation of a woman whose mental life he could share as well as her physical life. In the years when he had married, such companionship would have been unknown from a wife whose world was her home. Many men sought the geisha, but a geisha had been taught to converse with the patrons. It was an artificial approach, mimicking what they had been taught to think and say. He knew woman like Martha would be completely independent. Any woman who would travel halfway around the world to see an illegitimate child of her husband, who would face opposition at home had courage. *Guts* was the American word. He concluded life with Martha would never be dull.

Suddenly he stood up. He knew his line of thinking was unhealthy. It could not be concluded. He was already married. Then, because he was still as much Western in thought as he was Japanese, he decided to postpone any decision until another time. Had he been Japanese entirely, he would have remained in meditation until he had resolved an answer, however bitter it might be.

George replaced the narrow book containing the particular haiku he had read. He put the volume on a shelf. Then he opened a drawer and stood there, absolutely still for a moment while he inhaled the faint aroma of camphor emanating from the drawer where the scrolls were carefully kept. The pungent fragrance always gave him a ripple of anticipation, as he knew he would savor the joy of looking over the several minor masterpieces he had collected over the years. A colleague of his at the hospital had a priceless collection of *netsuke*, miniature carved ivories, which he would examine by the hour, using a magnifying glass to discern the finer-than-thread etched lines. But George preferred the scroll paintings with their purity of line, economy of design. The camphor fragrance evaporating, George looked carefully at the rolled *kakemono*. He could recognize them almost by the feel of the silk boxes in which they were encased. He selected one from the Kano dynasty, late seventeenth century. He held it in his hands, remembering when he had bought it. Since the rash moment of purchase, when he had spent far more than he could afford, shortly after his release from prison camp, George had often wondered why he had made this sizable purchase so impetuously—something he rarely did in decisions of importance. He had long ago concluded it was because the scroll was from the Kano dynasty that he had acquired it, apart from its intrinsic merits. The Kano dynasty was a family of artists, passing their talent from father to son through many generations, even through adopted sons. Thinking of this continuity and the blessings it had brought not only to the individuals of the Kano family but to the world at large, he had wondered if he could found a dynasty in medicine. His only son had been killed at Nagasaki, but he and Akiko were still young enough to have other children. If he could not be blessed again with a boy, but only with girls, perhaps they could adopt a boy child. On the other hand, perhaps he would wait until he had a son-in-law to carry on his name, a Japanese custom in which a son-in-law would take on the name of the wife's family, thus often filling a vacuum if there were no sons in the family. His mind racing years ahead, George had happily hurried home with the *kakemono* in its magnificent silk box wrapped in outer silk covering and held tightly in his hand. He would talk to Akiko.

But Akiko would not listen, breaking him off in the middle of his carefully prepared speech by her sudden departure. He remembered he had bent his head to light a cigarette; when he looked up, he caught a glimpse of her kimono already gliding through the fragile door. Upset, instead of trying to seek her out, he remembered crushing out the cigarette and leaving the house. He had spent the remainder of the night in his office.

Weeks, months proved that he would never have an opportunity to create another child with Akiko. She withdrew from him completely, finally leaving Tokyo to remain with her family on the island of Kyushu.

As he gently unrolled the scroll, preparatory to hanging it on the wall, he wondered if there was special reason why he had selected this particular painting tonight. He knew there was. Perhaps he would still have an opportunity to found a dynasty, but he broke off this thought. A child half-American, half-Japanese, half-caste, would have too many problems both in his own social strata in Tokyo and in Martha's background in the States. It was still too early in the history of Japanese and American culture. In Europe a merging would be accepted, but not in Japan or America.

He took down the *kakemono* that he had neglectfully let hang for many weeks, since before his trip to Korea. When he had hung the scroll there, he had not known of the existence of young Kate and her mother. George took a delicate brush made of white feathers and gently dusted the invisible flakes of soil from the hanging. Then he carefully wrapped the *kakemono* and put it in its silk-embroidered box, which he returned to the drawer. Gently, he hung the selected scroll in the empty spot. In doing this, he was calling a stop to any more meditation for the night.

CHAPTER X

Usually when Martha went to bed upon her return from a day and evening spent in Kate's room at the hospital, physical fatigue plus a desire to escape into the oblivion of sleep caused her to drop off almost immediately. At the time of Paul's death this had also been true. Sleep represented an escape from her problems, even for a few hours, like a temporary death.

Tonight when Martha returned, she lay down, but she could not sleep. Moreover she found herself wanting to stay awake, to think over and sort out all that she and George had talked about on the roof garden. They had been together for about two hours, but the time had no significance. Martha felt she knew more about this man, completely alien as he was, than she had really ever known about Paul. During the first years of her marriage she didn't know if Paul thought deeply but was not able to express himself, or perhaps if he just didn't think at all. Was it all surface, as his good humor and sparkling personality had been?

Tonight this man had dared to admit his failure as a husband, that he hadn't understood his wife, that he had turned away from her. He had made a mistake. Paul had never admitted his weaknesses, that he had made a mistake. It could have been that he had not considered his affair with Johnny's mother a mistake. Unless he had been a real coward, why had he not ever confided in her? She had been over this line of reasoning so many times, she now forcibly abandoned it. She could never find the answer.

She remembered reading that Japanese were taciturn, reticent to express their own emotions. Maybe this was evidence of George's Western upbringing that allowed him to speak freely so that she felt she had known him for many years. She concluded there were no general sweeping statements in categorizing individuals. The synthesis of the two cultures combined with his penetrating mind and scientific approach had created in George Tanaka a person unlike anyone she had ever met before.

She realized, too, that he was also, for her, an exciting person. He had attracted her physically as she had believed no one could again. She had decided since Paul's death that if she should marry again, it would be for companionship, not for any sexual attraction. The first blush, the nascence of romance were for the young. In Springfield there were no single, unattached men around. There were a few bachelors to fill in at dinner parties. One or two of these single men were summoned when an unattached lady visitor came to town, but this was only a token friendship. The several "eligible" bachelors would always do the right thing—flowers, dinner at the club, a theater if by chance a second- or third-rate company was bringing a belated Broadway play to town. If these escorts were not recognized openly as homosexuals, they were at least on the suspect list. Apart from them, in a narrow community made even narrower by the self-imposed stratum of the "best families" Martha could never hope to meet anyone. She had accepted her role as widow of the late Paul Montgomery.

Her thoughts about George Tanaka had rekindled a dormant excitement within her, and she remembered, like a schoolgirl thinking back over a date, how she had tingled when he had held her arm to guide her to the bench and when he had leaned over to kiss her. She smiled to herself that she was acting more like one of Kate's girlfriends than a mature woman. But she fell asleep pleased that he had asked her to the theater the next night.

The following evening Martha wondered if perhaps etiquette would require that she remain upstairs until the desk phoned to inform her of Dr. Tanaka's arrival. But she decided she was too old to be coy about such trivia; so she found herself with a few moments to spare, waiting in the lobby. She enjoyed just looking around, and the time passed quickly. It wasn't long before she saw Dr. Tanaka coming toward her. It was the first time she had seen him in a suit. For the past few weeks he had worn a white medical jacket, and she had almost forgotten their first meeting en route by taxi and plane to Seoul. She acknowledged the sense of pride she felt as she walked out the door of the Imperial Hotel with him.

The Noh play, which was held in the gardens of the Shinjuku Gyoen, was indeed interesting. But the elaborate costumes and masks used by the actors to indicate the characters they portrayed, plus the strange tones of the three-stringed *samisen* all made it difficult for Martha to understand. She was entranced at the setting, at the darkness of the open theater, with only the dim lights of fagots burning. George explained the action of the play to Martha, but much to her great embarrassment and to the doctor's amusement, the balmy night air, the almost-blackness of the theater and the monotone of the voices and music produced a soporific effect, and Martha dozed off.

They left long before the completion of the performance. At the entrance to the hotel, Martha, most apologetic, admitted she was too exhausted to invite George into the lounge for a drink. "Just breaking the routine of these days, I guess, has been too much for me," she said self-consciously.

"Probably it's the first time you've been sufficiently relaxed. Actually, I'm complimented. You won't be so tired the next time."

Martha felt guilty that she should enjoy herself while Kate was still hospitalized, but there was no doubt that the child was showing marked improvement. She was alert for longer periods during the day. She expressed herself as being thirsty or hungry. Although it was still an effort to chew her food, her menu now included such requests as lamb chops and hot dogs. Martha wondered how such Western foods were obtainable, but the nurse simply smiled, saying, "Dr. Tanaka patient always get what they want."

Dr. Tanaka and Martha were having dinner at a restaurant the doctor frequented. Having been there several times already, Martha felt a degree of familiarity with the place, although in point of fact there was a great similarity to many other restaurants, all built along the same general patterns. She was always amazed that a charming restaurant could be concealed behind the customary wooden fence that shielded the gardens and structures. Somehow, the moment she stepped past the fence and then slipped off her shoes at the entrance of the pavilion, she felt a sense of peace and tranquillity, which remained with her throughout the evening. By now she knew the architecture of these small, intimate *ryori,* a large pavilion and the tiny one-room structures where the diners could have privacy. No one came to stare or to be stared at, as in an American restaurant, she once remarked to George. He had answered that there were many, large, noisy, multistory restaurants in the Ginza, but he tried to avoid them.

They had been seated in a small, one-room pavilion. There was a low, lacquered table in one corner on which sat a rectangular, bronze container with an interesting flower arrangement. Martha was at ease and at peace here.

"What is bothering you?" George broke her reverie.

She looked up and smiled. "Nothing is bothering me." Looking around, gesturing at the walls, motioning to the low table at which they were eating, the *zabutons* on which they were sitting, she asked, "How could anything be troublesome in this peaceful place?" She sipped hot sake from delicate, porcelain cups, which the tiny waitress filled but never too full. "The other night when we were watching judo, you said many activities in Japan had almost esoteric values. I imagine you meant significance beyond what one sees, particularly what I, an American, see, or rather do not see."

"Not you alone, as an American, but almost all Westerners." George fingered the cup of the hot sake. "Let me try to make myself clear. Most physical activity, or for that matter any activity like flower-arrangement or the tea ceremony, when properly done is the result of years of learning, of self-discipline. Nothing in Japan is left to chance, done quickly, haphazardly or incompletely. Take that flower arrangement behind you."

Martha now turned around, since her back was to the low, lacquered table. George had once told her that the honored guest sits with his or her back to the *tokonoma,* which serves as a fitting background. George got up to help her, because she was experiencing difficulty in turning, with her legs bent under her as she sat on the *zabuton*. She looked at the flower arrangement, the unusual combination of a single calla lily and its green leaves, together with two slender reeds. "How simple, how beautiful it is," she remarked.

The doctor took several sips of sake. "Flower-arrangement, as you know, has been developed into a highly specialized art and refined in its most technical sense. My mother is a master of flower-arranging, just as she is of the tea ceremony. Young women used to learn the art. Nowadays I think they give streamlined versions, but there are professors who teach the art of flower-arrangement, which is called *ikebano*, and the tea ceremony, *cha-no-yu*.

"Both these arts, curiously enough, were started by a man, by a shogun who had tired of court life and had thus left for a beautiful spot at the foot of a mountain. He built a villa there, plus a two-story pavilion, which he ordered coated with silver foil. He spent his days thereafter viewing the scenery, the beautiful gardens on the outside, and the flower arrangements within. The flower-arrangement and tea ceremony are called 'elegant amusement.'" He smiled and nodded. "Quite a departure for the tired executive: not golf or cards, but contemplation of flower arrangements and sipping tea—elegant amusements all right."

Martha laughed. "That's a wonderful term, but I must say, I don't know how long I could enjoy it myself."

"I know," George said slowly. "When I returned from America, it seemed silly to me too. When Akiko and I were married, I was very impatient with her. I felt she spent too much time on such elegant amusements. I felt she should have improved her hours by reading about the world about her, current events, history. Martha, I didn't understand her at all; I didn't begin to understand her or the satisfaction she got from these activities. I simply wasn't mature enough to realize there are many ways of 'improving the mind and developing character,' as they used to say in school.

"I should have been more tolerant. But I was so bitter

about much of the traditionalism, which was so unrealistic to me, that I revolted against everything symbolic. It wasn't until much, much later—after Akiko and I were apart—that I began studying a little Zen. Then I began to understand—"

"Now I'm afraid I don't," Martha interrupted.

"Zen teaches you that man works best when he is not calculating or thinking, when he is relaxed, forgetting about himself. He finds his real enjoyment of life with the spirit of nature. At the same time that Zen advocates meditation and love of nature, it also teaches integration of Zen into everyday living. It is better to integrate Zen into daily living rather than to spend just a few hours of meditation and forget it the rest of the time. Look, I'm not being fair to Zen or to you in giving you what is not even a glimpse of its meaningfulness, of the help through meditation. There are some excellent books written in English about Zen. I'll get some for you."

"I'll read them, but I don't promise to understand."

George continued, "The nearest approach I can tell you is to read some of the English poets, Wordsworth, Keats, or even better, read Americans, Emerson, or Thoreau. They understood and lived the meaning of Zen, but, of course, they didn't call it by any name quite as esoteric. I really believe I like their variety the best. They were not extremists. As in so many beliefs, the true meaning of Zen has been taken over by zealots, who have become extremists, absorbed merely in more-metaphysical arguments." He stopped and uttered half-jokingly, "How did I ever get off on the subject of Zen?"

Martha thought back, then remembered, "You were telling me about the flower-arranging and the tea ceremony."

George spanked his hand on the table. "Enough lecturing tonight. Did you enjoy your dinner? I see you are doing better every time. I do not know whether your appetite is coming back or whether you are simply becoming used to Japanese food."

"Imagine serving this cuisine for Sunday dinner in Indiana!" Martha laughed, referring to the *nishime*, chopped pork with bamboo sprouts, taro root cooked in soy sauce; and *make*-sushi, rice cakes with ginger, pieces of eel and vegetables, all fried in seaweed. "It took the family years to accept barbecue shrimp."

He smiled. "And you have been eating only the more conservative of the dishes."

"The rice," Martha added, "Uncle Wilfred would say is good for his high blood pressure." She was enjoying the bowl of steaming white rice with which every Japanese meal is concluded.

"Martha," George said softly, "you're delightful. Everything you see, you do, even what you eat is translated in terms of Kate or Jimmy or the family. Paul must have been very content."

Reflecting on this remark later—as she had become accustomed to thinking over their conversations before dropping off to sleep—Martha wondered if Paul had been really content. He had never expressed himself one way or another. She assumed he had taken everything for granted, and she assumed also that most other husbands did. Would Dr. Tanaka respond differently? Was it because this kind of companionship they had been enjoying these past weeks was so unknown to him in his own marriage? He had carefully explained that a Japanese girl is trained from childhood to be a good and conscientious wife, but that in the rigid training, all spontaneous love and affection are stifled or, worse, are never there originally.

There was so much about Japanese culture that, as she had said many times, was incomprehensible to her. Dr. Tanaka had explained, on occasion, the sociological significance of Japanese culture, tradition and the vast changes that had taken place in the past sixty or seventy years, changes accelerated by the war and the new democracy.

Once, she had remarked that the Japanese seemed to be a happy people. He pointed out this was not the case. Actually he felt they were a pessimistic, unhappy people, even more so now that much had been taken away from them in their religion, in their traditions, in their attitude toward the emperor. Nothing real had taken the place of the things they had been taught to revere and obey. The superficialities and the materialism of Western civilization had brought only misery. "Postwar literature, for example, is particularly depressing," he had said.

"Beat generation over here too?" she had remarked.

He'd answered, "Beaten generation would be more like it. In America, in England 'beat generation' refers to a small, highly publicized segment of young people. But here in Japan there are far too many for the nation's good. In Japan melancholia has been bred in the blood. Any country that has lived with the thought of suicide as part of its accustomed thinking for so many generations can not suddenly erase this attitude of self-destruction from its mind."

"Is suicide an attempt to vanish from this life into a better one?"

"Exactly. The Japanese thought held that once past the door of death, the individual would emerge as a god, with better weapons and supernatural strength. If one held a grudge against another, the best way to seek revenge would be to commit suicide and thus be in a position to wreak vengeance from the vantage point of the spirit world. While these old thoughts are no longer held for the same purpose, too many still feel they can escape from life's bitterness and unhappiness."

In her thinking Martha realized what an un-Christian point of view this was, and then she remembered what he had said about Zen. She hadn't been wise enough to ask any questions about Zen, because it had seemed so entirely incomprehensible to her. Suddenly she smiled to herself in the dark. Zen in Springfield! In the fundamentalist Bible Belt in which she lived, even the Unitarians at one time had had all they could do to hold their own, and the few Jewish families had been held together by a congregation that had met in an empty storeroom whenever a rabbi from some other small community could be persuaded to come to conduct Holy Services. For a brief period there had been a group interested in Science of Mind, but they had long since dispersed. As for Zen, she knew it was unheard of. She doubted if one member of the family, with the probable exception of Sally, could identify Zen in a multiple-choice quiz.

The next day upon her return from the hospital—after a visit in which Martha had once again seen that Kate was showing rapid improvement—she found a large package awaiting her at the hotel. She eagerly undid the beautiful silk scarf that was wrapped around the gift. She found a collection of books: several beautifully illustrated ones on Japanese Flower-Arranging, an illustrated book on Judo, several books on Zen in English, a large cookbook of Japanese dishes and menus written in English—and the inscription inside the flyleaf, "For Sunday Dinner."

One evening Martha remarked to George that she felt like Alice on the other side of the *shoji* screen. Everything was still strange to her, whether she was in a Japanese tearoom or park or garden. She added that she hoped Kate could see the interior of a Japanese house or even tea house before they left Japan. Even as she mentioned leaving Japan, she felt as if she had stepped back once more to the Occidental side of the *shoji,* and the fleeting moment was poignant.

Dr. Tanaka replied, "My mother lives in Miyanoshita. We have a summer place there. Our home is entirely Japanese. It's done in true style with many objects not even seen in Tokyo today. You would enjoy it."

"I know I would." Then suddenly, impulsively, she asked, "Your apartment here in Tokyo, I'd love to see it. Is it done in Western or Japanese style?" She was instantly embarrassed at asking such a personal question, as if she were hinting to be invited.

"No, my apartment is Western. In fact, the building is quite modern. I have some pieces of antique art, tapestries, so forth, but the furniture is quite as you find at home." His voice became serious. "Martha, perhaps you have wondered why I have not invited you to my place. I have thought of it many times. I felt it was really necessary for you to see it. To understand a person, one must see how he chooses to live. But it wouldn't be proper for you to come. I wouldn't want to cause you any embarrassment if we should meet someone in the elevator. It . . . it isn't done here in Tokyo."

She nodded in understanding.

"Miyanoshita would be different," he continued. "You would be a guest of my mother." He stopped, then looked at Martha. "Let's see how things work out, Martha. You know, Kate is noticeably improved the last day or so. Perhaps it could be arranged."

Martha waited for him to continue, but he stopped and resumed eating, as the *nesan* served him from the small *habachi* near the table. Watching George closely, Martha had a feeling he was glad for the interruption from the waitress.

Several days later Martha came into Kate's hospital room. She looked at the bed as she usually did upon coming through the door, but Kate was not there. Her heart skipped a beat. Then from the corner of the room came Kate's voice. "Surprise!" Kate called out gleefully.

She was sitting in a chair, pleased as she could be. To Martha, she looked even more frail sitting up than she had lying down in bed, or even propped up in bed. Her face was tiny and peaked. Her hair, neatly combed back into a ponytail, accentuated her frailty. But she was wearing a *yukata* that Martha had bought her, and the blue pattern of the floral design brought out the blue of the girl's eyes.

Martha just stood there, caught her breath and said, "Well, I can't believe what I'm seeing."

Both the nurse and Kate were beaming at the surprise.

"Does . . ." Martha had to check herself, as she was about to say George, "does Dr. Tanaka know about this?"

Kate nodded. "Of course. He planned it as a surprise for you!"

"I must say, it was completely successful." Martha came over to the chair. "And, Kate, it seems to me you look much taller, even sitting up."

The nurse had all along been carefully timing Kate's debut. In a few moments an orderly came into the room. As if he were lifting a small child, he carried Kate back to bed. Kate protested she wasn't ready to go back yet, but the nurse reminded her of Dr. Tanaka's strict orders. Kate obeyed. And in a few moments she dozed off to sleep.

Martha had often wondered by what private semaphore system news traveled along a hospital corridor. For as soon as Kate was asleep, Martha decided to go up to the roof garden for a breath of air and to give thanks for this newest sign of Kate's recovery. She was waiting for the elevator when two of the floor nurses came up, smiling and bowing. They took her hands in warm salute. They did not need

English to express to Martha how glad they were about Kate's new accomplishment.

In a second, Mariko Ikeda came up to Martha, her face joyful. "Montgomery-san, I am do delighted Kate is recovered in a chair." She blushed. "I mean re-co-vered to sit back in a chair. It is very good news, and I am very happy for you."

"Thank you, Mariko. And I'm happy too. They surprised me when I came up from lunch. Wasn't that exciting?"

Mariko nodded her head. Her tiny white cap bounced up and down. Martha had a feeling Mariko had something else to say, since the nurse didn't make an attempt to leave, as she usually did. She always seemed to Martha to be darting down the corridor, in the direction of a patient's room, or to the charting office.

"How are things with you, Mariko?" Martha asked.

Mariko looked down at the immaculately scrubbed floor. "Montgomery-san, do you know where Detroi*th* is found?"

Martha was puzzled. "Detroith?"

"Yes, the city where all the automobiles are manufactured," Mariko supplied.

"Oh, Detroit." Martha saw the eagerness in Mariko's face. "I've never been there, but they say it's a beautiful city. Do you know someone from there?"

Mariko blushed. Her head was lowered so that Martha had to strain to hear. "I have a best friend who is in the American Air Force who is from Detroit." If possible, Mariko blushed even more.

"I've heard it is very busy and interesting, like Tokyo, but not as large," Martha said. "No city is as large."

Mariko looked up beaming. "I am so very happy for you and Kate-san." Then she scurried down the hall.

The elevator came, and Martha entered. She was smiling to herself at the great charm of these Japanese women.

Several nights later Martha and George were attending an exhibition of the Bon Dance Festival, a festival in which George explained that the spirits of the ancestors were supposed to revisit the household altars, but now, as with many Japanese customs, the dance had become almost theatrical.

In the courtyard of a Buddhist temple Martha watched, enchanted by the spectacle of all ages and sizes joining in the dance, their colorful kimonos fluttering in and out as they glided around in large circles, passing a huge drum, the largest she had ever seen. She noted that only several men took turns beating in rhythm on the side of the drum. She concluded that this was a rule of honor. The resonance echoed, and Martha, who was sitting some distance away, could feel the reverberation as of a distant cannon roaring. She looked at the colorful shoji lanterns hung on wires, and they, too, were swaying as if set in motion by the sound waves from the drum. Martha was conscious of a light drizzle, but the dancers never looked up. Even when the drizzle gave way to a downpour, the dancers kept on.

"Come." George pulled her away, and they ran to the shelter of the nearby Buddhist temple. They stood on the bottom step, with the ornate gold-canopied roof above them. "The rain's stopped a little. Let's make a run for the car." Taking her arm, George started running in the direction of the car, which was parked some distance away from the narrow alley leading to the temple.

Martha was breathless as she sat down in the front seat. "I wonder if the dancers even know it's raining."

"I doubt it. They become mesmerized by the rhythm, the solemnity of the dance."

Martha spoke softly, "All the tourists pouring in and out of the hotel think they have seen Japan when they've seen the Ginza and the Imperial Palace. You've given me an insight I don't suppose many Americans see."

"I wish I could show you other parts of Japan," he replied slowly. "Tokyo isn't even a fair glimpse of the country. In fact, there's far less difference between Tokyo and an American city than between Tokyo and many rural areas thirty miles away." He stopped speaking, and she, too, was quiet. Martha became aware of the motion of the windshield wipers and their singsong patterns.

Then George spoke. "Martha, I have to leave the city the day after tomorrow. I'll be gone only a few days, I hope."

"Oh!" Her gasp was audible above the sound of the wipers.

"Dr. Nishimura will take good care of Kate. She is in absolutely no danger now. He will watch her closely, and if there should be any unusual signs, he'll phone me. I'm going first to Kyushu, and from there to a medical meeting at Osaka."

In the darkness of the car Martha could feel her blush evidence itself as she said almost without thinking, "I'll miss you."

"I've been postponing this trip, but I feel now Kate is well enough for me to leave. And so are you."

Going into the lobby of the Imperial the next morning on her way to the hospital, Martha not only picked up several American magazines but, seeing a large tourist map of the four principal islands of Japan, she bought it too. The past week since Kate had been so much improved, Martha had been leaving for the hospital later in the morning and was accustomed to having a continental breakfast in the dining room of the hotel. Now, as she was having her morning tea and roll, she spread the map out on the table, true tourist fashion. She looked at once for Kyushu, which she knew was an island, but in what direction she wasn't too sure. She found it immediately. It was the southernmost island in the chain. Like a magnet, her eye was drawn to the name of Nagasaki on the map.

She was startled. Kyushu, then, might well be where Akiko was living with her family. As a matter of fact, she seemed to recall that George had once stated that his wife was living on Kyushu, but at that moment, disinterested and disoriented about location and his wife, Martha had paid little attention to the remark. Now the name of the island might just as well have been printed in neon. Undoubtedly he was going to see Akiko. Was this a customary visit, or did it have special meaning? Had he previously stated that he hadn't seen Akiko in five years or that she hadn't been in Tokyo in five years? She couldn't remember, and she couldn't ask. And since he hadn't mentioned Akiko specifically, Martha would in all probability never know.

A wife *in absentia* was one thing; a wife living somewhere on Kyushu was another. Then she recalled the previous night he said he had been postponing the trip until both she and Kate were well enough to leave. But this remark did not jibe with the statement that he was going to a medical meeting in Osaka. Suddenly she was angry at herself for being jealous. She had no right to be, nor to question whether he had postponed or planned the trip now. She hurriedly drank her tea, and then in her haste she left her pocketbook on the table. A busboy ran after her. He grinned and bowed very low, saying "*Hando baggu*," and pleased, handed Martha her purse.

"*Arigato gozai-masu*—thank you very much." Martha opened her bag and handed him some coins. He refused to accept them, again bowing low and grinning. But Martha insisted, and he finally accepted the money with another bow. The thought suddenly occurred to her: Kate had left her pocketbook on the table after their first meal in Japan. Had a busboy brought them the purse, they would in all probability have never met Dr. Tanaka. Perhaps the Oriental thought was correct: All in life has a pattern.

Because he was leaving early in the morning for his trip, George and Martha were having drinks in one of the lounge rooms of the hotel, rather than attending a theater or dining out. Martha felt uncomfortable in the cocktail room, which was like an Americanized island dropped in the middle of Tokyo. It was out of place with all she had come to know and admire. She was also displeased with herself for her own jealousy and her own doubts about George's trip.

Just as they were being seated at a table next to one occupied by two American couples, Martha could feel the eyes of the two women appraising both Dr. Tanaka and herself. She heard one of the women say to the other in a voice loud enough to penetrate the din of the lounge and also loud enough to carry to their table, "She's obviously an American. But did you ever see such an attractive man, even if he *is* Japanese? Most of them aren't good-looking, you know."

The other woman replied, "Yes, but would you marry him? Now, would you?"

Martha was deeply embarrassed, but if he heard, George gave no indication.

Later that evening, before going to bed, Martha realized

119

how relieved she had been when George had finally said good night. Then, unable to sleep, she took a sedative. But she was restless, and she woke up the next day with a severe headache along with a feeling of malaise and emptiness as she realized Dr. Tanaka would be out of town visiting his wife.

CHAPTER XI

George Tanaka had decided some time earlier to fly to Kyushu. He had felt for several days that Kate had been well enough for him to leave, but with her progress more noticeable each day, he decided he was now entirely safe in leaving. He also wanted to attend a medical meeting on contagious diseases in Osaka before returning to Tokyo. He had been asked to read a paper on the recent encephalitis epidemic in Korea, and because he was so thankful that Kate had made such beautiful improvement, he felt he had an obligation to share his knowledge and experience with his colleagues.

But Martha also had been right. The visit to Kyushu did concern Akiko, although seeing her in person was not the purpose of the trip there. He realized it had been five years since he had even talked with her. On his previous trips she had feigned one excuse or another for not seeing him. He had not pressed the matter out of deference to her.

This time he had written Akiko's brother, Yasuki Kataoka, for a meeting, explaining to Yasuki that inasmuch as Yasuki was head of the family, he had a matter of urgency to discuss with him. After he had mailed the letter, George realized he may have tipped his hand that the matter would be urgent to himself if not to Yasuki, who had always been opposed to George. His animosity had grown with the years.

George knew he'd been right about Yasuki's hostile mood, since Yasuki had arranged to meet him in his private office in the large shipping firm of which he was manager, rather than in a restaurant, which would have been more gracious. Yasuki clearly wanted it understood that this meeting was to be kept on a formal, business basis.

As he walked in to keep the appointment, George noted the larger outer office was filled with many workers, women as well as men, and there was a great deal of modern American office equipment. George thought that his wife's family was flexible when it suited its purposes in business. A high-speed copier was acceptable, but modern trends in thought and action were not. George had often felt and occasionally expressed the thought to his colleagues that if the more traditional Japanese had accepted democracy—*demokurasu*, as the shopkeepers called it—it was not because the Japanese accepted the ideology. But if democracy had helped the United States win the war, they were all for adopting it.

Yasuki bowed formally as George was ushered into the office. George took a quick look at him. Yasuki was even more homely than he had remembered him. Small in stature, overly precise in manner and dress, he wore huge, heavily framed glasses that obscured his small face. Three teeth protruded in the front of his mouth, giving him, as George had always felt, the look of the souvenir wooden badger one saw in novelty stores. George had deliberately chosen a tweed jacket and oxford slacks that had been made for him by an English tailor. He noted that Yasuki was wearing the traditional black suit, mark of respectability, which Yasuki always wore. George had asked him once many years ago if he had ever owned any other color suit. As he recalled, Yasuki did not answer directly but inferred that if something was suitable, there was no need to change one's tastes.

George had debated for some time as to the best method of directing the course of the meeting. The correct approach, according to Japanese custom, would be to discuss every subject possible before coming to the point of his visit, and then to arrive at the purpose in an oblique manner with much self-effacing and humility. George had to smile as he thought over the strategy for the meeting. If he referred to himself as "your most unworthy brother-in-law," Yasuki might indeed take him literally rather than consider it a term of politeness. George knew that Yasuki disliked him as much as he disliked Yasuki. George had only contempt for Yasuki's inflexibility. Yasuki was intolerant of George's Westernism, which he had accused George of flaunting.

Therefore, George decided on a direct approach. After a formal and very curt greeting, George said, "I shall be brief, Yasuki. I have come directly to you as spokesman for Akiko's family. I should like to obtain a divorce."

George could hear Yasuki suck in his breath and then exhale. Then Akiko's brother motioned him to a seat, not out of politeness, George knew, but because Yasuki resented George towering over him and looking down on him, since it placed Yasuki at a great disadvantage. George sat down. Yasuki took the chair behind the large, ornate, teak desk. "A . . . a divorce? But no one in our family has ever contemplated a divorce!" Yasuki said.

"No one in your family has ever used automatic calculating machines," George replied, jerking his head in the direction of the outside office.

"That is entirely different."

"Yes, you are quite right, Yasuki. It is. I apologize."

Yasuki nodded his head slightly. With precise, studied motions he put a cigarette in an ivory holder, then lit the cigarette. He paused. Looking at George with a face devoid of expression or reaction, he asked slowly, "Do I understand, honorable brother, you wish to marry a foreigner, an American lady?"

"I have said no such thing. It is true that I have met an American lady, a most gracious lady. Her very ill daughter has been a patient of mine."

Yasuki repeated, "It is my understanding, yes, that you wish to marry a *gai-jin*, a foreigner, from America."

George thought it was no wonder Yasuki had been one of the leading members of the *Kempetai*, the Japanese military intelligence, during the war. He knew everything and was unbending in making his point. George controlled his temper as Yasuki waited for his answer. "I have not asked the lady. I do not know if she would wish to marry me, but I would like to be in a position to find out."

Now Yasuki's eyes blazed; yet his voice was under control. "Honorable brother, only your face is Japanese. Your soul is not. For many years you have grossly insulted our family. You have caused the anguish of our dear, beloved sister." Here Yasuki bowed his head. "But if that were not enough, you now wish to insult us further by seeking a divorce—a divorce!—and in order to marry a foreigner, a Westerner, an American. You have disgraced us long enough," he hissed.

George's eyes were pinpointing the anger he was controlling. He said in steady tones, "Then, honorable brother, now is your opportunity to be rid of such a disgrace. Let me divorce Akiko, and I will be only an unpleasant memory."

Yasuki rose to indicate the meeting was at an end. He said, bowing low, "I regret you have come this distance to waste your time and mine. I can not grant your permission to divorce our beloved sister."

George looked down at the smaller man. "Yasuki, will you present my request before the honorable family council? Perhaps they will think differently."

Yasuki shook his head. "I regret, dear brother, but as head of the family council, my decision is sufficient just as it is final."

George himself bowed. "If that is your wish, Yasuki, there is nothing I can say."

Yasuki's words slithered through his teeth. "You are quite right. There is nothing more to be said, except for me to add that under no circumstance must you make an attempt to see Akiko. I will not allow her to be troubled."

George inclined his head slightly. Yasuki Kataoka bowed very low. The meeting was concluded.

George went back to his hotel room. He was defeated. He wondered if he had been wrong in his approach, too abrupt, too Western in coming directly to the point. Perhaps he should have been more prudent and less Western in observing the oblique, traditional method of arriving at his point. But he knew, regardless of the approach, when he would have broached the subject of a divorce, the answer would still have been an unequivocal no.

Actually he had realized there was little hope in having his request granted, but he was not prepared for the immediate denial. He had rather expected Yasuki to follow the Japanese custom of an evasive answer, but not an outright refusal. Yasuki had left no room for George to build his case, to say that perhaps a divorce would give Akiko an opportunity to remake her life. However, he knew full well that Akiko had remade her life: She was content with her escape. He wondered how he could have even hoped for a different response. He was like the family of a very ill patient: He could not accept the reality, and he clung to the one margin of hope that a miracle would occur.

Still, George had felt that if the proposal of a divorce could have been brought to the family council, there would have been some hope. One of the younger brothers of Akiko was more modern in his thinking than the others. If the family had suffered financial difficulties, the offer of a monetary settlement might have been held out as bait. But in the past few years, with the wave of financial recovery sweeping Japan, the family had prospered. Without the consent of Yasuki as the eldest brother and head of the family council, all hope of obtaining a divorce was gone.

George knew if he were to bring a judicial divorce, which he could do, there would be a formal trial in the District Court. His request would have to be on the grounds of something like unchastity, malicious desertion, incurable insanity or disappearance of spouse. He could, he thought, bring such a trial for desertion, since Akiko had left him. But this would be very difficult to prove to a court, since, as a husband, he had the right to demand the return of his wife. He had never done so.

In addition, he knew Yasuki would stop at nothing to prevent the divorce, accusing Martha and George of adultery. As a matter of fact, no doubt, Yasuki, with his intelligence training, had had George followed and knew exactly when and where he had met with Martha. George had been right in not bringing Martha to his apartment. Yasuki could have made an awkward situation for Martha and himself in retaliation.

George was despondent. He felt Yasuki's attitude was another case of the resistance of Japanese tradition to the realities of contemporary living. Divorce was still considered a disgrace. Yasuki could accept the best in mechanical inventions from the West, but institutions such as divorce he could not. A kabuki actor could put on the mask of a young girl, hiding his own ancient wrinkles, but the creases would still be there.

George had a medical paper to read at a meeting in Osaka. It was based on his recent research in Korea regarding the outbreak of encephalitis. He had termed the report, "Serological Evidences of Incidences of Japanese B Encephalitis Virus Infection in Korea Caused by Mosquito Parasites on Migratory Birds." As a case in point he had described in his paper the clinical picture of a young American girl who had been exposed to the disease just outside the city proper of Seoul, in a swampy area that attracted wild birds and was also a breeding ground for mosquitoes. Authorities had neglected to canvass the surrounding countryside for such infected areas, and it was unfortunate that the taxi in which the girl and her mother were riding had become mired in such an unhealthy spot.

In countless papers George had cited case histories of his patients. Each patient for him was an individual, not a medical case, and he, therefore, administered the optimum of medical care. However, because of the impersonal relationship that was particularly true in an illness in which the patient was usually in a comatose condition and therefore, lacking personality, George could without hesitation refer to the cases in terms of numbers, or letters of the alphabet. When George had begun dictating this particular paper for his secretary to type later, he had found, in the case of Kate Montgomery, that he could not call her merely by a letter of the alphabet, or a number. She was someone very dear to him. In describing her case, he had called her "Mary," covering with slight disguise the identity of the girl.

So moved had he been in the description of the case that his colleagues detected more than a medical interest in the patient. When, inadvertently, he had departed from the medical report, which he had carefully dictated to screen out anything personal, and had referred to the anxiety of the girl's mother, his voice for a brief moment had changed. But to some of his colleagues this was sufficient. Being tactful, they refrained from questioning him about it, but among themselves, being quite human and delighting to have a personal element to spark the meeting, they conjectured about Joji's interest in the patient and her family.

It was most unusual that he should have known the patient before she was attacked by the infected mosquitoes and that he should have had personal knowledge of her weakened condition because of a long, arduous plane trip from the United States. It was also most unusual that a specialist would have been called within twelve hours of the onslaught of the disease. There were indeed many extenuating circumstances to give reason for Joji's interest, and several of his colleagues smiled. "A ripple caused by a pebble thrown in a pond becomes a wave on the shore."

Dr. Kimpei Kimura decided at the last moment to attend the session at which Joji Tanaka would speak. He had not seen Joji in years, and he disliked him as much as he ever had. But still, Dr. Kimura figured Joji Tanaka was a doctor of importance, and it would do no harm to renew an acquaintance with him. But as he watched Dr. Tanaka address the group, standing tall on the podium in the front of the assembly, taller than any other doctor there, completely self-confident, Dr. Kimura felt a rush of hatred sweep over him, and he decided to indulge himself in the feeling. He closed his eyes to slits as one concentrating on the lecture, but he allowed his mind to return over the years to the time when he and Joji were classmates together at the University of Tokyo. Joji had returned from the United States, and they were taking a course together.

After a particularly difficult examination, Joji had remarked, "In the United States, if a student does not pass his medical examination, he is not made to feel a pariah for the rest of his life. You never hear of suicide for such a failure, unless the student is neurotic to begin with. In Japan too much emphasis is based on failure, and not enough on human dignity. Our concept is wrong."

Kimpei Kimura had swallowed hard. He could not think then of words to answer such an affront, such an insult to the emperor. He could not allow such heretic thoughts to go unchallenged. A man like Joji Tanaka was a menace, unworthy to carry the title of doctor. Kimura went immediately to the head of the department about these insulting statements.

The elderly head of the department to whom Kimpei Kimura told this scandalous defection of thought looked at young Kimura and said solemnly, "How strange for Tanaka-san to say that."

Kimura had been delighted to hear this. The elderly professor continued, "It is exactly what I have been saying for years. Too many of our bright young men are lost to society because they have not at one moment been the brightest to pass an examination." He sighed. "What a great loss in human resources, which Japan can ill afford." The professor had leaned his head forward to Kimura. "Maybe he will teach you more of his thoughts. You can learn something."

Kimura had felt his face sting with the rebuke. Not only had the professor not been angry with Joji Tanaka, but he had agreed with him. He had even suggested that he, Kimpei Kimura, pay more attention to Joji. Thus had Kimpei lost face completely to that rascal, Joji Tanaka. And now, listening to him speak, Kimpei Kimura considered that Joji had lost none of the arrogance of his youth. He was much too confident.

Soon after the medical meeting in Osaka was concluded, Kimpei Kimura, who lived in Fukuoka, a city on Kyushu, decided to return home via Nagasaki. Because Fukuoka had been spared the bomb, it had not received the worldwide attention that the smaller city of Nagasaki had. Although this stop was out of his way, Kimpei felt he would enjoy visiting with his good friend, Yasuki Kataoka, whom he had not seen in a long time.

Kataoka was pleased to see an old friend. He was flattered that as eminent a doctor as Dr. Kimura would still want to pass the time of day with him. Yasuki happily invited Dr. Kimura to a restaurant. There, over a specially ordered dinner or expensive and rare delicacies, they talked nostalgically of former times, when Japan had not been infected with Western ideas and customs, when *yamatodamashii*, the soul of Japan, was all-important, and no imported knowledge or techniques interfered with its maintenance, when the bushido spirit prevailed and when all paid allegiance to the emperor.

Waiting until the hostess serving them had momentarily

left the room, Dr. Kimura ventured the opinion that in retrospect it would have been better had the descendant of the sun goddess—and here he got up and made a slight bow—not survived to see the day when he would be looked upon as any other mortal man. For this apostatic thought, the doctor looked right and left, expecting instant retribution. Kataoka couldn't help but agree, adding that even within the family there was no more respect or allegiance to marriage ties.

Somehow Dr. Kimura felt this might be a propitious moment to add that, speaking of family, he had just seen Kataoka-san's honorable brother, Dr. Joji Tanaka.

"Ah, so. You were in Tokyo?"

"No, in Osaka, attending a regional medical meeting. Your honorable brother-in-law is a most capable man, growing in knowledge and stature constantly. His latest cause was a most interesting one." For dramatic effect Dr. Kimura sucked on a small *daiku*, savoring the taste of the pickled radish. "He described in a most . . . in an interesting and dedicated manner his recent case, that of a young girl, an American girl." Dr. Kimura bit the end of the radish most decisively, not glancing directly at Yasuki.

Kataoka did not show by the slightest change of expression that he had been touched to the quick by this remark. He sipped his tea. However, Dr. Kimura did notice a slight tremor in the little finger holding the porcelain cup, an involuntary quiver.

Dr. Kimura continued, "It seems this American girl and her mother—" Here he stopped like a Scheherazade. "If I bore you with this recital, please do not offend me by allowing me to continue."

Kataoka shook his head. "By all means, continue. I am always interested in medical reports. I have often wished if fate had so decreed, I might have studied medicine," He smiled, and three front teeth protruded to such a degree from his gums that Kimura wondered briefly if Yasuki could ever close his mouth.

Dr. Kimura went on. "To make a long story not too unbearable, this young American girl and her mother had been traveling in Korea, where the girl was afflicted by a mosquito bite—many bites, to be exact. Joji had seen the pair in Seoul before the child had been attacked by the mosquitoes, and then coincidentally enough . . ." he paused to let his remark light, "coincidentally enough, he was called in to the case in Tokyo almost immediately. A most fortunate stroke of destiny for both the American lady and also for Dr. Tanaka, since he was able to chart the disease almost from its inception. A most interesting case, is it not so? One so seldom knows previously the identity and personality of the patients involved, or is such prompt and skillful diagnosis usually made."

Dr. Kimura then spoke of the advances made in medical science, using obscure phrases a layman could not possibly understand. Having confused Kataoka, who had not been listening at all to the medical discussion, Dr. Kimura asked, "And don't you agree, Yasuki?"

Yasuki Kataoka had not been one of the leading agents in the *Kempetai* for nothing; so he replied immediately, "Why, Dr. Kimura, I would say that depends entirely on one's point of view, and I do not feel qualified to answer. There is so much that is intangible in medicine as in life, neither black nor white." Yasuki then closed his mouth to conclude his statements, and Dr. Kimura noticed that his lips did not quite cover his teeth.

The dinner was soon ended. Dr. Kimura expressed his happiness to have had this chance to visit with an old friend, and Yasuki Kataoka assured him he could not have been more pleased himself.

"*Domo, go-chiso-sama deshita.*" Dr. Kimura also thanked him for the excellent dinner, and then they parted.

Within twelve hours Yasuki Kataoka had sent out a summons for a family council.

CHAPTER XII

During the days of Dr. Tanaka's absence Martha found herself looking up every time the door to Kate's room opened, as if expecting Dr. Tanaka to walk in. After David Fletcher had left, there had been a void, because David had represented the realities of home. The absence of George had a deeper and, therefore, more frightening significance. She was afraid to acknowledge how much he had grown to mean to her, how much she had leaned on him, first as Kate's doctor, then as a friend and companion.

In her relationship with her husband, Paul, which had been marked by so many years of absence during the war, and then in her relationship with David she had always maintained a kind of independence in thought and spirit. She had somehow felt herself the equal of these men, intellectually and spiritually. However, with George Tanaka she felt she had at last found someone on whom she could lean and who could give her the support she needed. He represented the kind of strength, moral and spiritual as well as intellectual, that she had always wanted but had never found in either Paul or David. Without Dr. Tanaka, she found herself weak and in need of the quiet, competent strength he provided.

She also wanted George to share her joy in Kate's continuing recovery. Each day brought some new visible indication. George had said the physical improvements were there first; the apparent manifestations would come shortly.

Kate's hours of wakefulness increased. She was eager for news from home. Martha brought to the hospital stacks of letters both she and Kate had received from home. Martha made no pretense of keeping up a correspondence with her friends and all the well-wishers at home. She had neither the time, strength nor inclination. As a shortcut she had decided to write a community letter, which she had sent to David's office. One of his secretaries could then mimeograph it and distribute copies.

In the beginning the letters home had been only a few lines reporting the minimum about Kate's illness. She didn't want to worry the family any more than necessary, and she wanted to save herself the barrage of long-distance calls, cables and letters that would follow. Later she felt her letters were monotonous, since she had little new to add. Then as Kate improved and Martha began seeing Tokyo with Dr. Tanaka, she found she had to restrain herself from being too exuberant. At such a distance the family might criticize her severely for leaving Kate and enjoying herself; they had such rigid ideas of devotion and service to anyone ill. Then, too, she was afraid if she mentioned Dr. Tanaka's name too often, there might be more speculation and talk. Once, she had to tear up a letter, when upon rereading she found she had called him George. She was positive there was enough gossip as it was. However, trapped by the letters to the family, she could try to say only what she felt they should hear. She made it a habit to edit the letters carefully.

As for the correspondence she received, she could unfold the heavily monogrammed notepaper or scan the neatly navy-blue printed name and address in the center of the plain white paper and know what the letter would contain. "Can't tell you how concerned we are about you. . . . Are you sure you're all right? Don't overdo; try to relax. . . . If there is anything we can do, don't hesitate." She always smiled as she read that bit, remembering the similar statements when Paul had died. Martha always felt that everyone was sincere in a desire to help.

The letters to Kate were sparkling, as jumpy as the teen-age correspondents themselves. Kate couldn't wait to hear one particular letter. She would usually point to the one she wanted to hear first, the one from the latest boyfriend in her collection. Martha always said all these boys looked alike to her. Only their mothers and Kate could tell them apart. Nor were their letters vastly different; the emphasis usually rested on one sport or another, one elderly car being rebuilt, or one motor scooter. But even in spite of her initial enthusiasm, Kate was usually dozing by the end of the first or second page.

Dr. Nishimura suggested one day that Kate be allowed to walk a few steps. Martha would have preferred to wait until Dr. Tanaka's return, but she felt she could not contradict Dr. Nishimura. She held her breath as Kate, supported by a nurse and an orderly, tried a few steps. Kate was determined, and each day she tried standing a little longer, always trying one more step, until she could walk from the bed to the dresser, where she looked in the mirror. "*Eek!* A freak!" was her comment.

The next day Martha brought her a new lipstick, a trifle more brilliant than Kate would have worn at home, but it had the magic effect of bringing light to Kate's eyes, and a confident smile as she applied it too frequently. If it gave Kate the slightly bizarre look of a clown with white face and red lips, Martha refrained from comment, pleased at her daughter's obvious joy. Now that Kate was aware of her surroundings, even the night nurse brought a present— a screened bamboo container containing fireflies, a treat for a Japanese child.

Martha was almost tempted to buy a screened container of fireflies for her own hotel room, because her nights had become sleepless, confused, bewildered. "*Yes, but would you marry a Japanese?*" The woman's casual words in the cocktail lounge taunted Martha. Would she? Would she marry him? Would she be willing to be stared at, commented upon, speculated about? Would she become bitter, resentful, hostile, always on the defensive in Tokyo because she was an American—and in America, even more antagonistic because he was Oriental?

But she had no need to know the answer. The question was in the realm of supposition. George was already married; he was, no doubt, visiting with Akiko in Kyushu. Martha burned with the shameful thought that she was acting like a schoolgirl, an idiot for whom the fine line between reality and dreams had been swept away. Never had he even suggested any other kind of relationship than what she had enjoyed with him. She recalled he had once said affairs, as one called them in the States, between persons from the same caste or social structure were not known in Japan. There were many reasons for this. Above all was the sanctity of the home and the wife. Once a married woman had given birth to a son, she was sacrosanct, untouchable. No honorable man would contemplate her. In addition, a Japanese husband had the privilege of sexual pleasures other than at home without even being surreptitious about it. This would not, according to Japanese standards, infringe upon his wife's rights nor threaten the inviolability of his home. In fact, often the wife knew about a mistress, who would be selected from a lower social level. If the wife was consequently unhappy about her husband's actions, that was her own secret concern and heartache.

A wife, on the other hand, did not have the same privileges. Her primary duty was faithfulness to her husband. Even when she might consider an extramarital affair, few women would have sufficient privacy to carry on such a clandestine love. Besides, with whom would it be? Not one from her own social class, because any of the higher classes would consider such an arrangement with disdain.

Martha had jokingly remarked that maybe democracy would bring equal rights along all lines to women as well. George had shaken his head. There might be some, of course, who would defect from the accepted customs, but not many, and in due course, even though the younger generations did not feel the same impositions, there would undoubtedly be a swing of the culture pendulum to old established customs.

Then, when they had discussed the extramarital question, Martha had considered these statements to be an interesting sociological study of Japan. Now, she mused, how much of it applied to her? She was the mother of a son, but she was widowed. No home would be broken because of her action.

At times Martha ached to have George caress her. What would it be like to make love with him? Would his approach be Oriental or Western? What would the differences be? His complexion had a golden hue to it; yet he was not as dark or as ruddy as a suntanned American might be. His skin had a smoothness she found difficult to resist touching. When beads of perspiration dampened his forehead, she had difficulty in refraining from taking her handkerchief and stroking his brow. She wouldn't embarrass him in front of the nurse.

Would he be shocked if she spoke first about her feelings for him? Could she say something to him? She knew she never would. As much, as violently as she might wish it, she could never be the aggressor. Even with Paul she had never been. She recognized, too, how unsatisfactory such an affair would be. It would be far worse to leave George then. Perhaps this, too, was how he felt. Perhaps in his kindness he wanted to spare her any more problems, any more heartaches.

She knew now these past weeks with George had given her an understanding of Paul and Johnny's mother. Her sympathies had always been with little Johnny Kim, orphaned, a creation of war-time passion. Now she felt complete understanding and empathy with Paul and his oriental lover. As Helen Yang had said in Seoul, "There but for the grace of the gods go she."

One afternoon Martha went down to the lunch counter for a cup of tea. She saw Mariko sitting there and joined her. Mariko, blushing as usual, welcomed her.

"How's the young man from Detroit?" Martha asked Mariko.

Mariko replied softly, "I do not see him again."

"You didn't like him?"

Mariko looked shyly down at the counter. "I think I like him too much. I meet him, I like him. It is not good to like him too much." She stopped completely.

Martha said sympathetically, "Yes. . . ."

Mariko continued. "I am liking him too much, more and more." She sighed.

Martha paused and then said, "But he could marry you. The military law now allows it."

Blushing, the tiny nurse fingered the tea-cup. "Perhaps that would be worst of all," she said sadly. "He would not stay in Japan. He would return to the United States, and I go with him."

"The United States is a beautiful and wonderful country," Martha told her.

Mariko shook her head. "Not for a Japanese wife. I know. I have cousin who married very nice young man, American, in the Navy. She love him; he love her. They marry. She go with him to his home city. His parents pretend like her, but the rest of the family not even pretend. She never feel happy, never comfortable with them. The young man, her husband, he is not poor. He is not, of course, a *narikan*—millionaire—but he can afford to live in very nice house. They have trouble finding nice house, because she is Japanese. The little boy looks Japanese, like her. They, other neighbor children, make fun and throw stones and call him silly names. The little girl is fair like her father. Other children like her but still make fun, because her brother is very Japanese. So she can not like other children. It is good in school but not outside school. My poor cousin has many heartaches." There were tears in Mariko's eyes. "I shall not see any more my young friend from, how you say it, Detroi*th?*"

Martha was silent. Then she said slowly and meaningfully, "Perhaps you are right not to see him again."

The little nurse nodded her head. "I think so. I told him so yesterday night. We may never meet each other again. Now I like him, and it is already hard. Pretty soon I may love him very much, and it would be *warui*, very bad." Mariko looked at Martha. "Forgive me, Montgomery-san, for talking so much about myself. You are fortunate you are not faced with such problems."

"Yes, I am . . . fortunate." Martha picked up the check in spite of Mariko's protests. They walked out together. Again she had been told how fortunate she was, just as Helen Yang had told her in Seoul.

Serious, disturbed, Martha paused before entering Kate's room. Through the open door she saw Kate sitting in a big chair, a light blanket over her knees. And she was holding a new, beautiful Japanese doll. Kate was smiling. "I thought I was through with dolls ages ago, but I like this one."

Although Martha couldn't see him, obscured as he was by the door and screen, which protected the room, Martha heard the warm, rich voice of Dr. Tanaka saying, "Osaka is famous for its dolls, Kate. I thought you might like one for your collection."

Martha entered the room. Dr. Tanaka saw her come in and quickly crossed over to greet her, putting out his hands in a warm welcome, taking both of hers in his. He could feel her tremble. Martha hoped she was concealing from Kate and the nurse her joy and her anguish at seeing him again. After the visit with Mariko this was a particularly disturbing moment. But Martha scarcely had time to speak to George. She was interrupted by Kate's excitement about the doll as she held it up for her mother to see. Martha was grateful for the break, which would give her a moment to compose herself.

"In Japan," the nurse said, "we judge doll not by face, but by dress, the way is made. How you say, material is made up in small pattern just for doll dress." The nurse fingered the doll's costume. "This is very beautiful, very beautiful."

Kate pointed to a tiny container with an almost-minuscule firefly in it. "Look, Mom! She's carrying a firefly and cage." Martha examined the doll.

Dr. Tanaka volunteered, "Most Japanese dolls do carry something in their hands to give them a natural appearance, and usually each doll represents some person, either in history, or some caste, as a daughter of a Samurai, or a geisha."

Kate laughed. "I'll have to hide this when my cousins come for Sunday dinner. I don't want their cottonpickin' hands to spoil it. When I was small, I used to name all my dolls. What shall I call this one, Dr. Joji?"

He paused. "Let's see. The dress is yellow like a chrysanthemum. The Japanese borrowed the flower from the Chinese, who considered it an object of good omen. It is said a chrysanthemum is the flower of immortality."

"How do you say chrysanthemum in Japanese?" Kate asked.

"*Kiku*," Dr. Tanaka and the nurse replied almost in unison.

Kate repated it. "*Kiku*." Turning to her mother, she said, "Say *kiku*, Mom. Isn't it a wonderful name?"

"*Kiku*. Yes it's a beautiful name, Katie."

Turning to Dr. Tanaka, Kate said, "Now I have a surprise for you, Dr. Joji."

He laughed. "Look, you've given me quite a few surprises today. I left a sick little girl, and now I find a well one. I left a girl who hardly said more than 'good morning,' and now I find a chatterbox. I think I should be insulted, you did so well without me."

Kate was serious. "But I have another surprise for you." She threw aside the blanket and started to get up alone. The nurse rushed to her side. "Look," Kate said proudly, and as a toddler starting to walk, she took a few faltering steps alone. The nurse had her arms out ready to support her. Kate beamed with her accomplishment, but the nurse quietly took her arm. Kate did not object. "Just think, a few days ago I couldn't even do that." She was smiling. "I kept practicing . . . to surprise you."

George shook her hand solemnly. "You certainly did, and I congratulate you. It took a great deal of practice and—what's the slang?—guts. I'm proud of you, really proud." He turned to Martha to affirm his pride. "It really took courage."

"You know, it's funny." Kate became wistful. "Last summer I complained because I couldn't win a water-skiing race."

"Next year perhaps you can." Dr. Tanaka nodded his head.

Kate looked at him eagerly. "Do you think so, Dr. Joji? You promise?"

"Now, how can I promise? After all, you may break a leg skiing this coming winter."

CHAPTER XIII

Martha was disappointed when George asked her to step into the corridor after his visit with Kate. He apologized to Martha that he could not see her for dinner that evening, but he had some desk work to complete. A week's absence brought him more than a week behind in his schedule. He had clinic reports to check, and several articles for a medical journal to edit, both of which were long overdue. He hoped he could clear his desk for the next evening. Martha said she understood.

That night she ate an early supper of some sort of sandwich washed down with *chaa*—weak green tea. Then she visited with Kate, watching the fireflies glow in the darkened room. She returned early to the hotel. She felt petulant and frustrated. It had been some time—in fact since she had been in college and had begun to date Paul—since she'd had this feeling of keen disappointment. And once again she was ashamed of her attitudes. She knew the reasons for her unhappiness were the physical disappointment of not being with George as well as the doubts mounting during his entire absence about his visit to Kyushu. But how could she question him about his wife? It was hardly her right to do so. She was jealous.

She knew he was married. He had not mislead her or promised her anything. He had undoubtedly enjoyed the time spent with Martha as much as she had with him, or he would never have been as attentive. But her home would be Springfield, his Tokyo. Perhaps she was having the same problem with George that she had had with Paul. She wanted to possess, and to possess entirely. Then she stopped. This self-chastisement was neurotic. Paul, a husband, creating a child with another woman was one thing; a man going to see his wife was yet another, particularly a man who had never intimated anything beyond friendship. Angry at herself, angry in spite of herself, Martha was miserable and ashamed. Suddenly she realized she had faced disaster twice in the past year and a half, fatally with Paul, nearly fatally with Kate. She had withstood the shock and aftershocks of these catastrophes, but the absence of a dinner invitation was devasting. She laughed aloud at the incongruous analogy and at her attitude.

Martha was delighted, however, when George suggested the next evening that they have dinner together in the quiet *ryori* where they had been accustomed to going. At the entrance of the small room the waitress, who recognized them, smiled, bowing very low. Martha slipped out of her pumps, and the *nesan* placed them tidily on a shelf reserved for that purpose. Then the waitress knelt to untie the shoelaces on George's oxfords. As she stood up, blushing, she said something to George that made him laugh. He then told Martha that the waitress was afraid he and Martha had had an argument and were not seeing each other anymore. Laughingly, Martha said she trusted George had set the waitress right, that he had been out of town on business. She hoped her voice had betrayed nothing.

In the pavilion George pointed out that in their honor, when he had reserved the same room, the proprietor had changed the *kakemono* and had created a special flower arrangement, which signified "Welcome!" Looking at the several roses placed in the low bronze container, Martha exclaimed the flowers were beautifully arranged, but they did not speak any language she could understand.

They talked in general. George did not mention his visit to Kyushu, and Martha could not ask. After they had been served several courses, the waitress, who had been preparing the sukiyaki, finally left. George looked at Martha. "Martha, I was truly amazed at Kate's recovery yesterday. The encephalogram and myelograms have never indicated any permanent damage to the brain or nerves, but I wasn't sure to what extent her powers of locomotion might be affected. I know now the weakness in her legs is of secondary consequence. That is why I have a suggestion to make."

Martha nodded, not wanting to interrupt him.

"I told you once, I believe, Martha, that my family has for many years owned a summer home in Miyanoshita. This is a hot-springs resort in what is called the Alps of Japan. It's famous for its therapeutic baths. My mother lives there in summer, and she is there now. Martha, would you and Kate give my mother and me the honor of being guests in our home? For as long as it is necessary?"

Martha was overwhelmed. "Why. . . ."

He put his hand gently on her wrist. "No, let me finish before you answer. Arrangements can be made for Kate to go to the mineral springs daily for the baths. I can't promise they will affect an immediate and complete cure, but the baths have long been in use for a variety of illnesses for which hot springs are beneficial. I would recommend them for Kate, as I have for other patients, even if our own home were not located there."

"Isn't there a famous hotel at Miyanoshita? It seems to me I've read about one in a guidebook."

"Yes, there is a very famous resort hotel there. But, Martha dear, it would be our privilege and honor if you and Kate would be our guests."

Martha faltered, "I . . . I hardly know what to say. I'm quite overcome. We may be too much for your mother."

"I've already talked to my mother, and she, too, would be honored to help in any way she can. She's known all about the case and my interest in it. She is a very wise and knowing woman. We have competent servants and a reasonably large enough home to accommodate at least several guests."

Martha was disturbed. "George, please let me think this over. It seems almost too much to accept, this additional kindness. Everything you've done has been almost beyond comprehension."

George looked at Martha. "Martha, when you love someone, is there any limitation to what you do? To love is to give. Did you ever feel you were doing too much for Paul?"

Martha shook her head. He could feel her hand trembling.

"Martha, I have debated whether to tell you or not. In fact, that is why I postponed seeing you until tonight, to make up my mind. But I feel I should explain to you, to help you make up your mind about going to Miyanoshita."

She looked at him inquiringly, but said nothing.

"I have been hoping that I could be free to ask you to marry me. I don't know, of course, how you would feel about it, but I wanted at least to be in a position to ask you. On this trip I visited Kyushu to see my brother-in-law. That was the express purpose of my trip. I told him I wanted to divorce Akiko."

"I didn't know . . . I had no idea." All the former recriminations she had experienced swept over her, and she could feel herself getting pink with mortification, as if he could have known what had been in her mind.

"It is difficult to describe to a Westerner many of the Japanese customs and traditions. They are incomprehensible to any practical kind of thinking. First of all, there is the hierarchy of a Japanese family. The oldest male member is the chief. In my wife's family, since the death of her father many years ago, her oldest brother, Yasuki Kataoka, is the head of the family. I went to him to ask for a divorce from Akiko."

"I don't understand. You mean you didn't go directly to your wife?" Martha was confused.

"I didn't even see Akiko; I haven't seen her in over five years." He sipped the hot sake. "But at any event one would never approach the party concerned with a problem such as this. Just as a go-between arranges the marriage, so in a divorce the head of the family must be consulted in order to obtain an amicable, or consensual, divorce. The divorce itself, you see, is simple to obtain mechanically, if both parties agree. But it's the preliminary steps to reach such a mutual consent that are difficult, particularly in my case. First of all, I wanted Akiko to seek the divorce first, rather than have me instigate it, which I could do legally. But I wanted to save her the disgrace that is brought about in Japan when the husband seeks the separation. I therefore asked my brother-in-law. He could either decide himself to grant my wish, or he could call a family council."

"Which did he do?" Martha asked.

"Neither one. He decided himself, but the answer he gave me was unequivocally no. He knew, without my telling him, that I wanted to marry an American."

"Then what can you do now?"

For the first time since she had known him, George was depressed, despondent. "Nothing. There is literally nothing I can do now. Without consent, I could not start divorce proceedings. You see, divorce among, well, the higher classes is still considered an evil by most people. A proceeding not mutually agreed upon would take years and be most unpleasant. It is doubtful it would be successful."

"Couldn't you talk to Akiko herself?"

"No. That would do no good. She couldn't speak for herself. Her brother makes all her decisions."

"This is incredulous. It's . . . it's . . ." Martha sighed, trying to find an expression for the confusion she felt.

George interrupted, "Dearest, in Japanese culture much is difficult for a Western mind to grasp. It is hard for me, straddling both cultures as I have for so many years. But, Martha, if . . . if I were free, what about you? How do you feel?"

"I don't know, George. I don't know. I . . . I've never been so happy, so content with anyone, so stimulated. I was in love with Paul when we were married, but it was different, that first young love. It's so much a mixture of youth and romance, the unexpected, the anticipated. How can one define what it is? As we grew older, I would say I grew accustomed to him. I loved Paul; I was married to him. Sometimes I was bored. I knew what he would say. I used to say I knew what he was thinking, although I'm not so sure of that anymore. But it was just natural to be with him, not exciting, not stimulating, just natural—like breathing or anything else that becomes part of you. Yet he was gone so much of the time, I made those adjustments to his absence as part of my life too. Perhaps that is why his death for so long had no feeling of finality to it. I kept expecting him to come back."

She hesitated for a few seconds. "Being with you, George, has been a completely new experience for me. I can't separate in my own mind if it's because of the unusual conditions under which we met, if that's the reason for my great dependence on you. You know that I have leaned on you as I have never leaned on anyone before. I don't know. I haven't wanted to stop to think, to think things through, as the family would say. All I know is that . . . that," her boice dropped very low, "I've loved and treasured every moment with you. I don't know what you call it. But, oh, how I missed you this past week."

He had already crossed over to her side of the small lacquered table on which the dinner had been served. He had settled gracefully on the *zabuton* beside her. Martha looked up at him. He took her in his arms, kissing her, holding her. She could feel the strength of his arms, the delicacy of his hands caressing her. His head was very close to her, and almost fearfully she touched his hair. Even in the embrace she was aware of the quality of its fine, straight texture. Suddenly she remembered the bristling crew cut Paul had adopted the last year or so. She shuddered at the remembrance. Feeling her tremble, he released her, not understanding the cause.

She was embarrassed, not only at the moment itself, but at the remembrance of Paul. Was a memory to always obstruct her? "It's been a long time since a man has even kissed me like this," she answered. The affection David had always shown she'd put in the category of a devoted friend and relative.

"And for me," George said softly, "this whole time has been almost like a first time. You know, for my generation in Japan, romantic love is, well, something we know only in Western motion pictures or novels. Marriage is not based on it, as I have told you."

She was silent. Sometimes his reference to Japanese culture was so incomprehensible, she could say nothing.

George looked at her. "Martha dearest, believe me, I hadn't intended to speak of marriage, to ask you such a question, to cause you any problems, particularly after this negative meeting with Akiko's brother. But I felt I must tell you the truth about the impossibility of divorce. And if I asked you if you would marry me, it was because, I guess, I am human.

"I love, you, Martha. Believe me. This is the first time I have ever said it to anyone, ever experienced it. It's the first time I've known what it is like to have the companionship of a beautiful and intelligent woman, someone I can talk to, someone with whom I could share my life and my thoughts. For that reason I, too, wanted to be sure I wasn't confusing this emotion with the bizarre quality of our meeting. I know now, Martha, I know now, and I have for so long a time.

"I'm experiencing at this time of life what men in another culture know in their twenties, to fall in love." He smiled. "Perhaps like a childhood disease caught when you're older, it strikes harder."

"Maybe I should have taken immunization shots against love before I left home," Martha said. "I, too, have asked myself if George were free to ask me to marry him, what would I do? But then you hadn't asked me. I had no idea how you truly felt about me, and so I would push away any such questions and any answers."

"You still don't need to know the answer, but please think over the suggestion to go to Miyanoshita. I warn you, it will be a great sacrifice for me to have you that distance away. I'll be able to visit you only for weekends. But Miyanoshita is a beautiful scenic mountain spot."

"George, there is only one issue: Will it help Kate? Since you advise it, I know that answer too. The next question is when should we plan to leave? When do you think Kate will be able to travel?"

"I'll know more tomorrow after I take a few tests. Martha dearest, I'm glad you've made this decision. Kate isn't well enough to travel to the States, and yet she is convalescing too quickly to remain in the hospital. I know the baths will speed things along for her."

"I just hope we'll not be too much trouble for your mother."

"That is another reason I want you to go to Miyanoshita. I want you and my mother to meet. Knowing me, you know a quasi-American. But my mother, in spite of her

150

Western experiences, is still Japanese, representing the finest, gentlest qualities. Our home is entirely Japanese, as I told you. I want you to know me against my own background. This nomadic courtship of ours has been Tokyo, not really Japanese. When you return to your home and remember me, I want you to remember me as *Nihonjin*. Possibly, after all, it is fortunate you do not have to find your answer."

"No, George. It makes no difference, you know that. You must know that. I love you, George, so much, so very much."

Once again he held her tightly and kissed her. The *nesan* was waiting inconspicuously outside the door. When George and Martha left the place, Martha was crying softly. The tiny *nesan* found herself crying too.

Martha decided to write David Fletcher rather than cable her decision to go to the hot-springs resort as the guests of Madame Tanaka, George Tanaka's mother. Martha went into detail, explaining that George had recommended the mineral baths there as therapy for Kate, whose leg muscles had become spastic and weakened from lack of use, although organically there was no impairment. The baths at Miyanoshita were world-famous. She added that she did not know how long she would remain in Miyanoshita, but she would keep him informed.

Martha also wrote another letter to Helen Yang, explaining the continuing illness of Kate had postponed their return to the United States. She hoped that within the year she could send for Johnny and adopt him. What steps would be necessary from the Korean point of view? She, too, would investigate as soon as she returned to her home in Springfield.

CHAPTER XIV.

Dr. Tanaka felt Kate would be able to leave the hospital in ten days. He and Martha decided not to tell Kate the exact day so that if there was any postponement, she wouldn't be too disappointed.

David had cabled a reply to Martha's letter. It was worded in his usual legalistic terminology: "Advise follow George's recommendations re therapeutic baths. Proceed Miyanoshita long as necessary. Keep us informed. Love, David."

Martha decided to give up her room at the Imperial while she was to be at Miyanoshita rather than pay for an indefinite stay. The manager promised to find suitable accommodations when she returned. They would also gladly store whatever she wished them to keep for her.

Martha was puzzled as to what clothes would be appropriate for Miyanoshita. Did one dress formally or informally? Dr. Tanaka was no help. He said this was a department in which he was not at all knowledgeable. He would only suggest something warm for the evenings, such as a sweater and something cooler for the days, and to be sure to include rain garments, since there were showers or summer thunderstorms some part of each day.

The problem of clothes with Kate was more acute. Kate had lost so much weight, Martha knew nothing they had brought along would fit. Her daughter would need a complete wardrobe of dresses, underwear and night clothes. Martha left the hospital for a few hours of shopping. It was one of the few times she had been sightseeing during the day, and without George.

As she drove through the shopping area of the city, she was more amazed at its business, at the multitude of cars of every description. George had once said there were almost three quarters of a million automobiles in Tokyo, and she felt she had passed or been passed by at least a half-million. In fact, the kamikaze taxi drivers constantly amazed her, and she always arrived at her destination with a tiny prayer of thanks for a safe delivery.

She glanced at the store windows. The styles were Western, even copies of French designs, she was sure. Inside the store a young man came up to her, bowing low. He asked in English if she wished an interpreter. She replied she most certainly did. He bowed again and said it would be his honor to serve her. She explained that she wanted some dresses and other clothes for her daughter, but she wasn't sure of the comparative sizes. He bowed again, asking, "Will you favor coming with me together?" She followed him.

He was small and dressed in a black suit. George had once said the clerk class were the forgotten people of Japan. They had standards to maintain, but their salaries were infinitesimally small; yet they must keep up appearance. Positions such as this interpreter job were wanted by many equally qualified persons. Whenever she saw the average Japanese man, she was amazed at the contrast in appearance between him and George. George had said his height, no doubt, was inherited from his ancestors, who had probably come from one of the northern islands. That inheritance plus American food and boyhood athletics might have provided the extra inches.

Martha looked at the girls' dresses. She knew Kate's immediate reaction would be "kid stuff." Curiously, the clothes for a fifteen-year-old were of a style more suitable for an eight-year-old. The answer, no doubt, was found in the fact that daughters of customers who would shop in this higher-priced store were sheltered, guarded and chaperoned far longer than their American counterparts could possibly imagine. At this age the girls were still considered children, even though they were on the threshold of betrothal. Holding her breath, she did the best she could with the selection at hand.

Deciding to fortify herself if Kate objected too strenuously to her selections, Martha asked the interpreter if there were any kimonos at hand. She ended up buying several for Kate, for herself and for gifts back home. Although one of the nurses had told her she knew of a small shop where they could be made cheaper, Martha felt the saving was not worth the effort or time involved.

After Martha had finished her shopping, the young man asked if she had some extra time to look around the store. She said she had time; so he took her to the elevator and then up to the roof, where there was a large playground filled with children. She thought of Jimmy and of how Paul used to take him to Kiddieland on Saturday afternoon, letting him, even as a small child, go alone on the Ferris wheel and merry-go-round. She used to quarrel with Paul about his permissiveness with Jimmy. Suddenly she wondered if Paul ever thought of Johnny Kim while he was out with Jimmy, if he ever considered Johnny as his son too.

Then the young man took her back into the store, to a section apart from the rest and concealed by sliding doors. There she saw a magnificent display of antique porcelains and lacquer ware. She had seen enough exhibits with George to recognize their value. George was a good teacher. The realization that this was the beginning of the end, and that with the visit to Miyanoshita she would see him only on weekends brought an ache to her heart. She pushed away all thought of the permanent departure, wondering how she could bear the actual moment of leaving. The interpreter thought her silence was due to her interest in the lacquer box she was holding, an antique box with gold-lacquer design.

He suggested almost timorously, "Would Madame like to buy perhaps? It is expensive, but it is worth the value and will make a pleasurable memento of your visit, is it not so?"

Martha looked at the box. It was rectangular in shape. Dull gold lacquer covered the top and the sides, the top being a design of waves on a gold sea.

"Please to run your finger over the top's gold," the young man suggested.

Martha removed her glove and lightly ran her finger over the surface. It was as smooth as glass.

The young man bowed low. "This is very fine *makie*—"

"You mean that's the name of the wood." Martha asked.

"No. No. It mean pictures raised on boxes, lacquer. They take box out to sea to put on gold, miles out to sea where no dust can spoil. The box many years old maybe three hundred years."

Martha looked at the worn gold cord attached to the lock. There was an ancient key at one end of the cord. "How much is the box?" she asked.

The young man inquired of the salesman. Then he sucked in his breath. "Very expensive."

"How much would you say in American dollars?" Martha asked.

The interpreter took out a ball-point pen and figured on a scrap of paper. He looked at her sheepishly. "Ah, so, very expensive. Two hundred dollars. Very costly." He bowed low.

"Yes, yes, it is very costly." Then impulsively Martha replied, "I think I will take it." Suddenly she knew she wanted the box. She would omit buying pearls, although she could hear the family exclaim at her preference for a box, even one lacquered with gold and done at sea, to a double strand of pearls.

There were only two more days before the departure for Miyanoshita. Martha suggested to George that she stay in the hotel for the evening. She needed a few concentrated hours to finish packing. If she found she needed additional suitcases, there would still be time to buy them. She finished storing the clothes she was leaving at the hotel in a large bamboo case. She had already packed the miscellany. The room looked empty. She had always had a sentimental attachment to places. The weeks she had spent here, in spite of the trauma, now gave the room nostalgic quality, particularly because of Kate's miraculous recovery, and also because it was here she returned to think over the evenings spent with George. She had never kept a diary, even as a young girl, but she had made a habit of sorting in her memory the chronology of events.

In spite of the air conditioning, the room was warm, and she had become uncomfortable. She had taken off the *yukato*, finding its voluminous sleeves cumbersome to move in. She was standing in her slip when she spied on a top shelf of the closet a package she had overlooked. She brought a desk chair and climbed up, not even remembering when she had put the parcel on the shelf.

The brown-paper-wrapped package was still unopened. She immediately recognized the large handwriting, with the name and address scrawled in black crayon, as Sally's. The date indicated it had been sent within several days of the onslaught of Kate's illness. There were at least five dollars of airmail stamps on it.

Martha found a pair of scissors and opened the carefully wrapped package, the inside paper of which was a newspaper. Knowing Sally did nothing haphazardly, Martha glanced over the paper. It was a first page of the Springfield *Evening Times*. Centered in the paper was a picture of Kate and herself snapped at the airport. The accompanying story said that Kate Montgomery had been "stricken while traveling with her mother, Mrs. Paul Montgomery, in the Orient. Mrs. Montgomery was maintaining a constant vigil at her daughter's bedside." Martha remembered that when there had been a flood of messages from friends as well as people she hardly knew, she had marveled at how quickly the news had spread. Now she knew the semaphore for spreading the excitement: the newspaper article.

Wrapped inside, Martha found several tins of round butterscotch candies, her own favorites. She laughed. How like Sally to spend at least five dollars postage to forward three fifty-cent cans of candy! There was no one really like Sally. She bought candy by the bulk at the ten cent store and then would order special maple syrup from Manchester, Vermont, or expensive preserved fruits from the Farmer's Market in Santa Monica, California. She was always logically inconsistent.

Martha eagerly took the key attached to the bottom of the tin and started to open the container. In her rush and her excitement the key slipped on the tin cover and cut her finger. She felt nothing at first, but soon saw a gusher of blood spring from her finger. She rushed to the bathroom, turned on the tap and put her finger under it. She saw that the blood was spurting out, and she looking carefully at her finger. She could see she had cut the end of it so deeply, she was alarmed. She wondered if the tap water was safe to wash an open wound. She went back into the room for a thermos of drinking water she kept on the dresser.

The phone rang. At first she ignored it, but realizing that it might concern Kate, she rushed to answer it. Blood was now spilling onto her slip and making a path to the phone. She picked up the receiver and answered in an abrupt voice, "Yes."

It was George. "Hello. I'm in the lobby. I wanted to see if I could offer my services in packing. I'm pretty good at it, giving advice anyway." He could hear her sigh of relief, or of something more.

"George, I . . . I'm glad there's a doctor in the house. I just cut my finger rather badly, and I can't seem to stop the bleeding."

"My bag is in the car. I'll get it and be right up."

Martha was relieved to hear his voice. Now that the finger had started throbbing, she felt almost faint. She looked down and saw that her slip was covered with blood. She managed to get it over her head with one hand and put on the *yukata* she had been wearing. She rushed back to the bathroom to grab a towel to wrap around her finger.

In a few minutes she heard a knock on the door. She wasn't even sure how many times George had knocked before she was aware of it. She hurried to open the door and saw him standing there. He came in, his small black medical bag in his hand. She was pale and quite shaken. He kissed her, but as he started to hold her, she backed away, showing him the bloody towel.

She followed him into the bathroom, where he unwrapped the towel. He examined her finger. She had cut it badly, sufficiently to require stitches. As he opened his bag to get out the necessary medical equipment, Martha quipped, "All our internist at home carries in his bag is a stethoscope, the instrument for taking blood pressure, and the *Wall Street Journal*."

"If he has any good tips, let me know," George said. At the same time he took a rubber band from a bottle and placed it around the base of the injured finger. "Keep this on for a moment," he told her.

"A tourniquet. Never occurred to me."

George took out a large container of distilled water and poured it over the finger. Then he applied an antibiotic. "You've had tetanus?"

She nodded.

"I'll give you a booster in the morning." Then he deftly placed a small stainless-steel clamp at the end of the cut. He looked at her. "Hurt?"

She shook her head. "Not too much."

"I'm sure it hurts me more than it does you." Quickly he sutured the finger, taking about three stitches. Then he loosened the rubber band and deftly bandaged her up. "You'll make it." He smiled, then leaned over and kissed her.

"At home the pediatrician gives lollipops."

"I'll remind my nurse to put some in my bag."

"I like your sweets better," Martha said, and suddenly she felt herself blushing. "You really have a knack of arriving at the right psychological moment, Dr. Tanaka."

He put the things back into the bag. Then he washed his hands thoroughly. She handed him a fresh towel. She looked at his shirt; it was covered with blood stains. "Let me put some cold water on it before it stains," she said.

"Doesn't matter. Look, how do you feel? A little woozy?"

"Not particularly."

"Do you have any tranquilizers?" he asked. "I have some in my bag."

She opened the door of the medicine chest. "I haven't gotten around to packing these up. I have a new bottle. I thought I'd need a prescription, but the druggist downstairs in the pharmacy tells me you don't need one. What did he call it? tra—tranks, I believe. He says everybody seems to live on them here in Tokyo."

"I'm afraid that's so. Too many of them. Japanese have abandoned moderation, and I dare say there are more tranks, as your druggist calls them, sold in Tokyo than anywhere else in the world . . . probably also because there are more people." He added, "However, I think you better take one now."

She took a pill from the bottle and swallowed it down with water he poured from the thermos.

"Now tell me, what were you hacking when your ax slipped?"

"I'm embarrassed."

They walked back into the bedroom. She took the half-opened tin of candies and showed it to him. "Sally, David's wife, airmailed them to me when Kate was first ill. I never even opened the package."

He took the tin and, with a penknife, pried it open. "My favorites too."

"You know them?" Martha asked.

"I usually buy them at the drug store in my building." He smiled. "The world is quite small, you know."

"For butterscotch, George," she paused, "if not for me. It was the last package I had left in the closet." Suddenly, she started to cry. "Oh, no, George. It's almost all over. With all the horror, and the beauty, and the suffering—"

"And the love," he added. He walked over to her. As he took her in his arms, the *yukata* parted. He put his arms under the voluminous folds, and they walked together toward the empty bed. She lay down and closed her eyes for a moment. When she opened them, the ceiling light was off, and only the lamp on the desk was lit. He was there with her. She was aware of the throbbing in her finger, of the smoothness of George's back and shoulders, of a slightly spicy aroma of hair tonic, and then all sensations stopped as she entered into an experience unlike anything she had known.

It was as if in the release through love, all the anguish, worry and bone-tiredness of the past years dropped away. At last she found someone who could infuse her with the strength of love, on whom she could put down her burdens and say, "Take care of me. Love me. I need you." He was masterful; he was gentle; he was considerate; he was loving. In the act of love, the real nature of the man is shown, and George was exactly as she knew and wanted him to be.

George, too, knew he had found fulfillment, that this American woman was all he expected—responsive, giving, ardent and unabashed.

The soporific affect of love, along with the action of the tranquilizer, caused her to drop off to sleep. She was aware of George leaning over her. In the dim light she could see that he was now fully dressed. He kissed her gently. Then he left. Martha tried to rouse herself sufficiently to look at the time, but she was too sleepy to make the effort to turn her head to the night table. When she looked again, it was five o'clock the next morning. At some time George had put the silk comforter on her, but she did not know when. Now she felt chilly; so she drew the comforter around her neck and fell asleep again.

The alarm went off at the usual seven o'clock. Martha got up immediately. She did not allow herself the luxurious danger of thinking about the night.

CHAPTER XV

On the morning of the departure for Miyanoshita, Martha arrived at the hospital early. She went to the business office to settle her account. The elderly gentleman clerk behind the counter looked up from his large ledger and, seeing Martha, smiled and bowed low. He said nothing, but returned in a few moments accompanied by a younger man, who was dressed in the inevitable black suit. The young man also made a low bow. Could he be of service? Martha explained she had asked the day before to have the bill ready, since her daughter was leaving the hospital today.

Again the younger man bowed low and in carefully enunciated English said, "We are glad for yourself you are leaving, but whole hospital will miss you sorely and also your daughter. We have so greatly concerned about her and so pleased she is now recovered." The sentence had the cadence she found so intriguing. It was almost as if one were reading even the simplest sentence in rhythm.

Martha thanked him in turn for all the consideration that had been given both Kate and herself. The kindness of everyone had made a most difficult condition bearable.

The young man bowed again. "You will have a most beautiful day to drive to Miyanoshita, Montgomery-san."

The thought occurred to Martha that the whole hospital must know everything about her activities. Although realizing that one did not approach a problem directly, but also knowing that she was already pressed for time, Martha decided on a Western, direct attack. Taking out her checkbook, she asked, "Will you kindly accept my personal check for the hospital stay?" She was mentally prepared for any large sum. If it was more than she had in her checking account, she could wire David to transfer funds from her savings account.

The young man shook his head. Martha suddenly felt a quick rage. She wondered if she would have time to find a bank nearby that would cash her check. Perhaps she would have to return to the Imperial, but for such a large amount would they cash her check? She didn't want to bother George for his endorsement, but it could be necessary. All of these thoughts occurred to her, but before she could say anything, the young man spoke again. "Sorry, Montgomery-san, but we do not present you with a bill now at this moment. We mail it to you in your home in Indiana." The word "Indiana" was almost a question. He continued. "After you have returned once again to your home."

Martha was nonplussed. "But I would like to pay it now, if you will accept my check. At home one always pays hospital bills upon leaving."

He shook his head. "Montgomery-san, you have been guest in our country. You did not expect heavy illness. I assure you, our bill will arrive when you are once again in your own home. We know you are honest, and the hospital does not worry." He smiled. "You get bill all right, but not while guest in our country."

Martha could hardly speak. Impulsively she leaned over the counter and shook the young man's hand, to his embarrassment. "I . . . I don't know what to say, how to thank you."

The clerk came from behind the counter, and, bowing, he escorted her to the door of his office. "It is our humble privilege, Montgomery-san, to have served you." He paused. "*Yo daye ni.*" He closed the door gently after her.

Mollified by this experience, Martha arrived in Kate's room to find it filled with people. Floor nurses, private nurses from other rooms, orderlies, even the old lady selling newspapers, had come in to say good-bye to Kate, who was crying at the leave-taking. Martha had brought presents for Kate's nurses and for several of the floor nurses who had been attentive. But it had never occurred to her that the Japanese custom of bringing gifts to departing friends would result in such a deluge of things for Kate—paper lanterns with tops representing heads of small boys and with elongated paper bodies; the three "See No Evil, Hear No Evil, Speak No Evil," monkeys of Nara, done in wood; ceramic cats resembling feline Kewpie dolls; small trinket boxes; *ori-gama* or folding paper booklets. Martha realized some of the presents were too costly for the donors.

She was wondering how to make amends when George came in. With his presence the confusion seemed to vanish. He looked around at the hospital cart piled with boxes and luggage, and at the new assortment of gifts, which were on the bed, the bureau and the night table. "Looks like moving day at the farm," he said, smiling, to Kate.

"Looks more like Christmas to me," She replied.

The nurse added, "I'll order another cart right away."

Martha started to open several of the drawers in the bureau. "An old compulsive habit of mine." She smiled.

But as she pulled out one of the drawers, George noticed her finger, which was still bandaged and which she held stiffly. "I'm the one who's forgetting in all these farewells." George then spoke rapidly in Japanese to Kate's nurse, who had not yet left the room. She replied and scurried out. A nurse's aide next rolled in another cart for the gifts. And then Kate's nurse returned with a surgical tray complete with instruments and antiseptics.

Kate was alarmed. "Not for me, is it, Dr. Joji?"

"Not this time. It's for your mother?"

"For me?" Martha was puzzled.

"Another tetanus booster, and I want to look at your finger, see if it's unraveling." George went into the bathroom to wash his hands.

The nurse cleared a small table and put down the surgical tray. Martha held her finger out, and George cut the bandage.

"Finger bothering you?" he asked.

"No, I forgot about it—almost." She looked at him. He returned the look, but said nothing.

"Looks fine. Soon be reduced to a Band-Aid." He bandaged the finger again. "I suppose you'll have nothing to do with butterscotch again."

Martha said, "No, to the contrary." This moment, too, was another to recall, she knew.

166

At last the hospital carts were packed, almost precariously laden with gifts. Kate was in the wheelchair, with her doll, Kiku, on her lap. She was dressed in one of Martha's store purchases, a dress that the young interpreter had said was "very stylish." It hung on Kate without any shape, a pink-plaid gingham, tied with a huge sash. Her face was small, emaciated, her complexion pale, and her blond hair, unattended for so many weeks, hung over her shoulders like Alice in Wonderland. She was holding the doll in her lap. The incongruity of too much lipstick gave her the look of a child who had got into her mother's makeup box. Martha hoped that Kate's appearance would improve before they returned home; otherwise she could hear the family's remonstrations, not considering the fact that Kate's being alive was miracle enough.

Kate looked around the room as the nurse's aide was about to wheel her out the door. "Gee, I kinda hate to say good-bye to this place," she said.

Martha knew exactly what she meant.

Not until Kate commented that she didn't know Dr. Joji drove an American automobile was Martha aware that this was not his regular car. In the excitement of leaving the hospital, she hadn't been observant enough to notice.

"Thought you'd feel more at home, Kate. I also thought you'd have more room."

"You certainly think of everything," Kate said. Martha could only nod her head in agreement. She remembered Paul's last automotive purchase, a high-powered foreign two-seater car that could not accommodate a family. His explanation had been that every man is entitled to some freedom. She had agreed, but upon selling it after Paul's death, she was shocked at the exorbitant price he had paid for it.

Now Martha noticed the small sticker pasted on the dashboard indicating that the car had been rented from an American Auto-Drive. "I didn't know they had a branch even in Tokyo," she remarked.

"Wherever there's an American tourist." George smiled. "None of my friends could help me out; their cars are even smaller than mine."

The drive to Miyanoshita, through the Japanese countryside, was a source of wonder to Kate, as George pointed out places of interest. Although she had seen Tokyo as few visitors see it, Martha had not taken time to visit the country. She, too, was in constant amazement at the hillsides, which were all minutely worked, looking like enormous checkerboards of yellow, gold and green of every shade where corn and rice were cultivated.

When they finally arrived at Dr. Tanaka's home, George turned around to Kate, who was in the back seat. "Kate-chan, I didn't describe a Japanese home to you because words would not be enough. It is something that must be experienced. You will find it entirely different from anything you've known, but I hope you will be happy."

Kate's face was enraptured. Martha was pleased to see that the drive and excitement had brought color to the girl's cheeks. Somehow Kate had managed to tie a bright red-and-white-silk scarf, one of the gifts she had received, around her head. She had lost the almost-pathetic childlike appearance.

Martha looked at the outside wall and gate, which George opened. In Tokyo, George had driven her thought the residential sections, but it had been impossible to tell what the homes were like, each being shielded by an outside wall, as if the sanctity of the home was protected by a wooden fence. One could only surmise what lay beyond the foreboding and impersonal exterior.

They drove up a circular driveway to the entrance. From the drive, the main entrance to the house was hidden by an island constructed of huge rocks and trees to conceal the approach. He parked the car on the gravel outside the porte cochere, telling Kate this was called the *omote-genkan*, the main entrance for the use of guests. He added that he was a grown man before he could use this entrance instead of the *nai-genkan*, or side entrance reserved for family use.

Leaving Martha and Kate in the car, George went up to the entrance. In a few moments several tiny, immaculate Japanese maids, dressed in *yukata*—simple cotton summer kimonos—followed Dr. Tanaka to the car. They greeted Martha and Kate, bowing low, their sweet round faces in welcoming smiles. Kate was bouncing up and down on the car seat, overjoyed.

From the trunk of the car George started to take out a portable wheelchair. A gardener came up to assist, but George himself lifted Kate out of the car and placed her in the wheelchair.

She turned to him, smiling. "You really do think of everything, don't you, Dr. Joji?"

He patted her shoulder affectionately.

"Yes, Kate. Dr. Joji certainly thinks of everything." Martha's voice expressed her deep gratitude. She started to follow George up the gravel path, with her small cosmetic case in hand. But one of the *nesan* came up and gently took the case to carry.

At the door to the home George stopped, leaned over, untied his shoes and slipped out of them. Then he put on a pair of slippers. The *nesan* handed Martha a pair also, and Martha watched while the maid leaned over to remove Martha's shoes, carefully placing them to one side. Martha put on the slippers.

George said to Kate, "This stone is called a *kutsunugi-ishi*. It means 'shoe-removing stone.'" Leaning over, George started to pick Kate up from the wheelchair to carry her inside. Kate was pouting. She, too, wanted to leave her shoes outside and put on the cute little slippers. George spoke in Japanese to one of the maids, who, smiling broadly, disappeared into the house. In a brief moment she was back, holding a pair of slippers in her hand. She removed Kate's shoes, and Kate looked proudly down at the slippers she was now wearing.

They entered first into the *genkan*, or entrance room. Looking around, Kate gave an unceremonious whistle at the quaint, foreign charm of the home. Martha sighed and said, "How lovely. How simply lovely, and so tranquil."

From the room, they looked out onto another garden, an interior garden, which also included a small pool of water, stunted pine trees, old stone lanterns and several stone benches.

The room, barren by Western standards of decor, seemed larger and more spacious than its actual size indicated. White *tatami* mats with black borders, all of equal size, covered the floors. George explained to Kate the size of a room is described not by square feet, but by the number of mats it can accommodate. *Fusuma*, sliding doors of silk, separated one room from another. The walls were bare.

The next room they entered was what Westerners call the parlor. In a recessed alcove, which George pointed out to Kate, called the *tokonoma,* there was a delicate flower arrangement: pine branches and three chrysanthemum heads. These were in a low, slightly curved brass container placed on a waxed platform of a wood Martha could not identify. Above it hung the exquisite roll picture—the *kakemono.* Low tables, and cushions with armrests comprised the furnishings of the room. Kate was surprised to see in one corner of the room a small grand piano, seemingly out of place in the Japanese severity. "Who plays?" she asked.

George replied that he used to, when he was a boy. Then, pushing back a low silk door beneath a window shaped like a full moon, he showed Kate two deep shelves filled with books. "These are in English, Kate. Help yourself."

Still carrying Kate, who protested she must be too heavy, George walked down the corridor, to her room. There was a regulation hospital bed in the room.

Kate was unhappy. "Aren't I ever going to get away from one of these grown-up baby cribs?"

George laughed. "Kate, after you've tried the mineral baths and feel rested, we might even let you sleep on a *futon.*"

"What's that?" Kate asked.

"It's what the Japanese call a bedroll, or bedclothes that are put directly on the floor—no bedsprings or mattresses."

"Oh, a kind of sleeping bag!"

"Something, but not quite. Perhaps a glamorized sleeping bag, often made of silk," George added.

A maid, whose kimono was more elaborate than the others, came in to assist Kate. "Hinako will help you, Kate," George said. "She's had nurse's training; so you'll find her quite expert at assisting you."

Beaming, Kate said, "*Kibbuchi-wa.*" Then turning to

George, she said, "That means good afternoon, in Japanese."

He smiled. "Indeed it does, Kate. You'll probably be speaking Japanese fluently before you leave. Now, Kate, a good rest."

Kate nodded, and impulsively she put her arms up to grab him. Then she gave him a kiss. "You're simply wonderful to us, as good a friend as Uncle Dave."

Martha looked away and then hurried out of the room.

George caught up with her in the corridor. "Your room is to the right, Martha. The bath is here." He opened the door to the bathroom. A deep whitewood tub with two faucets above and a little row of gaslights below was the version of a bathtub.

"Does one just step into this tub?" Martha asked.

He smiled. "It just looks deep, because it is. A tub is called *o-furo*—honorable bath."

Carved towel hangers, shelves, and a big bamboo basket in one corner were all identifiable, but a large coil of garden hose intrigued Martha. "That looks like a plain garden hose."

"It is," George explained. "It's used to water the garden out here." A sliding panel revealed another tiny garden, complete with stepping stones, miniature pool and goldfish. "The water from the bathtub is used on the garden. "You see, you soap yourself before you get into the tub. The water in the tub is just for relaxing, not cleaning."

George showed her to her room, adjoining the bath. She looked around at the emptiness of the room—no bed, only cupboards built into the wall and a few cushions. He looked at the complete look of bewilderment on her face and started to laugh. "I wanted you to see just what life in Japan is really like, Martha. The maid will bring in the *futon* for you to sleep on. If you feel it is too difficult, we can order a Western bed for you."

Martha took a deep breath. "I feel like Kate, completely overwhelmed. I'm very grateful to you for giving me this opportunity."

He walked over to the cupboard and opened the doors. "Your bags will be brought in a moment." Then he showed her the *syoin*, a bay window with a fixed desk. "This is used for reading." He turned toward her. "Martha, I want you to be happy in a Japanese home."

"Oh, I will. I know I will."

"As soon as you feel rested, in about an hour, Mother will greet you for tea."

Martha felt a sudden start. She had forgoten about Madame Tanaka, since she had not been present. Now, suddenly, like an awkward girl, she became frightened. She hoped her voice would not betray her nervousness. "I'll change, and then be ready, George."

The *nesan* brought in her bags. Bowing to Martha, George left the room.

Not quite knowing where she would meet Madame Tanaka and feeling most ill at ease, Martha wandered into the garden adjoining the parlor. She sat down on one of the stone benches. The peace and tranquillity of this exquisite spot gave her a feeling of contentment she had not experienced before, and the strangeness of the whole household dropped away. She was wondering what there was about a Japanese garden that evoked this relaxed, meditative frame of mind. The little garden on the hospital roof induced the same kind of tranquillity, although not to the same degree, for there were strangers about. Finally she decided the mood resulted from the complete simplicity, the uncluttered design. Like the interior of the home, there was no confusion. Instead, beauty was created through the artistry of simplicity. The eye was not pulled in a thousand directions.

She was startled to hear George's voice. She was even more startled to see him. He had changed from his customary Western suit to a kimono. At the brief glimpse of him dressed as he was, he belonged in this completely Japanese background. She felt now she was looking at a complete stranger. She was talking to a complete stranger. Westernized Tokyo was one world; this was another. Now she was the complete alien.

George suggested they go in to meet his mother. Martha was not aware that her nervousness was so apparent, but as he slid his hand along the inside of her wrist in his accustomed fashion, he looked down at her, smiling. "Relax. Mother isn't that formidable, you know."

In another wing of the house, apart from that which

Martha and Kate were occupying, was the suite of Madame Tanaka. George rapped on the wooden strip attached to the silken door. A gentle voice answered in English, "Please enter."

Martha walked into the room. Although she did not have an opportunity to look around, she was aware of a different feeling to this room. It seemed at first glance more Western that Japanese. Even the Japanese features were more Westernized. There was a golden covering to the sliding panels, a variety of woods in the ceiling and woodwork. Martha quickly noticed there was a deep rug on the floor instead of the *tatami*, and there were Western chairs in the room. Madame Tanaka was seated in a large, comfortable easy chair. Next to her was a table and lamp, and on the table were Japanese and English newspapers.

George bowed low before his mother, and then leaned over to kiss her briefly on the forehead. He stepped back and presented Martha to her. Martha looked at this tiny, frail, older woman. In her kimono it was impossible to tell how tiny she really was. Martha hesitated for a brief second, not knowing whether to bow or shake hands. But then Madame Tanaka offered Martha her hand. Martha had a quick impression that the hand was so soft, so fragile, she was almost afraid to press it. In precise English, in the most beautifully modulated voice Martha had ever heard, she welcomed Martha and her young daughter to their humble home.

Martha, embarrassed and self-conscious, said she was afraid they were going to be too much bother.

Madame Tanaka smiled at her. She looked at Martha, but the look was kindly and sympathetic. "Not at all," she assured her. "We are honored to have you and your daughter as our guests. My son has told me of your great troubles with your daughter's recent illness. We are now eager to help her with her convalescence."

A maid appeared and brought the tea service. Madame served the tea, which she poured into a fragile white-porcelain cup. Martha put the cup to her lips, afraid that she might crush the cup just by holding it.

Madame Tanaka then told Martha that when they were first in the United States and George was a very small child, he had developed whooping cough while they were the houseguests of American friends. Every time Joji had whooped, Madame Tanaka said, she had ached, for she was afraid of troubling their host and hostess. She had wanted to place him in a hospital for children, but their very kind host and hostess would not hear of it. She had never forgotten their kindness and had always felt a great debt, which Martha could help her to repay.

The conversation then turned to Madame Tanaka's memory of the several universities with which her husband had been connected. She even described to Martha her great problem of remembering American names; those of colors like Mrs. Brown or Dr. White she could easily recall, but other names such as Jones she felt she could never master.

At a signal from George, Martha rose and bowed to Madame Tanaka. Martha said she must apologize in advance for all the mistakes she knew she and her daughter would inadvertently make, and she hoped that they would be put down to ignorance. But so much will be like "Jones" to her. Madame Tanaka smiled graciously, and George followed Martha out of the suite.

After they had left, Martha turned to Gerorge. "She is one of the most remarkable women I have ever met—so alive, so gracious, so feminine."

George smiled. "She's quite a person. In the States I'd say quite a girl, but I hardly think that fits Mother. But it was she who always urged me to accept the best of the two cultures. You may have noticed, she prefers Western chairs and beds. She says at her age they're more comfortable. Did you know what was behind that heavily embroidered silk screen? Guess what those white storks flying across the sky were hiding?"

Martha shook her head. "At first I was too frightened to look around the room; later I was too absorbed."

George laughed. "It was a television set. And do you know her favorite program?"

"I'd be afraid to guess."

"*I Love Lucy*. She looks at all American programs. Tokoyo has them all, you know, and she says she enjoys American humor."

174

Kate remained in bed for dinner—doctor's orders. Madame Tanaka had dinner served in her suite; so George and Martha were alone in the dining room, served by two of the *nesans*. The dinner was a combination of American and Japanese dishes.

Earlier in the day Geroge had shown Martha the dining room. The room had been empty of anything resembling a dining area. He had then slid back one of the panels and revealed a closet of many shelves on which were wooden bowls for rice, oval plates for fish, deep dishes for pickles, and many other plates and cups and dishes for various dishes. Beneath the shelves were lacquer tables, each a foot square and a foot high. Piled nearby were silk cushions.

Now, looking around at the room set for dinner, Martha remarked it was like a stage setting, an empty stage that had then been dressed for the performance.

After dinner Martha walked over to the grand piano in the parlor. She ran her finger idly over the key. The piano was in perfect tune. George explained that he brought a piano tuner up from Tokyo once a year, a former GI who had remained in Tokyo and had found he could have a good life as a piano turner.

For the first time in many months, almost in the year since Paul had died, Martha began to play. George seated himself on a *zabuton*, sitting cross-legged. At first, not being able to see him over the keyboard, Martha had the feeling she was playing to an empty room. But as soon as he saw her trying to look over at him, he moved the cushion nearer to her. She apologized for being rusty; her fingers felt awkward and clumsy. The acoustics in the low-ceilinged room were not good, and Martha found herself selecting numbers that were rather simple. As she played, her technique improved.

During a short break in which she smoked a cigarette, she told George she had majored in music at the university. She had wanted music as a career. She had even been offered a position with a symphony, but she had turned it down to marry Paul. After her marriage she had played with the local civic symphony group, but Paul had objected to the number of evening rehearsals required, and she had dropped out. At first she'd missed the music and being part of the interesting symphony group, but she soon became adjusted to doing without it. As her life filled up, she found less and less time for the piano. Looking back, she now realized it was because she had failed herself and her ambitions that she had departed entirely from her music. She used to blame Paul, but if she had really wanted to stay with the music, even practicing at home, she could have done so.

She played again. The hours sped by. Suddenly she struck a final chord. The sound lingered in the air. She felt she could not lift her hand again, and she sat there, almost numb. The physical efforts, the emotional catharsis of playing again in such a strange surrounding had fatigued her more than she realized. She sighed.

George looked at his watch. "Legitimate. Do you know that it's a quarter of one?"

"It isn't!" Martha looked down at the watch she was wearing—a rectangular gold shape with baguettes of diamonds on all four sides of the face. It had been the last gift from Paul. Upon seeing the time, she cried, "Oh, no!" But the sound was really less of a cry, and more of a moan.

George, who had already got up from the *zabuton*, came to her side.

When she looked at him, he could see the anguish in her face. "George, I forgot the date. I didn't even realize it until just now. This is the first time in all these years. George, today was our anniversary—Paul's and mine. Once he forgot, and I chided him. Even when he was away, he wrote or cabled. I never thought I'd forget, never in my whole life. I had planned our trip to be back home, in my own home, by this date. And now I forgot. The first anniversary since he's gone, and I forgot."

George wanted to hold her, caress her, but he felt this would only add to her guilt. He spoke softly, gently. He didn't remember later what words he had used to comfort her. "Martha dear, please listen to me. You haven't been leading a life, according to a calendar. These have been strange times for you. You can't reckon anything by what day, what week, what month. In abnormal surroundings, which I know all this is for you, how can you expect to remember what ever there has been to anchor you to a calendar on the wall. You have loved Paul; there never has been a time when I've been with you that you haven't referred to him. He lives in your heart every second that you breathe. And I love you all the more for that. Don't feel guilty about your feeling for me. Because a mother has one child doesn't mean there is a limit to her love. Love is expansive; there are no boundaries."

"I guess I'm simply exhausted. But when I realized the date, I felt I had lost my senses, to forget."

"Martha dearest, having you come up here, I felt, was not only beneficial for Kate. But I felt you needed a change, to get away from me, if you will. You needed time to think, to relax, to be rid of responsibility. But I think you needed something else. After Kate's been here and continues to improve, as I am sure she will, I want to show you something else of Japan—Kyoto, Nara, Osaka. We can plan it for the time just before you leave.

"But let's talk about it later. Now the doctor orders a good night's sleep."

"I think I need more than a trank, as they say in Tokyo."

"I have something in my bag. I'll get it. You'll find a thermos of ice water in your room."

A little later Martha was falling asleep. The foreign feeling of sleeping on the *futon* on the floor, the sight of the moon shining through the sliding door, all gave her a disembodied sensation. She wondered if she would ever feel whole again. Probably not until she returned to the familiarity of her own home. What was wrong, she asked herself, that she could not be flexible enough to accept whatever happened? In her own way she was as rigid as the family. They had left their mark on her, and she was too weak to resist. But the self-chastisement diminished as sleep came. Soon she was in a deep coma.

Lying down on the *futon* in his room, George, too, was speculating. Martha needed someone to look after her. She had done a remarkable job of simply keeping together during the ordeal in Tokyo, complicated, he realized, by her growing love for him. She needed love, physically and spiritually. He knew now he'd been right in bringing them here to Miyanoshita for Kate's convalescence. But he also felt before she returned home, she was entitled to see more of Japan, a vacation. He could even plan a week in Hong Kong, perhaps Bangkok, but he did not want to alarm her by suggesting what to her would be an extensive trip, although it was only about a four-hour flight from Tokyo to Hong Kong.

He knew full well the risk of Yasuki's probable ugly actions, but, George reasoned, by that time Martha would be out of the country and could not be hurt directly. It was unfortunate, but, as his countrymen always said, "*Shikata ga arimase*"—it can't be helped.

The next day George took Kate with Martha and Kinako, the nurse's aide, to the hot springs, where Kate was to have the mineral baths. George had previously told Martha that in certain sections of the spa both men and women bathed together nude, and it was quite customary, but he had, of course, arranged for a private bath for Kate.

On the drive over, George told Kate a little about the function of baths in general in Japan, that they were not used to get clean, as in America, but to relax. The Japanese considered as part of everyday routine a period in the early evening when they could relax in the bath. They washed and cleansed themselves outside the bath.

"Say, Mom, that's just like the sign on Aunt Sally's swimming pool at home. 'This pool is for enjoying, not for bathing. Take a shower first.'"

"That's just about it, Kate. But these mineral baths, of course, are medicinal and have real proven value," George said as they drove up to the entrance of a building, again surrounded by the ever-present wooden fence.

Kate was delighted with the baths, particularly when she found part of the treatment was being covered by what she called "mud-pie baths," a beneficial mud rubbed over the patients. Kate could hardly wait to start.

In the past, whenever she had seen George in a situation dealing with his profession, Martha had always been impressed by the respect and devotion shown him. And his own manner was friendly, competent and always dignified. Just as at St. Thomas's Hospital in Tokyo, Martha felt here at the spa Kate would receive care beyond that given the average patient.

Knowing that both Martha and Kate were happy in their new, if unusual, surroundings, George was ready to return to Tokyo. He would come back on the weekend.

The night before his departure he and Martha were in the car, returning from the Fujiya Hotel, where they had had dinner.

"You know how a plane comes in for a landing, it begins losing altitude considerably before the landing," George began. "My return to Tokyo is helping me lose altitude, preparing me for your departure."

"I know. It's all I think about. Soon it must come—next week, next month, whenever it is, it will be too soon."

"I shall write an opera and call it *Monsieur Butterfly*."

"Don't joke, even to make me smile. I can't tell you how I feel. When I leave Tokyo, I may never see you again. The thought haunts me, lurks behind everything I do and say. I can't enjoy this beautiful spot, your mother's wonderful hospitality, without thinking it will all soon be finished.

"Then part of me says this can't be happening to me. It's something I'm reading or a play I'm seeing, and I'm simply identifying with the characters. Do you have any idea how circumspect, how regulated my entire life has been? Now look at me! I've fallen in love. At my age. A mother of nearly grown children, with a man—"

"Of a different race, whose skin is another color," he interrupted her.

"No, don't say that. I've simply fallen in love with a man who is married, who couldn't possibly marry me, with a man who lives thousands of miles away, whom I may never see, except, if I'm lucky, on short visits."

He had parked the car along the road. It was pitch-black. There was scarcely any traffic. In the far distance she could see the lights of a village; it could have been Miyanoshita, but she didn't know or didn't care. Mt. Fuji was near at hand too, but in the dark she had no idea in what direction. As far as she was concerned, there were, at this moment, only the two of them in all of Japan.

"George, I don't want to go back. I could send for Jimmy, but I know I can't stay. Then I keep thinking of Paul and of Johnny Kim's mother. Don't you see, it was different with Paul? He did have a wife, children, responsibility to return to. His life in Korea was superimposed. But if Jimmy were here with me, I would have nothing meaningful to return to, nothing to keep me back home, only emptiness and widowhood."

"You mean, Martha, you would live here in Tokyo if . . . if I were free to ask you?"

"Yes, George, I would."

He had been holding a lighter in his hand. Now he took the lighter, flicked it and held it to her face. He could see her eyes, the love and the sadness, the confusion and the loneliness. He took her in his arms and kissed her and embraced her. She responded.

Then she broke away. He knew she was crying. "George, help me. Tell me what I can do. I love you so very much. And I know there is every obstacle between us. When Paul died, I accepted it. People said I was brave. I wasn't; there was nothing I could do. But now maybe there is. I rationalize, bring the chilfen here, let them go to school. But how could I live here alone, furtively waiting to see you at odd hours, sneaking away from the children. What can I do, George? Tell me, what is the answer, except to go back?"

He stroked her head. He bent his finger and slid it along her cheek. "Martha-chan, there is not an answer to everything in this life. There are not always answers that work out neatly. Maybe there is even purpose in that too. It would be too easy if one could find the right answer like a key to a lock."

"I know now, George, there are worse things than death."

A car came along. They could hear it chugging, since they were at the top of a hill. The reflection of the lights of the approaching car wove in and out of the front mirror. The car stopped as it pulled alongside them. A man said something in Japanese. George lowered his window to hear. For a brief moment Martha wondered if there were lover's-lane bandits in Japan as at home. Then she heard George say, *"Domo arigato gozai-masu"*—thank you very much.

He rolled the window up and started the car, laughing. "That nice farmer thought maybe my car was stalled. He wanted to push us. I told him the car was stopped, but I could get the engine started again. Certainly the truth."

Martha replied, "Evidently, cars don't park here, as we do at home."

"At least not by the side of a narrow two-lane road on a mountain," George answered.

They were silent on the way back. Martha noticed for the first time they had evidently been going up a steep grade. Beyond that she couldn't think.

George was asking himself if the decision to come to Miyonishita had been wise. He had thought it was best for both Kate and Martha, but now he wondered. Certainly the baths were beneficial for Kate. But he wondered about Martha. Sequestered in his mother's home, Martha's actions, her coming and going and any extended stay away from the home would be noticed. He could not embarrass her. He decided as soon as he saw improvement in Kate's condition, he would plan the trip to Kyoto, Nara and Hong Kong. Then the next thought came to him: This would mean Martha would soon be leaving for the States. Even for the joy of those few days he did not want to hurry the trip.

CHAPTER XVI

In her daily phone call from George, Martha reported on Kate's progress. One day Kate walked across the room, unaided. In a few days Martha excitedly described how her daughter had gone into the garden. But Martha did not say that with every step Kate took, Martha realized their leaving was coming closer.

Her ambivalent reactions—joy at Kate's progress, sadness at what the progress meant—gnawed continually at Martha. There was so much thankfulness, only to be snatched away at the same moment. Martha felt as if she were on a motor trip she once took with Paul when Kate was a small child. The car went up one hill, only to come down immediately. The series of undulating hills caused Kate to utter squeals of joy, but Martha became actively sick, and Paul had to stop the car by the side of the road. Now there was no comforting roadside to pull up to; her emotions would continue to careen up and down.

Martha also told George that Madame Tanaka and Kate were becoming fast friends, even in a few days. The older woman spent hours explaining Japanese customs to Kate, who was an apt pupil. Kate obviously had no awe of Madame Tanaka, and if the Western child's behavior seemed too fresh and unrestrained, Madame Tanaka gave no evidence of being annoyed by Kate's frankness of freedom of expression.

Martha did not tell George that if Kate had no inhibitions in her relationship with his mother, she herself felt most uncomfortable, constrained, inadequate, as if she could not measure up to Madame Tanaka. Martha felt unequaled to the older woman's soft spoken words, the artistry and grace in every gesture and movement.

One day, while Martha was idly opening a drawer in the cupboard in her room, she came across a scrapbook, a blue-embroidered cover on it. Not giving a thought that she might be prying, she opened the book and saw a series of snapshots. The early ones in the book had been taken of George and his family when they were in the United States, obviously in front of some college building. She could not identify it, but Professor Tanaka had on a cap and gown for a graduation exercise. George was a small boy—plump, curiously enough—his black hair standing straight up, dressed in knickers, with starched collar showing at the neck of a matching coat. Madame Tanaka was wearing a traditional kimono, although she said usually she wore Western dress, except when she felt her American friends expected her to be dressed in Japanese attire. This was evidently such an occasion.

Hurriedly, Martha looked through the book to see if there were any pictures of Akiko, but the scrapbook did not extend that far in time. She shut the book and wondered what Akiko looked like. She had no concept of her physical features, except that she was probably tiny, with very white skin and small features. Her manner of movement must have been the ultimate of feminity, as Madame Tanaka's was.

Suddenly Martha stopped. She realized this was probably why she felt self-conscious with the older woman. She imagined she was in competition with George's wife, not his mother. But there was an additional quality about Madame Tanaka that Akiko evidently had lacked—a brilliant, inquisitive mind. Martha knew from what George had said that his mother had given her husband mental companionship, something Akiko had never done. He had missed it in a wife. Then, coming full circle in her thoughts, Martha recognized that to George, mental and physical companionship had more significance than the mere automatonlike behavior of Akiko. The two women, Akiko and herself, represented the two poles of culture. George had now indicated his choice.

With this understanding of her own relationship with Madame Tanaka, Martha's awe diminished. Wholeheartedly, she joined Kate in what the girl called her flower-fixing class. Kate had remarked that if Aunt Sally knew there were flower-fixing lessons to be had, she would import someone to teach her children.

Martha soon found herself adept at handling the flowers. She had the dexterity necessary to manipulate the stems and wires; she had the patience demanded to bend a twig or turn a leaf. Through the flower-handling she lost her prepossession about herself. She also found out that nothing in Japanese art is done without purpose and meaning. Madame Tanaka was a most skillful teacher. She explained that at every American campus at which she had found herself, she had given classes in *ike-bano*. Madame Tanaka had told her the tea ceremony did not have the appeal for the American ladies.

Each step that Martha took into the labyrinth of Japanese culture brought her into closer understanding of George, but again it was paradoxical, because she realized she could never fully understand his actions beforehand. Only in retrospect could she see why something was done. She now understood thoroughly why he had insisted that she visit his home; not only to remove her from Tokyo, not only to help in Kate's recovery, not only to meet his most remarkable mother, but, above all, to see that he was basically Japanese, even for all his Western clothes, speech and mannerisms. Undoubtedly, he was a dichotomy: Western and Japanese.

In Tokyo, Dr. Tanaka received a visitor in his office, his brother-in-law, Yasuki Kataoka. Yasuki had written him a formal note, asking for an appointment, explaining that he would phone the exact hour upon his arrival in Tokyo. The letter was sent by regular mail, an understatement that was not lost on George, since under normal conditions Yasuki, like himself, would have wired or phoned.

At the precise minute of the appointment Yasuki was announced by the receptionist. George kept him waiting an appropriate length of time to indicate that he was not that eager to see his brother-in-law and on the other hand, that he was not that rude to keep him waiting unreasonably long.

When Yasuki, dressed in his black suit and neat dark tie, came into the office, George was wearing his white medical jacket. Yasuki bowed very low. George nodded his head and then offered Yasuki a chair and passed a box of cigars. Yasuki smiled and said that he still preferred cigarettes, in spite of all the medical warnings. He slowly and deliberately put a cigarette into his ivory holder and placed it between his jutting teeth.

Yasuki inquired after George's health and after his honorable mother, and here Yasuki rose a little from the seat to indicate respect. He talked about the weather, about political conditions, all as if he had not seen George in years. Then, just as George was beginning to wonder when Yasuki would come to the point of his visit, and what the reason was, Yasuki changed the tone of his voice slightly. It became a little more sharp, as he said he had a matter of great importance to discuss.

As head of the family he had felt for some time that a family council should be held to deliberate the important question concerning their most honorable sister, Akiko, wife of Dr. Tanaka. After a meeting of the family council, the family consider it incumbent to visit a lawyer for their sister so that Akiko may have the satisfaction of obtaining a legal divorce. While divorce has not been accepted generally among such social groups as theirs—and here Yasuki sucked in his breath—the family felt they could not, in point of fact, ignore the tools at hand. They must keep pace with democracy, progress and science. For a second, George wondered if his casual remark about business machines had penetrated farther than he'd thought.

If Dr. Tanaka would agree, Yasuki explained, the divorce would be consensual. They would avoid the formalities of complaints. While the family council is fully aware of the American lady, so that no scandal may touch the name of their beloved sister, they will omit any notice of this fact in the complaint. George felt a muscle in his cheek involuntarily contract at this reference to Martha, but he said nothing. The involuntary spasm was not lost on Yasuki, but the brother-in-law continued talking. The family council had already put the matter to their lawyers and suggest that Dr. Tanaka do the same. The consensual divorce would thus be completed immediately, and Akiko would be technically free of her manifold problems.

Without any reference to the fact that he himself had within the month approached Yasuki Kataoka with the same objectives of a divorce, Dr. Tanaka allowed his brother-in-law the face-saving gesture of not mentioning the fact. George hesitated and then said slowly he would give the matter his most earnest consideration and would arrive at a decision shortly. He did not indicate what his decision might be, thus allowing himself the face-saving gesture of indecision.

Bowing very low, Yasuki left.

Excited, happy, George could hardly wait until he was sure Yasuki Kataoka had left the building and would not return on some pretense. In addition, George left a message with his office nurse that he was not to be disturbed for a few minutes. He phoned Martha in Miyanoshita. Since he had never phoned early in the afternoon, Martha was at first alarmed. But at the sound of his joyful, exicted voice, Martha knew all was well.

"Martha-chan, I have news for you, such wonderful news that I am coming myself to tell it to you. I'll leave in the morning, right after rounds." George felt as if he were singing through the phone.

"George, George, I can't wait. What is it?"

"No. I want to see your face when I tell you. I'll even go to the hospital an hour earlier." Then he said, "Put some champagne on ice so that it will be chilled for a toast when I get there."

"In the middle of the day?"

"Why not?" His voice was solemn. "Martha-chan, you can not imagine the news!"

"Then give me a hint, just a clue. I can't wait twenty-four hours. Please, just a little hint?"

"Not a one. Martha, just believe me, it's too wonderful!"

"Well, I'll have to take your word for it, and I think you're mean not even to give me a kind of hint."

"See you tomorrow." And George hung up.

Martha wasn't sure about the champagne, since she'd only been served hot sake since her arrival. But one of the maids assured her there were many, many bottles; so Martha had not one but two put on ice.

Excited but puzzled over the teasing phone message,

speculating on what it could mean, overjoyed at new evidence of Kate's progress as she walked unattended around the outer garden, but again haunted at the thought that their departure could probably be reckoned in weeks, Martha could not sleep. She got up before dawn and, putting on a heavy coat, walked into the garden. The gravel of the path felt cold even through the soles of her bedroom slippers. She selected a stone bench and sat down. Looking around the garden, she wondered if she could live in such a home. Could she be flexible enough to adapt herself to the mysterious culture surrounding her, the nuances, the innuendos of a flower arrangement, of a tea ceremony, the circuitous way in which one asked even for theater tickets? She realized how much she knew of George, but how little of his environment.

Their courtship had taken place under the guise of showing Tokyo to a tourist. It was as if he was plucked out of the context of his ordinary living. If courtship among young people in America showed a false front with dating, sometimes almost an extravagance in entertaining, how much more false was her friendship with George? How did he live normally when he was in Tokyo? She suddenly was aware that she had never met any of his friends or colleagues in more than a passing moment of introduction. Why had he kept his friends and Martha apart? A rational answer could be, of course, that he did not want to create any embarrassing situations for her, since he was a married man.

The thought now occurred to her that perhaps his good news was that he had been appointed a delegate to an international medical meeting that was going to be held in Chicago in late fall. He would be coming to the United States. Should she meet him in Springfield, her home, or in another city? The answer would probably be that he would want to see Kate. She need not tell any of the family any more than that the doctor had been kind enough to come out of his way to examine Kate. She would have to be careful not to betray any emotion or unusual warmth. The family were eagle-eyed.

But again she was only speculating about this news he was bringing. The air seemed colder with the predawn dampness. A light was diffusing in the east. The walls of the house kept her from observing the rising of the sun. Suddenly she shuddered at the expression "the rising sun," which had brought such ugly connotations during the war. She remembered the insignia of the rising sun on kamikaze planes shown in newsreels.

Looking back now, she wondered if anyone had remained sane enough without the brainwashing of war propaganda to have kept a balance. Suppose America had been conquered and overrun with occupation soldiers, as Japan had been immediately after the war. Would Americans have been as ready to accept and forgive? Paul had always said the friendliness and generosity of the American soldier immediately endeared him to the populace, in spite of the excesses of many. She realized now, as she had so many times during this experience, there is no generalization where individuals are concerned. Who could have believed that she would have fallen in love at all, much less with a Japanese doctor? But this speculation only added to her bewilderment. She got up and went back to her room. Even the act of stooping and getting back under the comforters of the *futon*, which she had been accepting almost mechanically, now confused her.

The next morning Martha and Kate were at breakfast. Martha was amused. Kate, to whom even a few spoonfuls of cold cereal and a bite of toast were simply "Stuffing her" at home, now relished the Japanese breakfast of rice served in blue-and-white china bowls, broiled fish in oblong blue dishes, and the tiny ever-present teapot and cup. George had left word that Kate could have anything for breakfast she wanted to eat—cereals, eggs, anything. If it was not available in the local markets, he would send the food from Tokyo. Kate, however, was quite content to eat whatever the rest of the household was eating.

Looking into the garden through the sliding screen made of fine netting and a skirting of reeds, Martha remarked that it looked as if a storm were coming up. Almost at the same time one of the *nesan* came in and started to shut the wooden panels on the outside. As she deftly drew them closed, she announced, *"Cross amadoes.* Storm."

They were immediately aware of a sound that was growing in intensity. At first it was difficult to identify the noise, but another maid said, "The bells. Bells rings. Typhoon bells."

The sound of the bells was ominous, different in pitch and tone than any Martha had ever heard before. The little maid bowed low and scurried to the kitchen. Kate was alarmed; Martha was puzzled.

Madame Tanaka came in, dressed in her morning kimono. She reported in a matter-of-fact voice that she had just heard over the radio that typhoon Alice, the first of the season, was on the way. But there was no cause for alarm. Their area received much rain, some winds, but nothing like the other sections of Japan, even Tokyo. In fact, she continued in her calm manner, that is why they had originally selected Miyanoshita for a summer home.

Kate asked curtly, "Then why do they ring the typhoon bells if there isn't going to be a typhoon?"

"It is to warn anyone not to stray too far from home," Madame Tanaka replied quietly. "There will be heavy rains and winds, even if the storm does not reach the velocity of a typhoon." Madame Tanaka then suggested they would perhaps like to hear the reports of the storm on the transistor radio in her room.

In her suite, as placid as if she were listening to a morning concert, Madame Tanaka poured tea for Martha and Kate. She translated for them. They heard over the radio the announcement that more than four thousand prospective climbers on Mt. Fuji had been forced to turn back, and an estimated five hundred more determined climbers were huddled in mountain huts from the seventh station up on their descent from the summit, where they had gone to witness the sunrise.

Martha said lightly, "Good thing you're not mountainclimbing today, Kate." But Kate did not reply.

The winds increased in intensity and, mingled with the tolling of the typhoon bells, gave an eerie background to the increasing darkness. With the outer shutters, the *amadoes*, closed, the room became hot and humid. Madame Tanaka told one of the maids to bring in several electric fans, but no sooner were the fans installed than the electricity went off. A maid quietly appeared and lighted several oil lamps and candles. But there was nothing to relieve the oppressive heat.

Kate sat rigidly. Martha pulled her chair next to the girl's and, noting the frightened look in Kate's face, held her hand. Kate, in turn, squeezed Martha's hands so hard, she winced but said nothing to her daughter. The three women sat in the flickering light, listening to the voice of the announcer over the transistor describe the course of typhoon Alice, the first typhoon of the year.

The news of the storm reached Indiana as well. David Fletcher was driving home after a particularly harrowing day in court. He had his car radio turned on and was listening to the news. He was suddenly aware that the commentator was reporting about a typhoon that, coming out of the Taiwan Straits, had already hit Honshu earlier in the day.

" . . . The heart of the typhoon passed over the port city of Yokohoma at 9:31 a.m. and churned directly across it into the heart of Tokyo." David, trembling, pulled up to the curb to listen intently. The announcer continued, "National Police Headquarters in Tokyo listed six hundred persons already missing, and two hundred injured. It is estimated more than one hundred fifty thousand people will be homeless. Even in the business districts the heaviest deluge since the city began keeping weather records, in 1876, recorded seventeen inches of water within an eight-hour period."

As if he were trying to race the eye of the storm, David sped home. There he went at once to the television. There was no other report. He called the local radio and television stations as well as the newspaper, but they could add nothing.

Briefly he told Sally what he had heard, and in his worry blamed her for not listening to the radio "to know at least what is going on in the world outside your Goddamn rose garden."

"You should know as much," Sally muttered.

David immediately put in a phone call to Martha at the Imperial Hotel in Tokyo, as he had not yet received her letter from Miyanoshita. There was no telephonic communication with Tokyo. He urged the operator to keep trying, all night if necessary. Meanwhile, members of the family were phoning in to the Fletchers as they, too, heard reports of the typhoon. Many of the family dropped in to share in person their nervousness.

"Losing a night's sleep isn't going to help Martha in Japan," Sally announced succinctly as she left the room to go to bed. But she turned on the table radio on the nightstand.

David sent two cables, one to Martha at the Imperial, one to Dr. Tanaka. But Western Union soon phoned back to report that all service to Tokyo had been temporarily disrupted.

In Miyanoshita, although physically safe, tension was mounting for Martha. Madame Tanaka had tuned in on the one English-speaking station. Martha didn't know how much longer she could contain or conceal her nervousness about George. But, looking at the calm attitude of Madame Tanaka, she knew she could not say anything that would betray her fears. She had suggested phoning George, but Madame Tanaka had advised against it, explaining it was wrong to tie up a phone except in an emergency.

For the first time Kate spoke. "If this isn't an emergency, what is it? The biggest typhoon in all history."

Martha was too upset herself to correct Kate's childish exaggerations. If this is the first typhoon you have experienced, what difference does the degree of intensity make? Martha wondered.

Madame Tanaka answered Kate softly. "I do agree, it is a furious typhoon. But we must remember, Kate-chan, we are in no danger ourselves, and I am sure Dr. Tanaka is not either. There may be people who really need the communication of a telephone."

The three women were then silent, listening to the breathless, excited tones of the radio announcer report that this was the worst storm since the 1934 typhoon, which killed twenty-seven hundred people. Kate looked at Martha and then Madame Tanaka, feeling vindicated. The commentator described how the moat around the Imperial Palace was churning with whitecaps and overflowing the grounds. Tens of thousands of people on the streets were marooned as streetcars were stalled. Not one of the thirty thousand or more taxis, or any other vehicle, was on the street. Winds up to 140 miles an hour were toppling trees and power lines. Four persons had already been electrocuted by broken wires. Two bridges across the Sumida River had been swept away. Impossible to know how many lives have been lost. . . . The broadcast went on and on.

Martha abruptly left the room and went to the phone in the main part of the house. She found out there was no communication with Tokyo at all.

In Tokyo, George Tanaka had been in the hospital, making early-morning rounds before he left for Miyanoshita, when he learned the heart of the typhoon would strike Tokyo in a few hours. He tried immediately to phone Martha to find out if all was well with them and to say that he could not make the drive before the typhoon would hit. He could not get a line through to Miyanoshita. He left the message for his office nurse, but she found it was impossible to phone or wire. Meanwhile, he remained at the hospital in case he was needed.

David Fletcher heard the 6 a.m. news. He had been up almost all night. Now he heard the first report since the evening before: "Typhoon Alice has left death and destruction in Central Japan, with rescue crews working frantically to clear the damage. Although the eye of the typhoon has moved north, the winds and rain are still of violent intensity. National Police reported 341 known dead, 1,276 missing, and 442,548 homeless. The United States military crews are working with rescue teams as well as Tokyo police and firemen. Medical teams have been organized in major hospitals and health centers. Tetanus and typhoid vaccine are being flown in from U.S. bases in the Pacific."

The announcer then went on to give the national news. David turned the radio off with such a jerk, a vase of flowers quivered on the table. Sally looked at him. Powerless to act, he set himself and other forces in motion. David was like a caged animal.

"Looks like typhoon Alice is even bigger than you are, my love," she said.

David walked out of the room without answering.

CHAPTER XVII

Martha could not remember how long she, Madame Tanaka and Kate sat in the darkened room, listening to reports of the typhoon as it continued to hurl its massive destruction on Tokyo and the surrounding area. In spite of the wind, which she could hear whipping around the house, and the rain battering against the wooden *amadoe*, she knew they were in no danger. The heat, however, was oppressive, and her clothes were wet with perspiration. As she shifted her position, she could feel her dress clinging to the fabric of the chair. The excessive humidity caused difficulty in breathing. She wanted to cry out, but she controlled herself, murmuring comforting thoughts to Kate, who sat as one frozen.

Then, when a gale of wind struck some object, a tree perhaps, the noise rebounded like a sonic blast. At that sound, Kate let out a piercing yell, followed by another, and yet another. She jumped up from the chair and started running toward the shuttered door, screaming, "I can't breathe! I can't . . . give me air! Let me out of here! Let me out! . . ."

Martha ran to her side to grab the girl. Deftly Madame Tanaka moved toward the *amadoe*, speaking rapidly in Japanese to one of the maids, who came immediately to her side. But none of these motions was necessary, for Kate suddenly buckled up, her legs giving way, and she crumpled to the floor. She struggled to her knees and started crawling on all fours toward the doorway. Martha reached down to stop her, but Kate, with terrific force, pushed her aside.

"Let me go! Let me out! I want to get out of here, out of this silly paper house. I want to go home." Her hair was hanging like waving fringe in her face. The pupils of her eyes were dilated so that the eyes themselves seemed twice their normal size and were glaring, magnetized by the oil lamps in the room. She was like an animal ready to spring.

"I want to go home. I want to leave Japan. I hate it, everything about it. I want to go back to America." She tried to get onto her feet, but she did not have the strength to rise up. Martha bent over to pick her up, but again the girl struck out, shouting, "I want to go home!"

Then, almost immediately, she put out her arms and grabbed Martha around both legs, clinging to her, looking up at her mother. Kate's eyes had lost the look of a snarling animal's and had now narrowed down to slits. She began to cry, to take deep breaths, then sob. "Take me home. Please, take me home now. At once. I want to see my daddy. I want to see daddy. I want my daddy." In her aberrations she kept calling out for her father, the past and present being merged in her confusion.

With the help of a maid, Martha managed to get Kate to her feet, her arms supporting the girl. Madame Tanaka motioned to her own large armchair, and half carrying Kate, with the help of a maid, Martha managed to get Kate into it.

Madame Tanaka now came back into the room from an adjoining bathroom. She was holding a small bottle in her hand. The maid brought over a Thermos carafe and a glass on a tray. "This is phenobarbital. Give Kate-chan one," Madame Tanaka told Martha.

Martha took the bottle, and only the fact that Kate had misjudged the distance kept the girl from knocking the medicine out of Martha's hand. She swung out, missed, and then, angry, started to scream. "I won't take it! I won't! It's poison! I won't!" She shook her head back and forth, her blond hair swirling against her face.

In gentle tones Martha pleaded with Kate to take the medicine, but then, after realizing this approach was futile, she said in a stern voice, "Kate, take this at once. Do you hear? Open your mouth and swallow this pill."

Seeing the intensity of Martha's expression, Kate opened her mouth and obediently swallowed the pill. She took a few sips of water, with her mother holding the glass for her, as one would with a very small child. Then Kate drew her knees up under her and cowered in the chair.

Waiting a few moments for the girl to be calmed, Martha, together with the maid, started to half-support, half-carry Kate down the corridor to her own room. At that moment Hinako, who was drenched to the skin, came in. She had not taken time to remove her soaked clothing. Although it had been her day off, when the storm started, she felt she would be needed with Kate and had walked several miles from her sister's house to the Tanaka home. She quickly removed her wet coat and drenched head scarf and put them in a corner. Then she came over and helped the two other women with the girl. They placed Kate, who was beginning to doze, on her own bed and covered her with a blanket. Martha pulled up a chair and began stroking the child's forehead, as she had done when Kate was a child and had been terrified by a nightmare. The tactile feeling was as much a comfort to Martha as to Kate, the mother realized, as though by physical contact she could keep a psychological hold on the girl.

Measured by all reports that typhoon Alice had petered out into the sea east of the Kuriles, George felt it was safe for him to leave Tokyo and to attempt the drive to Miyanoshita. There was no telephone communication with the town, but according to checks he made with newspapers and radio stations, there was no substantial damage done in the resort area. George had wanted to take the train to Miyanoshita, but it was not running because of bridge washouts in several areas.

He left as early as possible in the morning after making his hospital rounds. He knew the drive would be difficult and tedious; he always chafed at the five hours it required along the slow, congested highways to traverse fifty-eight miles.

Now, as he started to drive, he felt as if he were part of a wartime evacuation. Flooded areas were congested by peasants pulling their few possessions in carts away from their damaged or destroyed homes. He knew they would remain with relatives in a nearby village until the water had drained away from their rice paddies. Then they would stoically move back to rebuild their small houses and repair the damage to the fields. There would be hard years ahead. There would also be another migration to Tokyo, whose population, now swollen to ten million, would have to encompass the thousands more eager to move to the city, away from the land.

But, he thought, the Japanese always seemed to be faced with one catastrophe after another—earthquake, flood, war. Nature's attempt to equate population and land seemed unfair to the population side, he felt, as he watched the pilgrimage on the roads. From his own personal observation it was, in fact, the survival of the fittest, plus a little luck on the side.

Luck, he thought, was as good a name as any for Yasuki's change of mind. He knew that some external event had caused this about-face, but in all probability he would never know the exact cause, nor was it important to know.

With all the congestion and innumerable detours, the drive stretched to ten hours, then to twelve. At times George felt he would run out on the road and abandon the car. But, of course, he realized he would do none of these things. He must sit patiently, waiting to inch up a few feet or maneuver a difficult detour over a muddy field. He hoped he would not be caught in the ooze, and then he recalled that it was such a detour in Korea that had caused Kate to be inflicted with encephalitis. The events of one's life were interlocking, like a clever design woven into a textile, but this was one of the first times he could see the design clearly set out. A child is stuck in the muddy earth in Korea; some months later he is almost equally marooned in a detour through a country lane as he rushes to propose marriage to the child's mother.

Now he recalled every word Martha had repeated on his last night in Miyanoshita. She would marry him; she would transfer her life to Tokyo. He realized, of course, that the marriage could not take place immediately; no doubt, she would have to return to Springfield to adjust her affairs. Or perhaps she would return to Indiana after the marriage, which he would prefer. They could honeymoon in Hawaii, half-way.

In view of the headlights he saw a signpost. He was almost to Miyanoshita. He looked at the radium dial of his watch. One o'clock in the morning. He had been driving eighteen hours.

Not knowing that George would be arriving, Martha had gone to bed early, exhausted by the trauma with Kate. Hearing unexpected voices in the *genka*, she got up, put on a kimono and went to the entrance room. Two of the maids had also come in. She did not know whether they had remained in the front of the home during the night or, hearing a noise, had also come out to investigate. Dr. Tanaka, his medicine bag in his hand, was standing there as one *nesan* helped him off with his raincoat. Another took his hat and bag. In Japanese he must have been apologizing for having awakened them, but the two little *nesans* were bowing and smiling, and Martha knew from their expression they were timidly assuring him it was no trouble at all.

Martha managed to restrain herself from rushing into his arms, but her expression told him what he needed to know. One maid went to his room with the bag, the other toward the kitchen, first stopping to light the *kotatsu* in the dining room for warmth and for tea.

Martha asked him to step into the parlor. She told him quickly but in detail the behavior problem with Kate, the girl's aberrations about her father, her fears, hysteria, and incessant desire to run away. George listened, nodding his head.

"Kate's recovery has gone too smoothly, Martha. I felt all along that somewhere we might run into this psychiatric sequela, but since we had not, I just counted it as one of our blessings. But aberration in sense of time, distortion of facts, hallucinations, all of these are frequent aftermaths of encephalitis. In this case the behavior problem was induced by fright over the storm. This episode can pass as quickly as it came, since it was brought on by a specific fact. Sometimes wall paper can upset a patient, or food, but this was real."

"George, will . . . will an episode like this happen again for Kate?"

He replied slowly, "Yes, it could. No one knows."

"You mean this could be a pattern of her life? These outbursts, aberrations—it could be chronic?"

"It could be chronic. We must remember, however, this

upset was caused by something very specific, a typhoon, which is frightening to even those accustomed to them. This was her first experience, and it was a particularly violent storm. And remember, Kate is also in strange surroundings."

"She seemed to be getting along so well," Martha said slowly.

"That is all to the good. Come, I want to take a look at her." Martha followed him to Kate's room. Hinako, who was sleeping on a *futon* alongside the bed, heard them and raised up. George shook his head and quietly left the room.

Over a cup of tea, scrambled eggs and toast, which George always liked to eat late at night, Martha apologized for the trouble they had caused Madame Tanaka. George said he knew his mother understood this was part of the sickness, since he had often discussed his cases with her.

Martha realized she still had a robe on, and laughed. "I've become so used to kimonos, I forgot I wasn't dressed."

George got up from the *zabuton*. "Put on a coat and come out into the garden. The night was wonderfully clear as I drove up."

Putting a heavy polo coat on over her kimono, and carrying a pair of *geta* to slip on outside, Martha joined George, and together they went into the inner garden. There was no trace of the turbulence of a few hours before. Moonlight was reflected in small puddles; the dwarf-pine trees and evergreens shimmered with the drops of rain gathered on the needles. The air was a fragrant mixture of rain, pine and flowers.

Looking around her and breathing deeply, Martha said, "Incredible that only a few hours ago all was darkness and destruction."

"I've learned in my medical experience one must never despair. Miracles do happen, albeit with scientific reason." He stopped and looked at her. Then he tilted her head up. "Martha-chan, a miracle happened yesterday, no, the day before. I've lost track of time. Yasuki Kataoka, my brother-in-law, came in to see me at the office. He told me he had called a family council to discuss divorce of Akiko and me. He feels we should be divorced."

Martha's face was eager. "How wonderful! Then he finally agreed to what you had asked."

George smiled. He ruffled her hair a little, playfully. "Martha-chan. Not at all. This idea was instigated by Yasuki, not be me."

"But George, I thought you went—"

"Darling," he interrupted, "this is not Illinois. What I said had nothing to do with it. It was all Yasuki's idea. And, of course, I agreed with him—after consideration. He accused me of deserting his sister."

Martha flared up, "How dare he, when it was she who left you!"

"Dearest, this is a face-saving technique for him, and I welcomed it. What difference does it make whose idea it was? He also accused me of being seen with a woman who was not geisha."

"A blond geisha, did he say?"

"Well, he inferred as much, but he won't bring in your name. He doesn't have to. Akiko has already started proceedings, and I have talked to my lawyer."

"How long will it take to get the divorce?"

"No time at all. There is no waiting period. We bring two witnesses and pay the charges. Finished." He stroked her head, lifted her face and kissed her. "Dearest, that means as soon as, or whenever you want to, we can be married."

"George, this is, well, about the last thing I could ever have dreamed of. But I can't believe it."

"But it's true. We can be married whenever, wherever you wish—if you still wish to."

"George, I do. Of course, I do. Only I don't know how to start to think."

"You mean about marrying me?" His voice was edgy.

"No, dearest, about when, how. I suppose I ought to go back to Indiana first, sell my house or put it on the market, arrange my affairs, bring Jimmy back with me. I can't leave him in school there. I guess there are good schools here for Kate and Jimmy. We can send for Johnny Kim—"

"Maybe if you go back, the family won't let you leave again."

"George, you know better than that. The family tried to keep me from coming the first time."

"You had David on your side then."

"What's David got to do with it?"

"He might have arguments why you shouldn't. He's a convincing lawyer." He decided not to say what he was thinking, that he was sure David was in love with her. He'd known it the moment he'd seen David gaze at her.

"Nonsense." She looked at him. "George, would you feel better if we married first, then I went back?"

"Frankly, yes. We could honeymoon in Hawaii."

"What about Kate?"

"She'd come too. Why not? Or she could stay here with mother."

"I think the family would expect to see her after her illness." Then she said softly, "Her outbursts this afternoon, what about the long trip?"

"We'll see how she is in the morning. I bet she never even remembers it. Sometimes these outbursts are like an electric shock for the patient; they remember nothing.

"But Martha-chan, as long as I know we can be married, that you haven't changed your mind, we can wait. Maybe it would be simpler and cleaner if you go back for a few weeks, as long as it would take, if you promise . . ." he held her very close, "promise that you'll not stay an extra day."

"I solemnly promise not to stay even an extra hour."

They held each other in an embrace. He slipped his hand under her coat, under her kimono, which he had loosened. They stood there in the garden.

"Before you go back to the States, I must show you a little more of Japan—Kyoto, Nara—so you'll have something to talk about."

"I don't need anything else but you," she whispered.

"Besides, a trip back and forth takes a long time, even by jet. I can't wait. I must be with you, alone."

She started to say, where the walls aren't so thin like this paper house, but she caught herself before she could repeat Kate's words. He felt her shiver.

"Cold?"

She shook her head. "No, but . . ." She stepped out of his embrace. "George, we've talked about me. What about you? What about marrying me, an American? What will it do to your practice? To your friends? Will they accept me?"

"It will do nothing to my practice but enhance it. My friends, if they are my friends, will accept you and love you. There is even an international group in Tokyo at the university. We can make a life for ourselves."

"The children? I couldn't let them stay back home, not now. Maybe later, when Kate goes to college."

"Martha-chan, if you are willing to marry me, to risk all the problems our marriage will bring, then any extra details can be ironed out. They're superficial. If you are sure—"

"Darling, I'm more sure of us than of anything in my whole life."

So absorbed in their new happiness, as Martha realized afterward, so numbed by the physical presence of each other, by the promise of a future almost too much to imagine, they did not hear Kate open the sliding door to the garden. Silhouetted on the *shoji* screen she saw her mother and Dr. Tanaka in an embrace. Quietly she walked through the sliding door and stood there in the silence, looking. Then, on her bare feet, she walked into the garden.

Martha happened to look up and saw her first. "Kate!"

Kate hissed her fury, her face now distorted in anger, venom. "My mother and her lover, her Jap boyfriend. You thought I was still sleeping; that's why you gave me the sleeping pill, to get me out of the way. My mother, the prim and proper Mrs. Montgomery, loving a Jap! In the memory of my father, how could you do this? How could you do this to him, to his memory." She started screaming. "I never want to see you again! Never, never, never! You and your Jap lover!"

Martha ran toward the girl. She tried to clutch her coat and kimono to bring them together with one hand. "Kate, you're ill. Go back to your room at once."

But as she approached the girl, Kate hit out at her. "Go away, you and your Jap lover. Go away." Then the girl started sobbing, bent over as if she were in great pain.

"How . . . how could you do this to the memory of my father, my dead father? How could you?" She collapsed to the ground.

George picked her up and started to carry her into the house. Regaining consciousness for a second, Kate recognized him. She kicked out and tried to bite him, all the while screaming, "Put me down! Put me down! Don't touch me! Don't you dare!"

Managing to hold her arms down at her side, he carried her into the room and placed her on the hospital bed. At his bidding, Martha had gone to get his medical bag, which was in his room.

Hinako came out of the bathroom, fully dressed. She was terrified at the sight of the child. In her fury Kate had bitten her own lip, and now it was bleeding. Taking the cue from Dr. Tanaka, who was putting up one side of the hospital bed, Hinako went quickly around to the other side.

Martha came back with the medical bag, which George took from her. He spoke quickly in Japanese to Hinako, who rolled up the sleeve of the girl's gown and rubbed a spot on the upper arm with cotton on which George had already poured alcohol. With Hinako grasping Kate's hand and keeping out of the way of the girl's kicking legs, George gave her a shot. "It'll take affect shortly. Hinako will watch her." He spoke to Hinako in Japanese.

Martha followed him out of the room, into the corridor, then into the parlor. She hardly had the strength to speak. "She was far, far worse now than she was today. George, I agreed with you that the earlier episode should not affect my life, your life. But this was different."

"The effect was different, not the cause," George said. "Martha dear, that child isn't responsible for what she's saying or doing. It's as much a part of the sickness as the coma, this irrational hysteria."

"But the irony, the irony of her accusing me of betraying Paul, and I can't tell her about Johnny Kim . . . George," she looked at him, "I wonder if she will always come between us. You said it could be chronic; she could have these episodes again, spew out these accusations. I can't do this to you. I can't bring this conflict to you. You don't deserve it."

"But I understand it. I will risk it."

"Maybe someday Jimmy will resent me. The family can poison him about me, you. They've done it to others."

"You can't let their narrow, provincial prejudices spoil our happiness."

"George, the children could come between us."

"Only if we let them. Isn't it possible that we would give them love, a good home, respect for each other? Martha-chan, if you do love me—if you want to marry me—everything else will fall into place."

"I don't know, George. I don't know. . . ."

"Dearest, don't judge your whole future by a sick child's hysteria. You don't have to make a decision now, tonight. I will wait as long as you wish . . . until you yourself know the right answers."

"Will I ever know the right answer?"

"Yes, in time. All I ask of you now is don't shut out your future and mine, our happiness, by any judgment you may make tonight. This isn't fair to you, to me, even to the children, because some day, if you decide not to marry me because of the children, you may resent them for having come between us."

"Why . . . why is everything so hard, so complicated?"

"Martha-chan, only those who merely exist, who have never lived or truly loved, they are the only ones who have no scar tissue on their souls."

"I'll try getting through once more," David told Sally at the breakfast table. For twenty-four hours David had been trying to phone Tokyo. At first there had been no lines in to Tokyo. Then, when he had finally reached the Imperial Hotel, he'd asked for Mrs. Paul Montgomery. After a pause he had heard the operator at the hotel say, "There is no Mrs. Paul Montgomery here."

"Try Mrs. Martha Montgomery," he had suggested. But there'd been no Mrs. Martha Montgomery registered.

"Maybe she's incognito," Sally said.

Not listening, David, still holding the receiver, said to the hotel operator, "Let me talk to the manager." After a pause he learned the manager was not in.

Daivd screamed, "The assistant manager then!"

A woman's voice softly explained she was the secretary to the assistant manager. David again asked for Mrs. Montgomery. The secretary replied, "Mrs. Montgomery checked out earlier in the week."

David, who had not yet received the letter that Martha was going to Miyanoshita, asked if she had left a forwarding address.

The secretary answered, "There is so much confusion, everything under water, I cannot find addresses." There was a pause. Then, "Sorry." The telephone operator came on brightly to announce that Mrs. Montgomery was not registered.

David now asked to put in a call to Dr. Tanaka. He reached in his black address book and gave the address and phone number. The operator promised to call him back. David remained near the phone. Finally the operator called back to say that they could not locate Dr. Tanaka, and his exchange did not know where he was.

Sally poked her head in the door. "Find Martha yet?"

He shook his head. "They can't locate Dr. Tanaka either."

"Um . . . maybe they've eloped. A little hanky-panky with an Oriental may be, well, diverting. You said yourself he's attractive."

"Leave me alone, for God's sake! Leave me alone." David got up and started toward the door. Sally, however, came into the room. She went over to his desk, took a cigarette and motioned for him to give her a light. When he didn't respond, she shrugged, took a match and flipped it under the table to light it.

"Thanks." Then she looked at him. "David, you love Martha, don't you?"

His lack of response gave her the answer she needed. "Do you want a divorce? Do you want to marry Martha? Is that what you want?" Her voice was low, even-toned.

David abruptly turned toward her. He shouted, "My God! I don't even know if she's alive, and you ask me that! She may be dead, missing. . . ."

Sally laughed. "Oh, don't be so melodramatic. If I know Martha, she's probably safe and warm and comfortable. Like the cat, Martha always lands on her feet."

"You're jealous," David accused.

"Naturally. I always have been. She's prettier. But that has nothing to do with it. Do you want a divorce? Do you want to marry her?"

"I've always wanted to marry her," David replied softly.

"Now's your chance. Better take me up on it, before I change my mind. After all, the presence of a man is better than no presence at all. I don't relish being a gay divorcee with six appendages. I'm rich, yes, but not beautiful. Do you want a divorce?"

David looked at her. "Sometimes I wonder if you're completely sane!"

"Why? Because I come directly to the point? What's the matter, are you afraid? Do you prefer living in your masochistic little cell, pining after your lost love?"

David started toward the door. He pulled it open. "Get out of here. For God's sake, get out of here. Now."

Sally ground out her cigarette into the bowl of a rare sandwich-glass vase, one of the first gifts she had given her husband. David had always considered the present a strange one, until he had found out the price of it from a client who had wanted to buy it. Now he kept it on a desk at home, away from the hurried hands of a janitor or careless secretary.

Sally moved slowly toward the door. "My, the learned jurist, always in control of any situation he can control. . . . Well, Mr. Smarty-pants, did you try to reach Kate at the hospital?"

David's face brightened. "I never thought of that."

Sally looked at him. "There's so much, my dear, you never thought of."

David hurried to the phone and put in a call to Tokyo for Miss Kate Montgomery at St. Thomas Hospital. In a few moments he heard the voice of the operator in Tokyo, speaking English, reach St. Thomas Hospital and ask for Miss Montgomery. The voice at the hospital announced that Miss Montgomery was dismissed from hospital earlier in week.

"Where?!" David shouted. "Where can Miss Montgomery be reached?"

"One minute," the operator said. She came back on the

phone. "Montgomery-san reached at home of Dr. Joji Tanaka, at Miyanoshita."

"Ask if they have the phone number," David said to the operator. The name, Miyanoshita, had been said so quickly, he could not understand it. The operator repeated the question, and David heard the voice at the hospital switchboard say, "Do you have phone number. Sorry."

Weary and frustrated, he once again tried Dr. Tanaka's exchange in Tokyo. When the operator had connected him, he asked where Dr. Tanaka could be reached. The exchange operator answered in Japanese. David felt it was a conspiracy to keep him from getting information. At length the English-speaking operator in Tokyo translated that Dr. Tanaka's mother lived in Miyanoshita, and she would give the phone number. David, impatient and angry, told the operator to connect him immediately. After more dialogue in Japanese with another voice, the operator explained in English that the lines were temporarily down between Tokyo and Miyanoshita because of the terrible storm. But as soon as they were repaired, would he still wish to speak?

"Yes, of course." David slammed down the receiver, only to pick it up at once, realizing he may have broken the connection. "Call me as soon as possible." He replaced the receiver, stared at it and then put his head in his hands and rocked back and forth. Sally, who had gone out when he had started to phone, now opened the door, saw him and quietly went out of the room. She shut the door behind her, saying nothing.

At first George did not hear the ringing of the telephone. Since untimely calls were always an emergency for him, he kept the phone near his bed. He woke now from a deep sleep, aware of its sound. How many times it had been ringing, he didn't know.

"Moshi-moshi," he said.

"Moshi-moshi," the operator answered. "Dr. Tanaka? One moment, the United States is calling. Springfield, Indiana." The voice spoke almost as if asking a question. There was a pause. "One moment for connections."

George reached over to the low table beside the *futon* and took a cigarette, which he put in his mouth. He opened the lighter, which automatically showed a small flame at the same time.

"George? George, this is Dave Fletcher."

"Hello, Dave. How are you?"

"Fine, fine. Are you all right?" Without waiting for an answer, David raced on. "How're Martha and Kate? Are they all right?"

"They're all right too."

"Are they with you?"

"Yes, they're here with us, my mother and me. Martha said she had written or cabled you."

"I . . . I hadn't gotten word. Storm, no doubt. May I speak to Martha, George?"

"Look, I don't know offhand what time, or even what day, it is in Springfield, but it's four in the morning here. Martha is asleep. I prefer not to wake her. Can she call you back?"

David's voice evidenced his disappointment. "George, when do you think Kate will be well enough to travel?"

"As soon as I can get plane reservations. I was going to see about it today, as a matter of fact."

"Do you really feel she's well enough to travel?" David's voice was anxious.

"Yes, I think she'll be better off with her family and own surroundings in Indiana for the rest of her convalescence."

David was not reassured. "I'm worried. You're sure she's all right?"

"Of course, she is. She can walk all over the place now."

"Good. Look, send a registered nurse back with them. I'll pay all expenses both ways for the nurse and whatever salary you arrange. Please get some qualified person."

"I'll tell Martha."

"No, I insist they have a nurse with them. It's a long flight. Would a ship be better?"

George hesitated. "No, I think not. The plane is more trying while it lasts, but in the end it'll be better for her than a longer voyage. I'll check into the situation and find a capable nurse. I'll have Martha try to call you back."

"Thanks, George. Thanks."

They both hung up.

210

George put out the cigarette and lit another. He knew Martha was completely unaware of David's frantic love for her. Undoubtedly, over the years, David had never given his scar tissue a chance to heal, but continually probed at it. Would he, too, do the same thing?

CHAPTER XVIII

Martha went to Madame Tanaka's suite to say good-bye. The elderly woman had kept in her rooms for the several days following Kate's outburst. Martha did not know whether it was from personal fatigue or to save Martha further embarrassment.

George had phoned long distance to Tokyo and made reservations for Martha and Kate for the end of the week. This would allow them several days in Tokyo and give Kate a few more days of recovery.

Martha knocked timidly on the door. She was in a bewildered state, feeling a complexity of emotions: deep gratitude, mortifying embarrassment because of the trouble she and Kate had caused, and solemn respect for this remarkable woman who could so easily adapt herself to two cultures.

Martha entered and stood there before her. Madame Tanaka put down the newspaper she was reading and took off her tortoise-rimmed glasses. In her serenity Madame Tanaka knew what to say. She motioned Martha to a chair, which Martha then pulled up alongside the larger one.

"There is nothing, dear friend, you need to say aloud to me that I do not already know. I, too, wish for your sake this visit could have been different. In fact, I could have wished that your whole trip to our country had been free from worry. But if your child had not been ill, you and George would never have met. One must always pay a price, for even the good things of life come high.

"George has told me for some time now of his love for you, and his desire to marry you. I have given my consent, since, old as he is, I am still his mother. In Japan a mother of a son has authority." She smiled. "But George is also

Western by education and instinct, and I do not really believe my consent has much significance anyway. But neither my desire nor his in this situation will prevail. The ultimate decision will be in your hands. And I do not believe you are ready to give an answer."

"I do not know the answer. I only pray that eventually it will come to me."

Madame Tanaka nodded her head. "It will come. Remember, Martha dear, there is a time for everything, or there is time for nothing." Then she got up and walked over to one of the built-in cupboards. Martha had never seen such grace or fluidity of movement as in Madame Tanaka's walk. It was ageless. Opening the door, Madame Tanaka selected several objects, which she placed on a table. She picked up one and, with a gentle smile, handed it to Martha.

"This is *Okami-san*. Although she is the face of a famous, ugly woman, she will bring luck during the year. Please give it to your daughter when you feel the time is opportune. She may not be ready to receive such an ugly one just now."

Before Martha could thank her, Madame Tanaka had handed her a package of material. She motioned for Martha to unwrap it. Martha carefully unfolded the cloth and saw a large measure of silk so carefully woven, it was like touching chinchilla, impossible to feel under the fingers. The fabric was so exquisitely embroidered that the colors blended as in a delicate watercolor. Against pale lavender were woven intermingling branches of pine, plum and bamboo. Martha had never seen anything as lovely.

"Yes, this is for Kate—in the future." Then Madame Tanaka explained, "Remember to tell her a young lady should always be like the pine, unchanging in all seasons of the year; like the swaying bamboo, yielding in gentle obedience; and like the fragrant plum, blossoming beneath the snow, never losing the gentle perseverance of loyal womanhood."

"But this is a museum piece, this material. It should be kept just this way, to admire and to treasure. I've never seen anything like it."

Once again Madame Tanaka walked to the cupboard.

She returned with a gift, which she handed to Martha. Martha held the box, wrapped in a silver covering, and was embarrassed, as she did not know what to do next. Gently, Madame Tanaka took the box from her, removed the cover and lifted out a scroll deftly unrolling it. Mounted on a rich brocade was the delicate hanging picture.

Madame Tanaka explained, "The scene on this *kakemono* is from the *Tale of the Gengi*. You have read the book?"

Martha shook her head. "I had never even heard of it before this summer."

"You must read it some time. It is a Japanese classic, said to have been written in the Eleventh Century, by Lady Murasaki. She wrote it in the three or four years that elapsed between the death of her husband and her arrival at court. Even widows in those days had their problems of filling time. The book has been translated into English for about thirty years."

"You said Eleventh Century! That was before England was even England, when it was still ruled by the Anglo-Saxons, if I remember my history. Madame Tanaka, how can we in the West ever hope to catch up with all you know in Japan? We have so much to learn."

"Both cultures have much to contribute to each other," Madame Tanaka replied quietly. "They complement, not rival, each other. But the trouble is that sometimes the wrong customs are copied, the trappings, not the essence of a culture."

"If I had seen only Tokyo, I would have been cheated, assuming that was Japan. But here, it's been like a wonderland. What can I say? How can I thank you? How can I express to you all I feel? It is I who should be showering you with gifts."

Madame Tanaka said, "But you have honored us by accepting our hospitality."

"Madame Tanaka, this summer has been a . . . a climax in my life. If I decide to return to Japan, certainly my life will never be the same. But if I decide not to return, I know it will never be the same again either."

"My dear friend, you never walk into the same river twice. Just as the river changes constantly, so must we."

Madame Tanaka got up slowly, gracefully to her feet, walked over to a piece of brocade that was suspended from a bell and rang the bell softly to summon a maid. In a brief moment or two a tiny maid appeared. Madame Tanaka spoke to her rapidly in Japanese, and, bowing low before Martha, the girl gently took the *kakemono* from her and replaced it in the box. Then she gathered up the other articles. Martha turned to say good-bye to Madame Tanaka, but in the second that Martha had been assisting the maid, the older woman had walked over to a vase in the far corner of the room. She was busy picking dead petals from a flower. In true Oriental courtesy she would not embarrass Martha by watching her leave. Martha hesitated a moment, debating whether to speak. But, judging that the decision had been made for her by Madame Tanaka, she turned and went out past the silk-screen door, which had been placed to one side. The tiny *nesan* followed her out.

At the Imperial Hotel in Tokyo, Martha found out that the guests had experienced many hardships during the typhoon, which she had been spared. They had no electricity, consequently no elevators; there had been a water shortage, broken sewer pipes and damaged plumbing. A large area of the first floor and basement had been flooded, and the luggage of many guests became waterlogged. Martha heard one woman complain that her mink stole now resembled a river rat. Martha was relieved to find her crates and cases that she had left for storage had been kept on a top shelf and were dry. The whistles, paper lanterns and other souvenir trivia were intact.

Throughout the train ride to Tokyo, Kate had been silent. She was in almost a catatonic state. The Imperial Hotel, which had delighted her before, now made no impression. She did not refer to her hysterical outbursts, and there was no hostility toward her mother or to George. In fact, there was scarcely any reaction. Martha told her repeatedly that she was going home, back to Springfield, where she would see all her friends, family and the dog—Sunday Dinner—but Kate nodded and made no comment. She had the power of speech; she could ask for a glass of water or request to go to the bathroom. She understood if Martha asked if she wanted to put on a sweater, or if she wanted something special to eat. But Kate showed no initiative, and beyond almost monosyllabic answers she did not respond.

Hinako had accompanied Martha and Kate from Miyanoshita to Tokyo and was now at the hotel with them. But George had not felt she was experienced enough as a nurse to accompany them on the flight back to the United States. While she had been discussing the problem of a nurse with George, Martha had suddenly remembered Mariko Ikeda, the little nurse at St. Thomas Hospital who had an Air Force friend from Detroi*th*. Mariko might welcome an opportunity to go to the United States, since she also had a married cousin living in Missouri and could visit her. George said he could probably pull some strings to get her an immediate passport, arrival and departure cards and whatever other papers would be necessary.

There was a question as to whether Martha should go herself to speak to Mariko, but on his hospital rounds the next morning George saw Mariko and spoke to her. After inquiring about Kate's health, to which George replied she was doing as well as one could expect, Mariko explained that she felt so sad, but she could not come to the United States at this time. Her married cousin with her two children were returning to Japan for a visit that might last a very long time. The cousin had been so unhappy in Missouri and was making her husband so unhappy too. Mariko felt she wanted to be in Tokyo to greet her cousin when she first arrived home again.

Martha asked George if he felt she should try to persuade Mariko this was a once-in-a-lifetime opportunity to come to America. But George just smiled. "Martha-chan, Japanese are very determined people. They give the resolution of an action without giving all the arguments. I don't think it would do much good to talk to Mariko. Frankly, I think she doesn't want to go."

So they decided to ask Hinako after all, since George reasoned the necessity of giving Kate any shots was remote. This time Martha and George found an entirely different response. Hinako, who was grinning from ear to ear, was overjoyed at the chance to see the wonderful United States.

Later, in Martha's bedroom, Hinako was looking in the long mirror. Her expression was sad, and Martha noticed the girl running her hands up and down her kimono.

"What's the matter, Hinako?" Martha asked softly.

Hinako turned toward Martha. "Montgomery-san, I could not go to America in kimono. I want to look like an American, in American clothes."

Martha put her hands on the girl's arms, relieved that that was the only trouble. "Of course, you should wear Western clothes. I'll give you money, and you take the afternoon off to shop."

Martha went over to her pocketbook and gave Hinako a generous amount. Hinako protested, "Not so much, Montgomery-san."

Martha said, "You may find you need many things, shoes, stockings, underwear, many things. A suit like mine, a skirt and a jacket may be nice."

Hinako's eyes were shining. "Always I have wanted a suit, but never before. My family not let me wear *yofuku*, Western clothes."

Hinako left for shopping, and Martha had some misgivings that she would be lost, but there was nothing else to do but let Hinako go by herself. Martha felt so protective of the little nurses she came in contact with—Mariko Ikeda and Hinako. No wonder American men fell in love with them, or with Korean girls.

Kate was taking a nap in her bedroom, and Martha sat at the desk in her own room to go over the large amount of mail that had accumulated at the Imperial while she was in Miyanoshita. She knew that her visit to Japan would always be equated with stacks of unopened mail. She was rifling through the envelopes, trying to summon enough energy and interest to read the letters, when she saw an envelope with a foreign stamp and unusual cramped handwriting. The words were very small, but the letters were perfectly formed. The envelope was postmarked Seoul, Korea.

Eagerly, Martha tore open the letter and saw first the neat, carefully penned signature of Helen Yang. Martha read the letter, then reread it several times. She felt the blood leave her face, and her legs and arms grew numb. As if the letter had been written in a foreign language, she studied each word carefully: "My very dear Mrs. Montgomery, I write you very good, happy news to tell you I marry soon, a very good gentleman whom I take care of as nurse in hospital. He is very good man and can provide good home. I do not need to work longer. He give Johnny Kim a very good home and send him to good school.

"I thank you. It happened because of you. One day at hospital I was very sad, and the old gentleman—my patient—he is not so young, asked me why I am sad. I tell him because Johnny Kim go one day to America forever. I tell him about Johnny Kim mother being dead and all that. He said if I marry him, he give Johnny good home, and I give him good life, because now he is lonely. His wife died two years ago.

"Johnny and I go to live with Mr. Yi as soon as we marry, as soon as Mr. Yi is out of hospital. Mr. Yi has grandchildren just like Johnny; so Johnny have boys and girls to play with. If you have not come to Seoul, and if you not want to adopt Johnny, and if I not be so sad that day, all would have been different.

"I thank you from my heart for coming to Seoul and seeing little Johnny and visit me. I hope that your dear daughter is well again and that you come some day back to Seoul to see Johnny Kim, who will soon be named Li, and to see me. Your friend, Helen Yang."

Martha started to cry—for Paul, for Johnny Kim, for Helen Yang. Helen Yang was marrying this older man to give Johnny Kim a home. She was protecting the child's future. She was keeping the promise she had made to Fay, Johnny's mother. She was relieving Martha of the responsibility for Johnny. Helen Yang was sacrificing her own future for the child. Martha's burden had been lifted, but there was an unfulfilled feeling about it. Helen Yang had taken the steps necessary; Martha had not. But yet Helen had said that but for Martha's visit to Seoul, all would not have happened. Martha reread that portion of the letter. If Martha had not come to Seoul, she would not have met George Tanaka. Was all life interwoven for everybody, or just for some?

Martha was eager to tell George about Johnny Kim, that

one of her problems had been solved. Was George correct when he had said pieces of life have a way of falling into place?

She wondered if she would ever see Johnny Kim again. If she lived in Tokyo, she could probably, from time to time, travel to Seoul. But if she remained in Indiana, perhaps someday Johnny Kim Li would attend college in the States. But that was a long time off. She would tell David to continue to send money to Johnny; it would be a nest egg for his future. A cry from Kate in the next room, asking for a glass of water, brought Martha back to the realities of her immediate problem.

Hinako returned from shopping. She had bought some Western clothes, and at Martha's suggestion she eagerly went into the bathroom to put them on. Smiling, proud, she came out and stood for inspection. Martha hoped that her disappointment at seeing how she looked did not show to mar the girl's happiness. The little figure so dainty in the kimono now looked awkward and clumsy in the tight-fitting skirt, which accentuated the short and slightly bowed legs of Hinako. The jacket was a little too long; the color of the suit too blue. However, Martha complimented her on how beautiful she looked. Hinako preened before the mirror. Suddenly she put her hand over her mouth, gave a little squeal and disappeared into the other room. When she came back, she was pointing at her shoes—high-heeled patent pumps. Hinako took a few faltering steps just as Kate had done with her first high heels last winter.

"Just like you now, Montgomery-chan." At this compliment, Martha hugged Hinako.

"Yes, now you're a real American," Martha said.

But the next morning Hinako looked a little ill. She started sneezing and finally admitted to Martha that she had a small sore throat and a much smaller headache. When George came in, he examined the girl and said she had a cold or probably the summer flu, but it would be better to get another room for Hinako and a relief nurse to care for Kate, who still needed someone with her.

After Hinako had been ordered to bed in another room down the hall, and the relief nurse was placed on duty with Kate, the thought came to both George and Martha as they were having tea in one of the restaurants downstairs that there was no one to accompany Kate to America. Hinako would not be well enough in two days to leave; the relief nurse, elderly and with only a limited knowledge of English, would only be a handicap.

George said, slapping the table with the palm of his hand, "I'll find someone if I have to go myself!"

"I didn't know you made house calls across the Pacific, Doctor," Martha responded lightly.

"Depends entirely on the case—and the patient and the patient's family," he answered.

But if Martha thought George was teasing, George took the idea seriously. He tried to find a competent nurse, but inquiries revealed no one who spoke sufficient English and was in a position to make the trip. The more he considered the possibility of accompanying them, the more he favored it. His passport was always in order. An arrival and departure card were all he needed.

Above all, he had thought that the extra few days with Martha might influence her decision. The strength of his love, the physical proximity of the few days might help at this time to black out the unpleasantness she had gone through at Miyanoshita. Then he even considered the possibility of breaking the flight in Honolulu. They could stay over a few days, depending, of course, on how Kate was feeling. As for Kate's hostility toward him, now she felt nothing at all toward him or toward anything else. He simply didn't exist as an object of hatred or even as a person.

He knew in the final analysis the trip could give him several more days with Martha. He had never believed in the existence of romantic love. Sex, loyalty, proximity, habit, all of these he had experienced, but the intangible void he felt at the thought of her departure, perhaps forever, left him with a feeling of misery and wretchedness beyond analysis or description.

He had faced death with the families of his patients; he had endured the death of his own son, softened by the fact that the news had reached him months later. But here was a separation made voluntarily by the decisions of human beings—Martha and himself. Why was this necessary? Why, why did they have to be separated? What barriers could there be that could not be overcome? What communication could he still keep open between them to convince her? But had he the right to convince her, since it involved not only her life but the children's as well? The circle was unending.

They had dinner the following evening at the Imperial. There was no point in going to the little *ryori*. By this time Martha had seen enough of Japanese life to have more than a fleeting impression; in addition, the effort to go there seemed to much for her. She felt as if these were the anxious hours before surgery—hours that seem endless and yet pass too quickly.

George looked at her downcast expression, and then, as soon as he had given the order for dinner, he spoke to her. His eyes were gleaming. "I have news for you."

"Good, I trust," Martha replied almost mechanically.

"That depends on the point of view." He took her hand across the table. "Martha-chan, I am going to America with you. I'm flying tomorrow too. I can not find a nurse to go with you, and for a few days I can be spared from the hospital. I have no critically ill patients at this moment. I am really coming—or is it going?" He was laughing.

"But I thought you were teasing when you suggested—"

"I was then, but the jest seemed to make good sense."

"George! George!" Her face was radiant, and George wanted to lean over to kiss her. Perhaps they should have gone to the *ryori* instead of this large Westernized dining room.

The waiter brought the soup, the clear soup with the water chestnuts floating in slivers on the surface.

"Are you hungry?" He looked at her, toying with his spoon.

"Not particularly, at least not now."

"Then let's not waste time now, eating." He called the waiter. "May I have the check, please?"

The waiter looked shocked. "But you have not yet eaten."

"The lady does not wish any more. Give me the bill for the two dinners." The waiter went over to confer with the headwaiter.

"Where are we going?"

"You have not seen my apartment, where I live. You must see it. You can help me pick out what suit is appropriate this time of year in San Francisco and maybe also, depending, as far as Springfield. But that we will see about later. Also a few days in Honolulu, if Kate is well enough."

"Well, that's a large order for a wardrobe, and for me too. Honolulu and Springfield—you will need entirely different clothes, I hasten to add."

The headwaiter came up, disturbed. "The lady will like to order something else?"

George answered, "No, she . . . she doesn't feel very well!"

The headwaiter bowed low. "I am very sorry." He totaled up the bill and placed it on the plate. "In that case we charge only for the soups."

George took out a large number of bills. "Not at all. We ordered the dinners. It is not your fault. He slipped a generous amount into the hands of the headwaiter and, taking Martha's arm, guided her quickly out of the dining room.

Martha turned to him. "You should have said the lady feels too well."

They entered the lobby of the apartment building in which George lived. It resembled the building in Chicago to which one of Martha's close friends had recently moved. It had the same impersonal feel of cleanliness and sterility imposed by interior decorators, but Martha smiled. Whereas the Chicago lobby was neo-Japanese, this one was neo-American. Both results had the same artificial quality.

The elevator, an efficient push-button, was empty; so George leaned over and kissed her. So far they had seen no one at close hand, and Martha felt that the danger George had mentioned previously about his brother-in-law spying had been exaggerated. But then, had the visit taken place previously, no doubt, they would have run into many persons.

As soon as George opened the door of the apartment and turned on the light switch, Martha gasped. Far from the barren, aesthetically simple mood of a Japanese room, the apartment radiated warmth and color and seemed at first glance almost crowded. As she entered the living room, she looked more closely at the objects. She closed her eyes as if clicking a camera shutter to photograph the picture. She wanted to remember each detail. She knew she could be happy living with him, sharing in his tastes—if not in this apartment, then in one perhaps larger. She was more in tune with his taste than with Paul's, who, if he had shown any interest in furnishings, had always preferred the garish.

"Want to see the rest?" George, too, was proud, for he knew that Martha was impressed. He showed her the kitchen, equipped with American gadgets. He explained that he didn't know whether to ask for a houseman who could cook or for one who was a mechanic. The dining room was small, but George explained he occasionally entertained small groups there.

"But you haven't seen anyone else, George, since I've been in Tokyo. You haven't seen any of your friends."

"Why should I?" he asked simply. "I didn't want to see anyone else."

He directed her down a corridor and opened the door to his bedroom. There was a Danish-modern set, in contrast to the rich woods of the living room and dining room. On the dresser were some photographs. She wanted to look at them, but felt a reluctance to examine them closely. To see what? she asked herself, knowing she was anxious to find out what Akiko looked like.

He seemed not to notice any hesitation on her part. "Later you can help me select some ties to go with dark suits." He showed her the bathroom off the bedroom; it was immaculately clean and uncluttered. She recalled the messy bath Paul had always maintained, with half-used shaving-cream cans, half-empty bottles of lotion, spilled talc. Neat about his person, Paul had been always untidy. But apart from teasing him about it, she thought, she had never made a fuss about cleaning up after him.

Then George led her to the closet where his apartment linen was stored. Luggage was placed on one of the shelves. "I'll take this one," and he reached up and took down a plaid folding case, similar to the thousands one sees when traveling.

Then he hesitated before the next door. He took out a key and unlocked it, but before standing aside to let her enter, he said, "Martha, no one else has ever been in this room, but I feel you should see it." He turned on the switch, and the large cylindrical globe in the center cast its shadows on this completely Japanese setting.

"This is my retreat room." George looked at her. "This is the Japanese part of me; this is the other part of me. Just as my mother keeps a Western room in her Japanese home, so I keep this in my Western apartment."

Without consciously thinking, she slipped out of her pumps and left them at the entrance of the room. She entered, and the *tatami* felt cool under her stockinged feet. Although she had been living in a Japanese home at Miyanoshita, she felt completely alien in this retreat. It was more severe, more aesthetic, like a private shrine. She saw the *tokonoma* and above it the *kakemono*, but the light from the ceiling illuminated it in a diffused fashion. Looking up, she noticed there was a small lamp focused on the elaborate picture, the kind used in an art gallery. She stepped up to the *tokonoma* and looked closely at the scroll. He saw her looking at it and remembered his thoughts the night he had hung it there. Now she was standing next to him. . . .

"That one is very old. I must take it down soon. I have had it hanging a number of weeks now."

She wondered if a "number of weeks" was before or after they had met.

"I want to show you some of the other hanging pictures I have." He went over to the built-in cupboard, and she followed. When he opened a lower drawer, she was aware of the aroma of camphor. He lifted out one of the fragile cases. "This is a very nice one." He took out a handkerchief from his breast pocket and dusted it lightly over the top of the cupboard before he unwrapped the picture. She watched his long, sensitive fingers carefully unroll the *kakemono*. He pointed out the carved ivory ends of the rollers. "Curiously, these ivory ends help make this picture so valuable. Look at this work."

She bent down to see it. "I must need glasses."

He laughed and opened a small drawer from which he took a magnifying glass. "Now look."

With the aid of the magnifying glass, she could see a

whole world open up. There were minuscule figures of men, probably priests. "Can you imagine a lifetime spent carving these ivories?" she asked him.

"But think of the joy when they had completed their labors. Each line, each turn of whatever instrument they used expressed the individual. What do we have today to compare with it?"

"You're right." She put down the magnifying glass. "I'm going back, George, and I will see everything in America as through a magnifying glass. I wonder how it will look." She ran a finger along the ivory roller. "For the first time in my life I feel rootless."

"Need you . . . need you feel rootless?" He hadn't intended to ask, to pressure her to a reply, but it was too late. Suddenly he put his arms around her. She clung to him. He lowered his head even with her cheek, and she felt the smoothness of his skin. In the light there was a golden luster to it.

Without saying a word, he went over to the closet and took out his kimono, a heavy brown silk, and handed it to her. She held it in her hands for a second. There was a fragrance of tobacco, of camphor and of a shaving lotion he used. She turned around, but he had left the room. She took off her clothes and hung them in the closet. Then she put on the kimono, which was far too large for her. It swirled at her feet. She wrapped it around her. The feel of the silk against her skin was unlike any other silk she had ever worn. Once on Christmas, Paul had bought an extravagantly expensive silk nightgown, which had torn at the seams the first night she'd worn it. Practically, she had told Paul to get his money back from the store. But he had replied, "It had been worth the tears."

Now she looked at the kimono. The lining was even softer than the outside. She rubbed her hands against it. How many times had George worn it? Only in this room? She was the first one to come in here, he had said.

He knocked on the door, and she said, "Come."

He had on a summer cotton kimono. Smiling, he apologized. "First one I could grab."

He came over to her and slid his arm under the brown kimono. He then turned off the switch. The spotlight on the *tokonoma* gave a low, diffused light. He led her to the *tatami* near it. He helped her down. She felt the hardness of the mat under her head, and automatically she put her hand under it.

He knelt down beside her. "Would you do something?"

She nodded.

Gently he slipped her arms out of the kimono and pulled it from under her, tossing it to one side. "I have dreamed of seeing you on this love mat, and I don't want the robe to spoil it."

He looked down at her, marveling at the supple, lithe body; yet she had borne two children, she had been married many years. He put his hand on her stomach, firm, flat, like a healthy young woman's, not a child's. He shook his head as if to wipe out the first memory of Akiko.

In the light she could see his skin, glistening, smooth, golden honey. She held her arms out to him, and now she felt his strength, his eagerness, his warmth. She closed her eyes, and she could feel the grain of the *tatami* under her bare skin as she was pressed against it, but it had no more an abrasive quality than that of warm sand. Soon she was no longer aware of the *tatami*, of the overhead light or of the *kakemono*, which she had momentarily glimpsed over his shoulder.

He took the brown kimono and, gently lifting her, put it under her and then placed one fold over her body. He put his arm under her head to pillow it, and for a brief second she had the sensation of the blood rushing back into her head as it was released from the hard surface of the mat. Then she felt his body stretched alongside hers. It was cool. She wanted to ask if he wanted part of the kimono, but she couldn't speak.

They said nothing. She had never been aware of such silence before. There was not even the familiar tick of a clock or a bracelet watch. Nothing in the room but peace and contentment. This feeling of relaxation was so pronounced, she knew she would always remember it as if it had been outlined like a portrait sketched in a heavy line, cutting it off from anything else.

Because it seemed an intrusion they would not accept at first, they were unaware of the ringing of the phone. She sat up first, then he jumped up, grabbing the cotton kimono. She heard him go barefoot down the corridor to the bedroom.

She heard his voice, but she was unable to understand what he was saying. He was speaking Japanese. Suddenly the thought that it might have something to do with Kate prompted her to get up quickly. She put on the silk kimono, putting the sleeves in even as she went through the doorway and down the hall.

She saw his face, tense, almost as if he was in pain. She knew immediately that this was not an ordinary call about a patient.

"Kate? Is it Kate?" She went over to him.

Abruptly, he shook his head and almost brushed her away with his elbow.

"Your mother?" She looked at him, but again he shook his head.

She had never seen such an expression on his face in all the weeks she had known him. Anger fused with grief contorted his features into something resembling the picture of a Samurai, transforming him for a brief moment into someone entirely different than the gentle lover of a few moments ago.

He spoke rapidly in Japanese. Then he hung up. "That was my brother-in-law, Yasuki. It was about my wife, Akiko." He paused. The fact that he'd said my wife did not occur to him, but Martha felt herself gasping. "Akiko tried to kill herself. She did not quite succeed. Yasuki says she is calling for me. She felt she no longer had to keep her promise to me about suicide. She had no further obligations of a promise."

"You must go to her at once." Martha looked at him. She could scarcely understand her own words. "You must go."

"How can I? I am leaving for America in a few hours. I can not."

"George, you must. You must go to Akiko. She is asking for you. She needs you."

George stood there. He was silent. He knew as long as he lived, he would always remember this moment, this moment of indecision, of decision.

Martha spoke quickly, "What time does a plane leave for Nagasaki?"

George went into the retreat room, gathered up Martha's clothes and handed them to her. She went to the bathroom to dress, but first she put her head under the cold tap and let the water run over her face.

When she came back into the bedroom, George was dressed. "I've called a taxi."

"You don't need to take me back to the hotel, George."

He looked at her and said matter-of-factly, "This isn't Springfield. It's Tokyo, Martha."

In the cab he turned to her. "Martha, would you, could you postpone your flight until I get back from Nagasaki?"

But he knew her answer before he heard it. "No, George, I can not. We have our plans. . . ."

She got out at the hotel. He stood at the taxi entrance and took off his hat while he spoke. How long ago was it she had first seen him at this very taxi entrance? Was his hat on or off then? She could not remember what she thought when she'd first seen him standing there with the other Japanese doctor.

Now, for a second, they stood there looking at each other. A lifetime of things they wanted to say, to remember, but how can words spoken in a second at a busy taxi entrance convey the essence of one's innermost feeling?

"Good-bye, George."

"Good-bye, Martha."

She turned away, toward the entrance door of the hotel. Thank God, she thought, he had had the sensitivity not to say *sayonara*.

She went up to her room, looked in on Kate, who was sleeping, and at the relief nurse, whose name she hadn't bothered to learn. She could not think clearly enough, but in a hazy way she felt she would have to fly alone with Kate. Perhaps they could manage without anyone else, if she could pull herself together.

Then she went into the bedroom. She turned off the light and sat down in a chair and remained there, staring straight ahead, for the rest of the night, until the first rays of morning came in through the window. *Akebono*, sunrise, one of the few Japanese words she remembered, came to her as she watched the gray light come through the drawn curtains.

George had gone back to his apartment. He had spent the rest of the night phoning his colleagues, not caring that he was awakening them, not caring what they might think, trying desperately to find a nurse or young intern, someone who could take his place on the plane. Then he remembered an American colonel connected with an air-base hospital for whom he had once done a favor. The colonel, awakened in the middle of the night, knew immediately that only panic could have induced a Japanese doctor to lose face by such a call. He got on the project immediately and within an hour called back to say he had found an American nurse who would welcome a trip back to the States.

George waited until five in the morning to call Martha. He kept looking at watch every fifteen minutes from 3:30 a.m. on. He had wanted to jump in a taxi and drive to the Imperial. But he had argued with himself not to upset her any more because of any selfishness on his part.

Then at precisely five o'clock he phoned the Imperial. "Did I awaken you, Martha?" he asked.

"No, I haven't been asleep, George," she said, not adding that she had not even gone to bed.

"Nor I. Martha, I found a nurse, an American woman, a Mrs. Henderson, who is coming along with you. An American colonel located her for me. She must be reliable, or he wouldn't have recommended her."

"I'm sure she is, George." She knew her voice lacked response, even warmth, but she was too drained to speak.

"Martha, I'll leave her ticket at the airline window. Martha . . . Martha my dearest, I haven't time . . . I haven't time," she could hear him trying to control himself, "I haven't time to come to the hotel. My plane leaves at 7:30."

"That's all right, George. It's better this way." She wanted to say don't, for God's sake, don't put me in double jeopardy by saying good-bye again.

"Do you think you can manage to get Hinako to go back to Miyanoshita? Check out of the hotel? Get to the airport? All?

"I'll manage."

"Mrs. Henderson will be at the hotel in about an hour." There was a long pause. "Martha . . ." In panic he spoke again. "Martha? . . ."

"Yes."

"I was afraid you had hung up."

"No, I'm still on the line, George."

"Martha-chan my dearest, I don't know what I can say. I don't know if I am doing the right thing. I don't know."

"You are doing the right thing, George. You have no choice." She started to add, Your wife is calling for you, but she checked herself and said simply, "You have no choice."

"Martha . . . Martha, when you get back to Springfield, will you write me how things are?"

"Yes, of course, I will. I'll have the doctor write you about Kate's condition."

"Will you write me, if I should come to Springfield, if you will come back . . . I don't know what I'm saying."

"I'll write you when I know, George. George, I think we better hang up now . . . for both our sakes."

"Yes, yes, you're right. If I lived a hundred years, I could never say all I want to."

"Nor I, George. Good-bye."

"Take care, Martha." He hung up the phone and stood there, looking at it.

The phone rang a second later, and Martha was afraid to answer it, afraid George might be calling back. She let it ring several times and then finally picked up the receiver. A voice said, "There is a lady to see you . . . Mrs. Henderson."

"Will you ask her to come up, please?" Martha asked the receptionist.

The moment Martha saw Mrs. Henderson, she took a deep sigh. Mrs. Henderson, middle-aged, in her starched white uniform under a dark-blue coat, looked the classic example of friendliness and competency. As Martha found out later, she held the rank of captain but had come along because Colonel Waterbury had had such a note of urgency in his voice. Mrs. Henderson seemed to take over completely. She resembled one of Kate's own childhood nurses. And as soon as Kate was awake, she established an immediate rapport with the girl, who smiled at her as if welcoming an old friend. It was the first overt sign of emotion Kate had shown since the episode at Miyanoshita.

In addition, Mrs. Henderson could understand and speak a little Japanese. As she said to Martha, "It would be foolish of me not to take advantage of everything I can. Knowing Japanese helps."

Martha—with Mrs. Henderson as interpreter—paid the relief nurse, who, bowing and smiling and repeating *"Domo arigato gozai-masu,"* left the rooms. Then Martha went down the hall to Hinako's room. She had purchased the rail ticket for Miyanoshita through the porter at the desk, and now she handed it to Hinako along with money for a taxi and extras. She hoped that Hinako would make it all right to the depot and board the correct train. Hinako was in tears, ashamed at her inability to go with them, and feeling that she had dishonored Dr. Tanaka, Motgomery-san, herself, her family, everyone.

As Mrs. Henderson and Martha left Hinako and walked down the corridor, Martha shook her head. "It's amazing that on home ground Hinako was so efficient, but she's like a baby away from home. It's as if her training were part of her background and not part of her own personality."

"That sometimes happens with Japanese women. They are not—at least those raised in traditional backgrounds—they are not flexible, and wearing Western dress isn't going to make them so," Mrs. Henderson said. "And yet they have come a long way. A short time ago, and I mean just a few years ago, a girl in Hinako's place might have killed herself over mortification of letting someone down. Japanese always lived with the idea of suicide. But I don't think Hinako will do anything foolish. For that matter, one doesn't hear so much of suicide any more."

Out of the corner of her eye Mrs. Henderson saw Martha turn pale. She wondered what she had said, but wisely she didn't ask.

Like an automaton, Martha paid the hotel bill and managed to have the luggage sent down. From somewhere the head porter found a wheelchair for Kate, and the trio—Mrs. Henderson, Martha and Kate—waited at the entrance as the doorman called a taxi. A black limousine came up immediately. This one was empty, and they got in.

"Where are we going, Mama?" On the one hand, Martha was elated that Kate had even asked a question; on the other she was dismayed that, with all the preparations, Kate had no idea they were leaving, completely unaware of all that had taken place.

"We're going to the airport." Martha paused. "We're flying home, Kate. We're going back to Springfield."

"That's nice," Kate replied, and like a child, she wiggled back against the upholstery of the car.

At 11:45 in the morning Mrs. Henderson and Martha walked down the red carpet to the plane. A porter was pushing Kate in the wheelchair. They were escorted by an official of the airlines who not only waived them through customs, but now assisted them in boarding ahead of the other passengers. George's influence was still being felt.

They were shown four seats, two on either side of the aisle—with an empty one next to Martha for extra pillows, books and things, the official explained.

"But this is such an extravagance," Martha couldn't help saying.

The official bowed low and smiled. "You do not pay. We rearrange other passengers' sitting. No obligation."

Martha started to thank him profusely, but he bowed low again. "Thank you, and good-bye. You have fine trip." He bowed low to Mrs. Henderson and to Kate and then was gone. An American stewardess came up to them. George had selected an American airlines rather than Japanese. No detail escaped him, Martha knew. She also knew that for all intents and purposes they were at this moment back in the United States, only the wheels of the huge plane touched Japan.

At 11:45 a.m. George walked into the entrance of the hotel in Nagasaki. He had flown to Omura and then come the forty-five minutes by taxi to Nagasaki. There were no messages waiting for him at the hotel. He had no idea what hospital, if any, Akiko was in. He tried to reach the family home, but whatever servant answered feigned ignorance of anything, as servants are often instructed to do. He called Yasuki's office, and the secretary, in the customary circuitous way, announced that Kataoka-san would be gone for several days.

Uneasy, George took a taxi to Yasuki's home. He tried to remember what Yasuki's wife had looked life, but he could not recall her face. He had seen her last at the funeral of Akiko's father, soon after he and Akiko were married. George tried but could not remember how many children Yasuki had, nor could he remember in what age group they would be. Everything about Yasuki was blotted from his memory.

George arrived at Yasuki's home. He went through the entrance gate and, seeing the large number of bereavement lanterns hanging in the courtyard, and noting the large number of both men's and women's shoes placed neatly at the entrance, he knew immediately what had occurred. He was prepared when Yasuki told him sorrowfully that Akiko had gone on the long journey.

George bowed his head in reverence, as was expected of him. Then he looked at Yasuki. He was about to say, She was already dead when you phoned me last night, but he resisted giving Yasuki the satisfaction. The thought had occurred to him on the plane coming over that Akiko was dead already. It was too late then, and it was too late now to do anything about it.

George knew that Yasuki was still using the tactics of his Kempetai days. He had deliberately phoned the night before George was to leave for the States, having ferreted out somehow that George had planned to go. George looked steadily at Yasuki. At least Yasuki would never know how well he had timed his call. Then, watching Yasuki's eyes narrow beneath the heavy-rimmed glasses, George had an intuitive flash, the kind that comes in a difficult medical case. Yasuki had planted the thought for Akiko to kill herself. There was no doubt, George now felt, that Yasuki had stressed, subtly, of course, that Akiko no longer owed any obligation to Joji. She would be free to do with herself whatever she wanted in the manner of living. And promise made to anyone was no longer valid.

George looked around at the family. In the matter of death he was as far removed from these traditionalists as he was in the matter of living. If Yasuki had suggested suicide to Akiko, he was not an accomplice to murder, as a Western mind might conceive it. Yasuki probably realized that Akiko preferred dying to living, and only her sacred promise to her husband had kept her alive. George realized also that he felt more guilty than Yasuki ever would, and he knew also that Martha would always share this feeling of guilt. He could write to her, explaining the Japanese point of view, but he could not begin to express in the letter the Shinto philosophy of death.

Yasuki had won the battle that had been going on between them for so many years, George acknowledged, and Martha had been one of the victims.

George wondered if he shouldn't leave immediately rather than remain for the three days of observance following a death. But then Yasuki asked him in front of other members of the family, "Can you be spared, oh honorable brother-in-law, or do you have a very sick patient who requires your presence?"

Deciding not to give Yasuki the satisfaction of gossip among the family, George answered, "No, I have no very sick patient at the moment. I shall remain."

Yasuki was sly enough to pretend ignorance of Martha and Kate's departure, for his reference to a "very sick patient" was most pointed.

But why not remain? Martha was gone. He looked at his watch. In another few hours she would be approaching Honolulu. Perhaps these days would help him think through some of the problems by taking him out of his normal routine. He joined the family in their traditional observances. He followed the swaying death kago carried by white-robed bearers; he heard the mournful throbs of the drums, the chants of the priests announcing the arrival of the dead at the gates of heaven, asking for mercy; he sat with the family in the immaculately clean home, greeting the more distant members of the family, who allegedly did not know of the divorce. Yasuki was extracting his last ounce of revenge.

The orthodox observance of the ceremony, performed ritualistically as it had been for hundreds of years, and the inane conversation of the family, who were unaware of any world outside the fenced compound of their houses, all of this made George want to cry out in frustration and anger. Had he ever been part of this group? Had these same people, older ones, now dead, replaced by younger ones, been in attendance at his wedding, the funerals of Akiko's parents, the celebration of the birth of his son? Why hadn't he rebelled then? He tried to recall his attitudes on these previous occasions, but they could not have been hostile, or he would have remembered. Undoubtedly he had accepted them as part of living—acceptance with complacency.

But when had he started to change his attitude? After the war, perhaps, when he had returned to try to take up his life with Akiko? But not immediately then, because he'd been too engulfed in trying to reestablish his career. Perhaps the change had been so gradual, he had not been aware of it. There had not been the slightest thought that he and Akiko would not be compatible when they were married. His parents wanted the wedding; they had arranged it; he had acquiesced. There had been no doubt in his mind then.

But now he realized whatever he had been, he no longer was the same. He was farther removed from these people than he could ever be from Martha. Only the language was similar; the meaning was not. The color of his skin, his features were like these people's, but he was not one of them. He was, as Yasuki had said, a Japanese superimposed on the personality of a Westerner. Then, pursuing the thought farther, he wondered if this attraction to Martha had been not only physical desire for a most charming lady, but also because she represented the West. She was the essence of America, particularly with her Midwestern background. She was actually the only American woman with whom he had any close association. During his college days, and later his internship and residency in America, he had been concentrating on his medical career. Then, too, who would have been interested in a gangly, immature Japanese man?

His thoughts continued: Was Martha attracted to him because of the unusual surroundings in which they had met? He had asked himself if her feeling for an Oriental was simply to avenge Paul's affair with the Korean girl? Martha would not, of course, be aware of any thought of vengeance. But the human mind and its motives could not be analyzed under a microscope. There was no encephalogram, no mylogram to give the answers.

Would Martha come back or send for him? Would her return to her environment evoke more or less feeling for him? He felt that the longer she would wait, the less chance there would be for a marriage. She would accept again the status of widow in the community. He had no answers, and he was in the depths of despair. He contemplated suicide himself. He knew that would be the easy way. In addition, he had no right to take his own life. He had been trained to be an expert in the field in which his knowledge could save the lives of others. He had a debt to society to share his talents. What right would he have to destroy them. The easiest way of all was closed to him.

At the airport at Omura, on his way back home, he took down a schedule of transpacific flights. He could easily catch the plane and arrive in Springfield in less than two days and nights. He put the timetable in his pocket.

In his office in Tokyo there was a cable from Martha in San Francisco: "Arrived safely. Kate stood trip well. David and Sally met us at the airport. All send regards."

He pondered at the message. There was not "love," no other term of endearment except the perfunctory "all send regards." Perhaps she had not wanted to embarrass him if his office nurse should receive the message. Perhaps David had sent the cable for her. But what difference would the addition or omission of a simple word mean?

As he took off his jacket to put on his white examining coat, he automatically reached into his pocket and found the timetable he had picked up at Omura. He took it out, tore it up and watched the pieces fall into the wastebasket.

Kate had stood the trip well. As Mrs. Henderson said later to her sister, whom she visited in Scranton, Pennsylvania, "To tell you the truth, I was more worried about the mother than the daughter."

Martha had remained in an almost-static position during

the entire trip. She did not touch her meals; she had kept her eyes closed. The stewardess had brought her a glass of champagne with her dinner, the mark of the deluxe flight. But Martha had taken only a sip and put it down. Once, Mrs. Henderson, alarmed at looking across the aisle and seeing Martha's pallor, had moved into the empty seat next to Martha and had taken her pulse. It had been faint but regular. Mrs. Henderson had noticed deep marks on Marth's left wrist, made by fingernails clawing into the skin.

"Do these hurt?" she'd asked Martha, and Martha had shaken her head. Mrs. Henderson had gone back to her small traveling bag, taken out a first-aid kit and had applied some antiseptic to the almost-bleeding abrasions. When the nurse looked again at Martha some time later, she noticed that Martha had put on her gloves.

The strength that Martha had summoned over the past year was now drained away. She knew she was in a void, a vacuum requiring no action, not even understanding. Martha would close her eyes and then open them quickly, as if to blot out the memory of George's face as she saw him standing there at the phone. The rapid Japanese he was speaking contradicted the anguish on his face. Then when he had turned to her and said, "Akiko, my wife," she knew that the few lines of the consensual divorce could not erase his marriage. Except for her, George would have continued in his marriage. Akiko would have felt an obligation to keep her promise of no suicide.

Martha looked through half-open eyes at Kate. Her daughter was really enjoying the company of the nurse. Mrs. Henderson was the personification of security for Kate, someone she could relate to, a person out of her own background. It was best that Hinako or Mariko had not come along. But was it best also that George had not accompanied them? Martha shut out this thought.

She saw a few seats ahead of her, several Air Force officers. They looked secure, confident, victorious. She wondered about soliders and officers coming home from a battle, beaten, defeated, unsuccessful. Glad to get home, but knowing that part of their souls had been buried in the defeat. Not everyone could be the winner in a battle, or in the ordinary skirmishes of living. She had been defeated. But then there was one saving thought: She had gone to the Orient to provide for Johnny Kim. In this the trip was not in vain. Helen Yang had written, "Without your visit here, this probably would never have happened."

At home, near the fireplace, Martha recalled that she had huge, brass scales on which she liked to put pots of flowers. Her great difficulty had always been in trying to balance the scales so that one side would not spill. But this was hard to do. How could one balance the lives of people? Was one small Korean boy able to put into proper balance the misery of all the others involved in this odyssey of hers? Martha looked down at her hands. The red of the Merthiolate had stained the beige of her left glove.

David and Sally were at the airport in San Francisco to welcome them. Sally had insisted on coming with David. There were no measles at home, no broken water pipes. Annoyed at first, David was, upon second thought, glad that Sally had decided to come. And when it had looked as if an important meeting of the National League for Municipal Betterment, which Sally had organized, might keep her from making the trip, he had coaxed her to come. She'd wisely refrained from asking him, as she was on the verge of asking, Scared to go alone?

Martha came down the plane ramp, gaunt, pale and with an expression of misery and sorrow. David wanted to cry out. Sally glanced at him. Again she held her tongue. Instead she rushed up, past the gate, and grabbed Martha in her arms. David had seized Kate, who was laughing and hugging him as if afraid to let go.

In the suite at the Fairmont, on top of Knob Hill, Mrs. Henderson was standing by the window, watching the lights go on across the Golden Gate. "Well, for six weeks I'll be on this side, watching the sun set, and then I'll go back and watch it rise. To tell you the truth, I don't know any more on which side of the Pacific I'd rather be. It gets you over there all right, their way of life."

David casually turned to Martha. "Well, Martha, I suppose that's one place you never want to go back to, isn't it?"

The question, casual as it was, was not lost on Sally. "You don't have to answer, you know, Martha," she said.

"No," Martha spoke slowly, "I don't know. I may go back some day." She paused. "But I don't know when—if ever."

Paula Fairman

Romantic intrigue at its finest—
over four million copies in print!

☐ 41-795-0 **FORBIDDEN DESTINY** $2.95
A helpless stowaway aboard the whaling ship *Gray Ghost*, Kate McCrae was in no position to refuse the lecherous advances of Captain Steele.

☐ 41-798-5 **THE FURY AND THE PASSION** $2.95
From the glitter of Denver society to the lawlessness of the wild West, Stacey Pendarrow stalks the trail of her elusive lover for one reason: to kill him.

☐ 41-783-7 **JASMINE PASSION** $2.95
Raised in a temple and trained in the art of love, the beautiful Eurasian Le' Sing searches California's Barbary Coast for the father she has never met and for a man who can win her heart.

☐ 40-697-5 **PORTS·OF PASSION** $2.50
Abducted aboard the *Morning Star*, heiress Kristen Chalmers must come to terms not only with immediate danger, but the desperate awakening of her own carnal desires

☐ 41-800-0 **SOUTHERN ROSE** $2.95
Amidst the raging furor of the Civil War, the beautiful actress Jaylene Cooper is torn between her passion for a dashing Southern rebel and the devoted love of a handsome Yankee officer.

☐ 41-797-7 **STORM OF DESIRE** $2.95
The only woman in a rough and brutal railroad camp in the wild Southwest, young Reesa Flowers becomes enmeshed in a web of greed, sabotage, and lust.

☐ 41-006-9 **THE TENDER AND THE SAVAGE** $2.75
In the wild and ravaged plains of the Dakota Territory, beautiful young Crimson Royale is torn between her savage lust for a Sioux Indian and her tender desires for his worst enemy—a captain in Custer's Army.

☐ 41-749-7 **VALLEY OF THE PASSIONS** $3.25
Forging her destiny in the harsh Oregon wilderness, Sara Landers must choose between the love of two men—a powerful rancher and the muscle-bound foreman who murdered her father.

☐ 41-415-3 **WILDEST PASSION** $2.95
Wrenched from the wealthy embrace of New York society, beautiful Courtney O'Neil sells herself as a mail-order bride in the untamed Northwest—never forsaking her dream of triumphant love.

Buy them at your local bookstore or use this handy coupon
Clip and mail this page with your order

PINNACLE BOOKS, INC.—Reader Service Dept.
1430 Broadway, New York, NY 10018

Please send me the book(s) I have checked above. I am enclosing $_____
(please add 75¢ to cover postage and handling). Send check or money order only—no cash or C.O.D.'s.

Mr./Mrs./Miss _____

Address _____

City _____ State/Zip _____

Please allow six weeks for delivery. Prices subject to change without notice.

The Windhaven Saga
by Marie de Jourlet

AMERICA'S #1 PLANTATION SAGA — OVER 8 MILLION COPIES IN PRINT!

☐ **42-006-4 WINDHAVEN PLANTATION** $3.50
The epic novel of the Bouchard family, who dared to cross the boundaries of society and create a bold new heritage.

☐ **41-967-8 STORM OVER WINDHAVEN** $3.50
Windhaven Plantation and the Bouchard dream are shaken to their very roots in this torrid story of men and women driven by ambition and damned by desire.

☐ **41-784-5 LEGACY OF WINDHAVEN** $3.50
After the Civil War the Bouchards move west to Texas—a rugged, untamed land where they must battle Indians, bandits and cattle rustlers to insure the legacy of Windhaven.

☐ **41-858-2 RETURN TO WINDHAVEN** $3.50
Amid the turbulent Reconstruction years, the determined Bouchards fight to hold on to Windhaven Range while struggling to regain an old but never forgotten plantation.

☐ **41-968-6 WINDHAVEN'S PERIL** $3.50
Luke Bouchard and his family launch a new life at Windhaven Plantation—but the past returns to haunt them.

☐ **41-690-3 TRIALS OF WINDHAVEN** $2.95
Luke and Laure Bouchard face their most bitter trial yet, as their joyful life at Windhaven Plantation is threatened by an unscrupulous carpetbagger.

☐ **40-723-8 DEFENDERS OF WINDHAVEN** $2.75
Out of the ashes of the Civil War, the South rebuilds. Laure and Luke Bouchard continue to uphold Windhaven Plantation as Frank's niece and her husband forge a new frontier in Texas.

☐ **41-748-9 WINDHAVEN'S CRISIS** $3.50
With the fires of civil war still smoldering, our nation prepares for its first Centennial—as the proud Bouchards struggle to preserve the legacy that is Windhaven.

☐ **41-110-3 WINDHAVEN'S BOUNTY** $3.50
Left alone by a tragic twist of fate, Laure Bouchard opens a casino in New Orleans and struggles to defend the house of Windhaven against those who would bring it down.

☐ **41-111-1 WINDHAVEN'S TRIUMPH** $3.50
As the proud South once again raises its head up high, the heirs of Windhaven must sow the seeds of a legacy that is both their birthright and their obsession.

☐ **41-112-X WINDHAVEN'S FURY** $3.50
As a new age dawns in America, the Bouchards face new opportunities and dangers—and struggle to reconcile destiny with desire.

Buy them at your local bookstore or use this handy coupon
Clip and mail this page with your order

PINNACLE BOOKS, INC.—Reader Service Dept.
1430 Broadway, New York, NY 10018

Please send me the book(s) I have checked above. I am enclosing $_____
(please add 75¢ to cover postage and handling). Send check or money order only—no cash or C.O.D.'s.

Mr./Mrs./Miss _____

Address _____

City _____ State/Zip _____

Please allow six weeks for delivery. Prices subject to change without notice.

Patricia Matthews

America's leading lady of historical romance.
Over 20,000,000 copies in print!

☐ **41-857-4 LOVE, FOREVER MORE** $3.25
The tumultuous story of spirited Serena Foster and her determination to survive the raw, untamed West.

☐ **41-513-3 LOVE'S AVENGING HEART** $2.95
Life with her brutal stepfather in colonial Williamsburg was cruel, but Hannah McCambridge would survive—and learn to love with a consuming passion.

☐ **40-661-4 LOVE'S BOLD JOURNEY** $2.95
Beautiful Rachel Bonner forged a new life for herself in the savage West—but can she surrender to the man who won her heart?

☐ **41-517-6 LOVE'S DARING DREAM** $2.95
The turbulent story of indomitable Maggie Donnevan, who fled the poverty of Ireland to begin a new life in the American Northwest.

☐ **41-835-3 LOVE'S GOLDEN DESTINY** $3.25
It was a lust for gold that brought Belinda Lee together with three men in the Klondike, only to be trapped by the wildest of passions.

☐ **41-873-6 LOVE'S MAGIC MOMENT** $3.25
Evil and ecstasy are entwined in the steaming jungles of Mexico, where Meredith Longley searches for a lost city but finds greed, lust, and seduction.

☐ **41-834-5 LOVE'S PAGAN HEART** $3.25
An exquisite Hawaiian princess is torn between love for her homeland and the only man who can tame her pagan heart.

☐ **41-064-6 LOVE'S RAGING TIDE** $2.75
Melissa Huntoon seethed with humiliation as her ancestral plantation home was auctioned away—then learned to survive the lust and greed of a man's world.

☐ **40-660-6 LOVE'S SWEET AGONY** $2.75
Amid the colorful world of thoroughbred farms that gave birth to the first Kentucky Derby, Rebecca Hawkins learns that horses are more easily handled than men.

☐ **41-514-1 LOVE'S WILDEST PROMISE** $2.95
Abducted aboard a ship bound for the Colonies, innocent Sarah Moody faces a dark voyage of violence and unbridled lust.

PINNACLE BOOKS, INC.—Reader Service Dept.
1430 Broadway, New York, NY 10018

Please send me the book(s) I have checked above. I am enclosing $ _____ (please add 75¢ to cover postage and handling). Send check or money order only—no cash or C.O.D.'s.

Mr./Mrs./Miss _____

Address _____

City _____ State/Zip _____

Please allow six weeks for delivery. Prices subject to change without notice.

**THE TOWERING SAGA
OF A PROUD, PASSIONATE FAMILY
AND THE MIGHTY PETROLEUM EMPIRE
THAT MADE THEM GREAT**

"Marvelous..."—*West Coast Review of Books*

THE OKLAHOMANS
WHITNEY STINE

Driven by pride and ambition to wrest their fortune from the dark riches that lay deep beneath the sun-baked Oklahoma soil, five generations of Herons struggle against a backdrop of some of the most turbulent—and fascinating—chapters in American history, forging one of the largest oil dynasties in the world.

☐ 41-886-8 THE OKLAHOMANS $2.95

☐ 41-488-9 THE OKLAHOMANS:
    THE SECOND GENERATION $2.95

☐ 41-662-8 THE OKLAHOMANS III:
    THE THIRD GENERATION $3.50

Buy them at your local bookstore or use this handy coupon
Clip and mail this page with your order

PINNACLE BOOKS, INC. — Reader Service Dept.
1430 Broadway, New York, N.Y. 10018

Please send me the book(s) I have checked above. I am enclosing $_____
(please add 75¢ to cover postage and handling). Send check or money order only—
no cash or C.O.D.'s.

Mr./Mrs./Miss_____

Address_____

City_____ State/Zip_____

Please allow six weeks for delivery. Prices subject to change without notice.